OTHER BOOKS BY KIM BOYKIN

Palmetto Moon: A Lowcountry Novel

A Peach of a Pair

The Wisdom of Hair

ECHOES
of MERCY

ECHOES OF MERCY
By Kim Boykin

www.RiversEdgeMedia.com
Published by River's Edge Media, LLC
100 Morgan Keegan Drive, Ste. 305
Little Rock, AR 72202

Cover design by Paula Guajardo
Manufactured in the United States of America.

ISBN-13: 978-1-940595-57-3 softback
ISBN-13: 978-1-940595-58-0 ebook

ECHOES
of MERCY

KIM BOYKIN

RIVER'S EDGE
—— **MEDIA** ——
Little Rock, Arkansas
2016

For Kaley, a fierce and wonderful mother.

ACKNOWLEDGMENTS

I love Billie Warren's story, and wanted to publish this book after my first novel, *The Wisdom of Hair* came out in 2013. My editor in NY loved the story too, but said the protagonist was too old at 49. Really? But what did I know? I was 54 and brand new to the publishing business. So I turned out two more books with 20-something-year-old protagonists, and hoped that the world would be ready for Billie Warren some day. Thanks to Kerry Brooks and the team at River's Edge Media, that day has come.

The strange thing is, I wrote this story about a woman who has a mom with Alzheimer's and a teenage daughter who is a single mom years ago. Today, my dad has Alzheimer's, and my daughter, who is 29, is a single mom. In some ways, I think Billie prepared me for my place in this sandwich generation.

I am sincerely grateful to Donna Ciriello, my favorite librarian in the whole world, for her keen eye, but most of all for her friendship. Thanks to the many adoptees I interviewed who shared what it was like to search for and sometimes reconnect with their birth mothers. Thanks to Hugh McAngus who always answers my legal questions or directs me to someone who can. Thanks to my critique group who, no matter what I brought to group all these years, always asked when I was going to do something with Billie's story.

But most of all, thank you for reading my books. You make it possible for me to do what I love, and if I could, I would hug each and every one of you.

CHAPTER ONE

Forty years of atonement ought to count for something. After all, Billie Warren was just nine years old when she did what she did. She'd hoped the memory of that one horrible act would be diluted by time, by the birth of her daughter, and the death of her father. But the recollection was always there, following her around like a pack of lost dogs.

Lately, the dogs hadn't stirred, and, if they did, Billie didn't have time to notice them. At forty-nine, she considered herself too young to have a grandson and too old to deal with his teenage mother, both of whom lived with her. She was the police chief of Stanton, which really meant she was the glorified mom of a tiny Lowcountry town near Charleston that was barely a speck on a map. Throw in her mother's Alzheimer's, and Billie was in the middle of a shit storm that had no end in sight.

The admission yanked hard at the left side of her chest, and the landscape was nearly black by the time she jerked the squad car onto the shoulder that overlooked the marsh. She threw the car in park, her finger stabbing wildly at the button until the window was all the way down. She gulped at the thick salty air and pressed her palm into the tight spot on her chest, her thumb digging into the muscle like she could push clean through to her heart.

God, she used to love riding patrol because it gave her time to think. Now she hated it for the same reason. But riding patrol also gave her moments like this, with the full moon suspended just above the creek like a giant dollop of butter. The silvery glow illuminated the marsh grass and bathed the pluff mud in a dreamy light that made the oyster shells laced across the surface glow like rhinestones.

Billie drew in a long steady breath and let the sweet musty smell of the marsh take her mind away the way a dog-eared black-and-white photo from a dresser drawer could, the way an old beach tune always did. It took a while, but the tightness in her chest began to ease. Her breathing was near normal until the police radio sent all that flying with a garbled message. Billie fiddled with the knobs until she caught the tail end of the dispatcher's message. "Come again?"

"911 call, Chief," Delores snapped. "Melvin Gifford's wife has winged him good. County dispatcher sent the sheriff for back up. Ambulance is on its way."

"Shit," Billie hissed.

"Copy that," Delores said.

Billie flipped the light on as she pulled onto the highway and headed back toward town. Delores had said winged, hadn't she? Billie couldn't remember, so she turned on the siren and picked up speed. She hung a left on Cherry Vale Lane and proceeded down the street lined with neat white-washed clapboard houses until she reached the tiny red brick home that was the crime scene. The ambulance and the county's boys were already there. Jimmy Malden, old Chief Malden's nephew, was holding court on the front porch with two other cops who were barely wet behind the ears.

The screen door flew open and two hefty medics navigated the gurney onto the porch. Melvin Gifford was lying on his belly as they wheeled him toward the ambulance, his backside full of lead. He wasn't dead, but as often as he had knocked his wife around, he ought to be. The front door was open and Billie could see Penny Gifford sitting on the edge of a tattered blue Lazy Boy with a lace doily where Melvin's greasy head had lain for most of his sorry life.

The hairs on the back of Billie's neck prickled as she got out of the car and walked toward the front porch. She ignored the smirk on Jimmy's face over the fact that he'd beaten her to the scene of the crime. She recognized only one of the other cops. Donnie Shepherd was boy band cute and had always had a thing for Billie.

Jimmy had shared that little tidbit over more beers than Billie cared to count and then laughed his ass off over the very idea of Billie with a twenty-three-year-old. But Jimmy wasn't laughing several beers later when he confessed that after his uncle disappeared, he'd wanted to be the police chief of Stanton more than anything. Jimmy Malden was a natural born smug bastard, so it had thrilled Billie's soul that he'd actually cried when he confessed that a Malden belonged in her job.

"Hey, Billie." Donnie was the only one of the three officers with his hat in his hands. "We all tried to talk to Mrs. Gifford. Sergeant Malden even acted like he was going to put the cuffs on her, but she says she's not talking to anybody but you."

"He's exaggerating," Jimmy said. "I'm just letting her simmer down."

Billie didn't speak, just nodded to them and opened the screen door. Before it closed, a bleary-eyed Penny was up and out of the Lazy Boy.

"I know," Billie said, and she did know. Billie wrapped her arms around the sobbing woman. She'd been called to the Gifford home too many times to count over the past twenty years, mostly by the neighbors who feared for Penny's life. Penny was always glad when Billie responded to the call, but she was too afraid to press charges. Too afraid that some good old boy judge would turn Melvin loose, and he would kill her for putting him away.

Billie couldn't blame Penny for not sending Melvin to jail. Judicial wisdom in domestic cases like Penny's was legendary, and not just in little podunk towns in South Carolina. But if anything had kept Penny Gifford in her place all those years, it was the raw power that a man like Melvin Gifford wields that makes women like Penny believe there is no place they can go where they won't be found. No wonder she shot him.

"Oh, Billie." Penny sputtered and held tight while Billie stroked her hair and the cop in her looked around the room. Blood was splattered on the wall behind the easy chair. Just off the living room of the tiny house, the kitchen was spotless. There were two plates and two jelly jar glasses in the dish drain, a pair of wire spectacles on top of a well-worn Bible on the dinette.

Best guess, Penny cleaned up the supper dishes, did her daily devotional before she got the same shot gun Melvin had shoved up under her chin a thousand times, and shot him as he was treading toward his sacred chair.

"Oh, Billie—I just couldn't—"

"Shhh. You're alright now."

"No." Penny pulled away and looked at Billie like she was back to believing she was worthless, a know-nothing who couldn't do anything right. "I was aiming at his head," she sobbed as Billie pulled her close again.

Jimmy took a long draw off his cigarette and threw it down on the concrete stoop. "Billie." The smugness was gone, but he didn't sound like he was going to throw his arms around them for a group hug.

Billie looked Jimmy Malden straight in the eyes to let him know he had better take good care of Penny Gifford if he knew what was good for him. Maybe he half-nodded his head as he snuffed out his cigarette with the heel of his boot; Billie wasn't sure. But it tore at her gut when Penny took a deep breath and pulled away like she was ready to go anywhere, even to hell if it was better than the one she'd been living in for the past thirty-four years.

"They told you they have to take you to the sheriff's office for processing?" Billie asked. Penny nodded at the floor. "I'm so sorry."

"Chief Warren doesn't have a jailhouse in Stanton, Miss Gifford, or she'd take you herself," Donnie said.

"I know." Penny wiped her eyes. "I don't mean to be no trouble."

Donnie gave Billie a sheepish look as he led Penny Gifford to the squad car. They didn't cuff her, even though procedure said they should. Jimmy's sidekicks were young, but Billie knew between the four officers, they'd seen enough women like Penny to know they were carting the wrong person off to jail. If things went the way they normally did during domestic calls, Melvin wouldn't file charges; men like Melvin Gifford prefer to administer their own brand of justice.

"We didn't cuff her," Jimmy said, like that was some big consolation. "There aren't any kids to take to social services."

"No, they're all grown and gone," Billie said. "And you can bet wherever they are, they're carrying on the proud family tradition of beating the shit out of their loved ones."

Jimmy was quiet for once as Billie leaned in the driver's side window of the squad car. Penny's hands were folded in her lap. She was whispering the Twenty-third Psalm. Billie knew she didn't have to remind Donnie how to treat Penny and appreciated the way he'd handled the situation. She started to tell him so until she noticed him staring down her shirt.

Billie rose up enough to stop the peep show. "Penny, whether you're at home or—you're going to be okay. I'll call you tomorrow."

Jimmy rapped on the top of the squad car, and Donnie obediently pulled out of the yard. "We got this one covered, Billie." Even with all the drama, he was smiling over one of his young pups trying to sneak a peek. "He must like little tits."

"Jesus, Jimmy, don't you read? They're ample breasts."

"It's no fun to give you shit, Billie Warren. Nothing gets to you."

Jimmy was half-flirting, but he was dead wrong. Things did get to Billie in a big way, especially lately. Seeing Penny Gifford carted away in a squad car was an undeniably hard pill to swallow. If she added up all the other shit in her life, the odds that she could muster enough objectivity and detachment to do her job were impossible.

She got back into her piece of crap Ford and radioed Delores.

"Penny okay?"

"Yes," Billie said, "but it's a damn shame her daddy never taught her how to shoot a gun."

"They arrest her?"

"She shot the man, Delores. Not much anybody can do to pretty that up."

"Penny ought to know better than to just wing the bastard. Tell her next time, make that bullet count."

Billie's lips tipped up. "Thinking I'll let you pass that tip along to her."

"Glad to," Delores snorted. "Half an hour 'til the day is done. You be careful out there."

"Will do."

The squad car meandered through the city streets and then seemed to have a mind of its own as it headed out past the city limits. This was Jimmy Malden's territory, but Billie always came out this way after her shift was over. The Ford followed the highway toward Rainbow Row. Not the pristine Row fifty miles away in Charleston. The one just nine miles outside the Stanton City limits where funky old houses painted electric shades of eggplant and fuchsia, chameleon green and sunshine yellow dotted the Edisto riverbank.

The lights of the Row came into sight. She turned off the county highway and onto a dirt road that wound its way toward the homes of folks who had found a way to make a living out of their art. Tiny houses and workshops filled with creativity spilling over into front yards and into the back eased the knot in Billie's stomach that had tightened hard when Donnie put Penny in the squad car. Although she still felt like somebody, maybe a small toddler, was standing on her chest.

The headlights flashed across the Devil Oak, the centerpiece of the Row and a counterpart to the famous Angel Oak on Johns Island, near Charleston. While neither of them had anything to do with the angel or the devil, both were southern live oaks as old as time, with branches sixty yards long. The Devil Oak was the most prized work of art on the riverbank and was said to be sculpted by God himself. But Billie was more interested in the other sculptor on the Row.

The thought of letting the car follow the slight hill into Cole Sullivan's front yard was tempting, not to see if he had anything new displayed or because he was a great artist. Her favorite pieces weren't the pricey burled wood or metal ones in the shop or on his front lawn. She loved the ones in the garden, just off his bedroom, people made out of old fence posts that looked real in the early morning shadows.

For six months, Billie had had the good sense to turn around before she got within sight of Cole's house. Shoot, with all that had been going on with Mama and Amber, the last thing Billie Warren needed was man troubles. But something inside begged her to take her foot off the brake. The road was slightly downhill. If she let it, the car would roll right into Cole's front yard. He would meet her on the porch with a smile that said he was glad she was back. It would feel good to put her arms around him, to wake up with him and look out at those fence post people.

To be fair, Cole was no trouble. He was one of the best things that had ever happened to her, and yet she denied herself. Why was that? Why couldn't she just save the world five days a week from three to eleven and then fall into his arms? Why does any woman do that—reject the very things she knows are best for her, whether it's a man, a little extra sleep, copious amounts of chocolate? If she could answer that question Oprah would offer Billie her own show. If she could answer that question, she could *be* Oprah.

The key was a good excuse, and the one that worked best for Billie was that she didn't have time for Cole. Granted, it wasn't real sexy, but it sounded good and kept people like Delores and Amber off her back. The lack of time made so much sense to Delores, she'd taken it upon herself lately to check in on Mama for Billie because it was on her way home from work. Billie was grateful for Delores's little gift, but not so she could slip between the sheets with Cole. It stung that Mama never called her by her name anymore and never recognized her face.

Before she could fall down that rabbit hole again, the clock on the dashboard blinked 11:00. She pulled the squad car back onto the highway and was headed toward home when her radio chirped.

"You ain't gonna believe this. You close by?"

"I'm done, Delores." Beyond done. "Unless there's been another shooting, whatever it is will keep until tomorrow."

"Honest to God, Billie, you better get to the station," Delores hissed. "Now."

CHAPTER TWO

The screen door to the cracker-box-sized police station was still bouncing in the jamb when Billie walked into the station house and stopped dead in her tracks. When she saw the old woman sitting in the battered folding chair beside Delores's desk, those dogs that had lay quiet for so long began to howl, and Billie wanted nothing more than to turn tail and run like she had when she was nine.

"You remember me?" the woman asked, like the two of them were chatting over potato salad at a family reunion. Billie knew her all right, but couldn't speak, couldn't even nod. The old woman asked the question again, louder, enunciating each word slowly with the hard twang of the Lowcountry.

Billie's stomach pulsed. She wanted to retch, run and then keep running from the former town crazy who'd disappeared after the only murder in Stanton's history, but she willed herself to stay put. "Yes, ma'am, I know who you are."

"I remember you weren't the little lady your mama wanted you to be." The truth hurt, not because it hit home, which it did. Billie had never been what her mother thought she should be, which never bothered her much until lately. "You used to run with that pack of boys," the old woman continued, cocking her head to the side, her brow creased like her mind was sifting through time. "And what was that song you all used to sing?"

Billie shook her head mechanically. *Please. Don't.*

The woman's words came out flat and monotone. She punched the words the way Billie and the Wild Boys had when she was a child.

"*Crazy Sadie* sold her babies; don't you never *tell.* Crazy Sadie sold her babies; she's going straight to *hell.*"

"Sadie Byrd." Billie barely got the words out.

The haggard appearance of Miss Sadie was permanently etched in Billie's mind, the constant look of sadness, the desperation on her face, the thick smell of baby powder that always followed the woman, even when she wasn't pregnant, which was rare. Yet, here she was in the Stanton Police Department four decades after skipping town, well cared for, with a big Coach bag that matched her burgundy flats. Her hair was a yellowish gray color and worn in a bob that looked stylish for someone her age. Her eyes were clear and bright, not unlike Billie's mother's on a good day, before the Old Timers' disease turned ugly.

The old woman put her big pocketbook on the counter and pulled out a Kleenex. "Well, that's all done and gone." Her friendly smile faded. "I've come about Caroline Norris's murder."

Delores gave Billie an I-told-you-so look. The hard undertow of Billie's past brought back images of that horrible day before Caroline Norris was found dead, the day Billie on a dare to become a Wild Boy and crushed Sadie Byrd to the core. Billie shook her head like she could erase the indelible memory and told herself to get a grip. She was a cop, for God's sake.

The old woman looked tired and as sleepy as Billie's grandson when her daughter, Amber, woke him up to see if he was still alive or wet or hungry. "That nice lady said you're taking me home with you tonight since it's so late."

Billie's eyes shot to Delores and then back to Miss Sadie. The last thing she wanted was to be under the same roof with a boatload of guilt and the one soul Billie had wronged so that nothing could make up for it. During a dare, Billie and the rest of the Wild Boys, had watched the woman lose her mind. The dare had been Billie's initiation into their club, her chance to finally fit in, to belong.

"Excuse us a minute," she said, yanking Delores out the screen door.

"What in the hell is going on?" Billie hissed.

Delores pulled away and righted her sleeve. "You got to hear her story, Billie."

Billie's chest went tight. Her breath was rapid and shallow and not nearly adequate enough to fill her lungs. "Did it ever occur to you that she might have escaped from some old folk's home? Somebody's probably looking for her right now. But forget that. You told her I'd take her home with me?"

Delores planted her hands on her hips. "Well, I've only got the one bed at the trailer, and my back don't let me sleep on the couch."

"How long has she been at the station?"

"Couple of hours, maybe three."

"And you didn't think you should mention this?"

"Not after Penny Gifford filled her husband full of lead. And, yes, Miss Smarty Britches, I did check to see if anyone had reported her missing.

"Her son, Cecil, was her only legal relative. I say *was* because she buried him today.

"The daughter has six priors in Columbia, all drug related. Cecil filed two of them for the same old, same old. Junkie steals anything that's not nailed down. Then he turned around and posted bail. After the last time, she skipped town for good. Couldn't find anything else on her. Somebody with a jones that bad usually ends up dead."

Shit. Delores wasn't on the defensive anymore and that look in her eyes said she knew something was up. She was ten years younger than Billie and didn't know what Billie had done to Miss Sadie, or if she did she'd never mentioned it. "I reckon I can take the couch, but don't count on me coming in tomorrow unless I can get to the chiropractor."

"Fine. I'll take her home with me." Billie ran her hand through her short blond hair. "At this point, I don't care; I've just got to get some sleep."

"You're gonna need it. She told me all about Caroline Norris's murder, and it's a doozy." Delores shifted her giant pocketbook to the opposite shoulder and glanced back into the station house. "Poor woman is so worn out. You're doing the right thing, Billie."

There was no denying Billie owed Miss Sadie. She rubbed her eyes and let out a tired sigh. "God, what a shitty night."

"You get some rest. Hear?" Delores gave her a warm hug. "Tomorrow is another day. Whatever the hell that means."

"Okay, and thanks for looking in on Mama for me."

"I don't do nothing for you that you wouldn't do for me." Delores waved over her shoulder and headed for her car.

Miss Sadie dozed the five minutes or so it took to get to Billie's house. It was just after midnight and the house was dark. Billie had forgotten to call Amber and let her know she'd be late. She wondered if Amber thought she'd gone out for a beer or that she had broken down and gone to see Cole.

The motion detector light was supposed to come on when Billie pulled into the carport. It was burned out again. Her ex-husband was always good about stuff like changing the oil and replacing lightbulbs, but not much else. She used the flashlight on her belt to light the way and helped Miss Sadie up the steps to the kitchen door. It was unlocked, which didn't mean anything in a town where hardly anybody locked their doors.

"You got a baby?" Even dog-tired, Billie could hear the excitement in Miss Sadie's voice.

"My daughter Amber does. He's cute. His name is Tyson—Junior." Named after his whore-dogging daddy who moved on to greener pastures after Amber announced she was pregnant. "But I call him Little Man. Have a seat at the kitchen table. It won't take more than a couple of minutes to get your bed ready."

"I'm so tired, if I sit down, I might not be able to get up." Miss Sadie acted like she didn't see the dozen or so dirty baby bottles in the sink and picked up the Fisher-Price keychain on the counter. She smiled at Billie and jingled the plastic keys, but Billie couldn't hear them over the music blaring from Amber's room. "I wish you wouldn't go to any trouble for me."

"It's no trouble at all."

Miss Sadie followed Billie out of the kitchen and down the hallway of the tiny three-bedroom ranch. Billie opened the linen closet and pulled out a set of white, eyelet sheets for Amber's bed and hoped Miss Sadie didn't notice that nobody in her household could fold a bottom sheet if their life depended on it. The singer of the rock band was pleading "motivate me." Billie wished someone would motivate Amber to get off her ass and get on with her life. Little Man's daddy wasn't coming back.

There were only two things on Billie's mind when she turned the doorknob to Amber's room—putting Amber on the futon in the nursery so Miss Sadie could sleep on Amber's bed and then collapsing into her own. She threw open the door and groped for the boom box to turn it off, the only sure way to wake Amber from a dead sleep.

She stopped short of turning on the lamp and wished Miss Sadie wasn't standing right beside her when the light from the hallway flooded Amber's bedroom. Tyson Cantrell stood beside the bed with his clothes wadded up over his private parts, his good-looking face a cross between embarrassed and terrified, knowing Billie kept more than one gun in the house.

"Tyson Cantrell, unless you have a U-Haul parked out back and big plans to start providing for your son, you better get the hell out of my house."

He turned his back on Billie and slipped his jeans on, looking over his shoulder every half second at the gun on Billie's belt. There was no need to remind him it was loaded. Amber pulled the sheet around her chin and looked at Billie with big teary cow eyes, crying. But Billie was hardened from years of Amber whining her way onto her well-worn soapbox where she lived to remind Billie that she was a teenager and should be able to do as she pleased.

Tyson scooped up his shirt and shoes. "Sorry, Ms. Warren," he whispered under his breath. "Ma'am." He nodded at Miss Sadie with his jeans half buttoned and his shirt in hand as he brushed past her with his Abercrombie & Fitch body. Amber let out a wail when she heard the screen door screech open and then bounce shut in the frame.

"*You,*" Billie growled. "Out of here. I'll deal with you in the morning."

Amber whipped the sheet around her in grand dramatic fashion and quit sobbing just long enough to give Billie her best go-to-hell look as she stormed passed.

"I'm sorry, Miss Sadie—" Billie began.

"Don't think nothing of it." She reached for her end of the bottom sheet and slipped it over the corner of the bed. "Ain't nothing I haven't seen before." Billie snapped the crisp white sheet twice until it floated almost perfectly onto the mattress. Miss Sadie tucked it under the foot of the bed and was breathing hard, like making the bed, along with the rest of the day, had done her in. Billie put some extra blankets on top of the comforter and one of Mama's nightgowns from when she used to sleep over.

Miss Sadie sat down on the bed and slipped her shoes off, wiggling her toes like a little girl just freed from stiff patent leather. "Well," she looked at Billie with a shy smile. "He sure was a pretty thing."

CHAPTER THREE

Billie was bone weary, an odd feeling that competed with the adrenalin inside her from the whole Amber–Tyson thing. She took off her belt, trying not to think about the fallout that was sure to come her way from teenage drama. Better to just unload her gun and put it in the lock box. She returned the metal box back to the top shelf, behind an old hat box in her closet. The same place she'd hidden it since the day Tyson found out Amber was pregnant and dumped her.

Amber was one of those kids who always expressed herself by wearing out a song ad nauseam. One day she was a cheerleader blaring "Brave New Girl" and the next she had "Suicidal Lyrics" on replay. God, how Billie had wanted to shoot that boy skank for crushing Amber like she didn't matter. She continued to push away the real reason she'd kept the gun hidden; Amber had been depressed after Little Man was born —scary depressed.

Billie pulled on a Braves T-shirt and washed her face. She was brushing her teeth when the cell phone she'd tossed onto the nightstand buzzed and vibrated around like a dying beetle.

It stopped abruptly and began chiming Nat King Cole's "Unforgettable." Being the least technically savvy person on the planet, Billie knew her daughter had downloaded the song as Cole Sullivan's ring tone. Amber had done that once before after a huge fight she and Billie had, only "Ding Dong the Witch Is Dead" was her calling card.

Even through the tiny speaker of the half-ass cell phone, Nat sounded good. The song played through and started over. Cole Sullivan was a patient man. If she let the water run and didn't look herself in the eyes while she finished brushing her teeth, she could ignore the urge to grab the phone, to tell him what he already knew. She felt lost, she was tired, and she needed him.

The phone went mercifully silent. Billie turned out the light and let out a tired sigh as her head settled onto the pillow. A green pulsing glow from the cell phone let her know that Cole had left a message. If she had any sense, she'd just go to sleep.

Billie closed her eyes and listened to his silky voice. "I know it's late, and you're tired, but I miss you, Billie. So damn bad."

She'd met him at a party her best friend, Abby, threw to welcome him to the Row. That was almost three years ago when things weren't so crazy, before Amber got pregnant and before Mama graduated from dementia to Alzheimer's. She'd been excited when he'd asked her out, the kind of excitement a girl feels when she's in her twenties and she's met a guy that makes every cell in her body scream, *he's the one*. Of course when a girl is forty-six and has that reaction to a man, she takes it with a grain of salt. Still, Billie couldn't wait for their first date.

It was a hundred and two degrees that day and Billie knew it wouldn't get much cooler after the sun went down. She went through the entire contents of her closet and settled on a short white denim skirt, a black cotton tank, and a pair of sandals she didn't want to admit she'd bought for the occasion.

Cole had wanted to impress her, too. He showed up in an expensive-looking suit and a crisp white shirt. His dark hair was slicked back, setting off his rugged face and those piercing dark chocolate eyes that made her all gooey at her center. He was tall enough so that when he hugged her hello, his chin rested on top of her head. His scent was light, citrus with a hint of something woodsy, and musky. "I hope you don't mind," he said as she was grabbing her purse, "I made reservations at the Charleston Grill."

The great thing about the Lowcountry is even the finest restaurant in Charleston is casual, albeit dressy casual. Billie knew nobody from the fashion police would even think of cutting their eye around at a woman doing what she had to do to keep cool in that kind of heat. Still, out of the slew of phenomenal restaurants in Charleston, the Grill was considered to be the best, a fancy place in a hotel with a grander staircase than the one Leonardo DiCaprio perched on in *Titanic*. The restaurant was part of a small mall with shops like Gucci and St. John, and, Billie's favorite designer, Godiva.

She'd never eaten at The Grill or played dress up in clothes she couldn't afford there, but whenever she was down King Street way, she always made a point to treat herself to at least one hazelnut praline truffle. With Cole dressed up like he belonged on the cover of *GQ*, Billie felt like she was wearing a parka in August or, at the very least, mismatched shoes. "Then I should change," she'd said. "Compared to you, I look ridiculous."

He shook his head, slight smile, as his eyes moved across her body, making her smooth her skirt nervously. "Don't change. You're beautiful."

The words took her aback. While Billie liked the way she looked and thought she was holding her own at forty-six, nobody had said those words to her in a long time. So she didn't change, but she didn't say much during the short drive to Charleston. She could feel him observing her, noticing things about her the way he might study a model for one of his sculptures.

The Cooper River Bridge was barely visible in the distance, a sign that they were close to the Holy City. The bridge made Billie uncomfortable. She crossed and recrossed her legs and pulled at the hem of her skirt. Cole seemed to sense her uneasiness. He put his hand on hers. "Is there someplace else you want to go?" It had been even longer since someone asked Billie what she wanted. She pointed to the Sullivan's Island exit up ahead and asked him if he'd ever been to Poe's Tavern.

Billie had always laughed at the girls on the MTV shows Amber loved to watch. Especially the ones who chirped to their BFF's and the cameras on a daily basis about "the best date *ever.*" But that's what that night was.

Cole stopped at a gas station in Mount Pleasant, got something out of his trunk, and went inside. He left the radio on and the bluesy sound of B.B. King worked its magic, loosening Billie up, awakening the woman who'd gotten pushed aside by the mother in her, by the daughter in her.

A few minutes later, he came out of the store, his suit folded up. He was wearing his killer smile and a pair of baggies. The shirttail of his white dress shirt was out, and his sleeves were rolled up. He had on his swanky black Italian loafers but no socks. He got in the car, looked at her with those eyes that melted her to the core. "Who looks ridiculous now?"

She was already in lust with him, but at that moment, she fell a little bit in love.

Anybody who's ever been to Poe's knows it's impossible to get in. You can never find a parking place, or a table, and they don't take reservations. A lot of people, mostly tourists, see the crowd out the door and the cars cruising for parking spots and just give up. While Cole had to park down past the post office, luck smiled on them when they walked into the old tavern and were immediately seated.

With her a small-time cop and him a big-time sculptor, she'd been a little worried they wouldn't have much to talk about, but the conversation was easy. Turned out Cole was an anomaly, a Chicago boy who loved to surf the puny waves of the Atlantic, but said he preferred Malibu. He said he surfed the Pipeline once, and the midwesterner in him said that was enough.

He ordered beers for both of them and fish tacos for himself. Billie ordered her usual, the best burger on the planet, the Amontillado with guacamole, pepper jack cheese, Pico de Gallo, chipotle sour cream—and Poe's thin hand-cut fries, the only ones she allowed herself to eat.

The waitress returned with two glasses of Blue Moon. It was a pretty beer, set off with an orange wedge on the side of the glass, and, at the end of such a hot day, it tasted like nectar. As always, the food was excellent, and even when the conversation lagged, there was a comfortable silence between them. She loved the way he looked at her, the way he listened so intently. She loved his laugh.

She didn't have to ask him to walk down to the beach after dinner, he just took her hand and they headed down Station 22 Street. The bright full moon was veiled by clouds and glistened off the smooth flat shoreline. They stood facing the ocean, bare feet in the sand, taking it in without the obligation of words. He put his arm around her and pulled her close and she surprised herself by wrapping her arms around his middle.

She pressed her face into his chest and breathed in the thick night air along with his scent. "If this never goes anywhere," she thought, "the night, this moment—best date ever."

But it did go somewhere. She fell hard for Cole and then her world changed. They'd been together almost a year when Billie's mother got in the car to go to the Piggly Wiggly for a gallon of milk and wound up three states away, stranded on the West Virginia Turnpike.

Mama didn't have a clue as to who she was or how she got there. It was like one day she was a sweet, forgetful old lady and the next her mind was wiped clean of Billie, of her brother John, of the history Mama had made with them. And then Billie's all-American teenage daughter was pregnant, dumped, and scary unstable. The one-two punch had doubled Billie over, pummeling her until she forgot herself, until she was struggling just to keep her head above the shit in her life. To be sure, the last thing she wanted was to lose Cole Sullivan, but somewhere in all that, she had to let him go.

She had no business listening to the message on her cell phone again. She closed her eyes and felt the same pang in her gut she felt when she stopped returning his phone calls, didn't answer the door when he showed up on her doorstep wanting answers.

"Let me buy you a Blue Moon and a burger and we'll figure things out."

Cole deserved a better girlfriend, a fun one without any problems.

"Come on Billie give me a chance." He was superhuman. "Give us a chance."

She turned the phone off and cussed herself for being so stupid, but even dog tired, there was still a part of her that defended her self-denial. Together, Amber and Little Man were a handful. Mama's Alzheimer's took more of Billie's mind and soul than when her father was in hospice. Besides, didn't Cole deserve to be happy with someone who could give all of herself to him? She pretended not to hear the last question in her mind as she drifted off to sleep—didn't she deserve to be happy, too?

———◆◆◆———

On most nights, Billie's sleep was hard and dreamless; exhaustion was her friend. But with Sadie Byrd sleeping in the next bedroom, Billie's reoccurring childhood nightmare ran in her head all night long.

She was the leader of the Wild Boys, stripped down to her underwear like the others, her nine-year-old body covered in war paint. Feathers from a greedy buzzard some of the boys had once pelted to death because it was too stupid to fly away from the road kill it had claimed were stuck in Billie's yellow blond hair and cascaded down her back to make an impressive war bonnet. Billie screamed and raised a spear in the air; the Wild Boys did likewise. The Lone Ranger and Tonto tom-tom drum Slick Johnson had gotten for Christmas played in the background, sounding like a hundred authentic ones. The drumbeats became louder and louder, competing with the war cries, as Billie led the dance around a pole encircled by fire. A terrified Sadie Byrd was strapped to the pole, crying, her eyes searching for someone to help her. Just like she had that day in the park when Billie stole the tattered old baby doll the woman always clung to like it was a real baby.

The dance went on forever. Billie's insides battled like separate warriors, the savage and the good girl tearing each other apart until the morning light saved her from herself, and Billie snorted herself awake.

She wiped her mouth with the back of her hand and looked at the clock—six a.m. She could barely hear Amber in the nursery talking to the baby. She got up, went to the door, and opened it without knocking. Amber shot her a look, then looked back down at her son and stroked his head as he nursed like he hadn't eaten in a week. The ravenous sucking noise made Billie want to laugh, and then Amber would laugh. Then Billie might be able to let go of what happened last night.

"Amber—"

"Don't start Mama."

"Honey, what were you thinking? Especially after Tyson left you to fend for yourself."

Amber was silent for a long time before she set the little chunker on her knee and leaned him slightly forward. Little Man let out a monster burp as a thin stream of drool ran down his chin. He caught sight of Billie and smiled gloriously before attacking the other breast Amber had loosened from her gown.

"I'm *thinking* that Tyson is my baby's daddy." Little Man reached up and yanked her hair. She pried it lose from his grip and flipped it back over her shoulder before readjusting herself in the rocker; the wide-eyed child latched on for all he was worth. "I'm nineteen, Mama. Nineteen. I loved Tyson. I still love him."

"God, no, Amber. You're just lonely."

"Hell, yes, I'm lonely. I'm here all the time with the baby. All of my friends went off to college, and I—"

"In time, you can do those things, but you don't have to settle, honey. Not for somebody who's going to come and go as he sees fit."

"Like Daddy did?" Billie ignored the dig. "Besides, how do you know that Tyson doesn't love me?"

"How do you know that he does?" Billie shot back.

As soon as the words left her mouth, she felt sick inside, the way she did when she and Amber's daddy used to go at it over money or his inability to hold down a job. And then the realization came out of nowhere, slamming into her, the ultimate sucker punch.

"Did he use anything?" Amber shot Billie another go-to-hell look. "Please tell me you've gone out and gotten some birth control pills. Hell, a whole case of condoms. Please." Another look. "Answer me."

"Everybody knows you can't get pregnant if you're nursing, Mama."

Shit.

Amber ought to know better than to let Tyson back into her life. But who was Billie to talk? It had taken her until her midthirties to wise up enough to get rid of her ex, and he still came back from time to time for the same reason Tyson Cantrell did. Regardless, if there was ever a time for the *wake up and smell the Starbucks* lecture, this was it.

Little Man looked up at his mama with her nipple between his gums, rubbed his eyes, and smiled at her. "You never said anything about bringing home company. Who was that old lady?"

"Somebody who came into the station last night—hell, Amber, it doesn't matter who she is. This is my house and as long as you're living here you'll live by my rules. Now, Tyson has a legal right to see his son. I can't do anything about that, but as far as you're concerned, he had better keep his pecker in his pocket unless he's planning on taking care of you and this baby for good."

Amber unlatched Little Man who seemed awfully proud when he let out another belch without being coaxed. She buttoned her gown with one hand and then handed the baby his clown blanket, which he promptly crumpled up around his face. Billie stood there watching her grandson, waiting for her daughter to say something.

Wasn't that how the dance always went? Billie would bitch, then Amber would make a pissy whine fest until Billie was tempted to throw her hands up. And on too many occasions lately, Billie had surrendered to the ancient art of teenage torture. But the silence was scary. It was gut wrenchingly hard to watch Amber seething in denial over Tyson Cantrell. But Billie knew better than to waste another breath on that argument unless she wanted Amber to dig in even deeper.

Amber leaned back in the old ladder back rocker that Billie had rocked her in when she was a baby and closed her eyes like she hoped Billie would just go away. Lord, how Billie wished it was that easy. When Billie was growing up, men were the only ones who were allowed to pick up and go when they wanted a different life. Now it wasn't uncommon for women to change out of their old lives like a pair of dirty underwear.

Back when Amber was a colicky baby, *Kramer vs. Kramer* seemed to be the movie HBO aired with the frequency of *The Shawshank Redemption* or *My Cousin Vinny*. One night when her ex-husband was off trying to find himself, the crying, the work at home, her job made Billie feel like she was going to implode. She wanted to look at somebody the way Meryl Streep looked at Dustin Hoffman and say, "I'm leaving. I just can't do this anymore." But who would she say it to? The stuffed animals in the nursery? The baby?

Things weren't much different today, but she didn't have that luxury. For her own sanity, Billie left the nursery and knocked softly on the guest bedroom door before opening it. Miss Sadie was still asleep and, judging from the other side of the bed, she hadn't moved all night. Billie closed the door and went into the kitchen to put a pot of coffee on before she went to the mailbox for the newspaper.

Normally there'd be a half dozen or so neighbors headed off to work, but the tire plant's closing one county over had hit Stanton hard. Several houses on Billie's street were vacant, some for sale, some foreclosed, leaving just a few retired neighbors. It was sad to see the block full of overgrown yards and "For Sale" signs, but she had enough on her plate. Not that she could do anything about Stanton's economy or world peace even if she wanted to. Still there was always this tension inside her that made her feel like she was responsible for everything, even things she had no control over—especially things she had no control over.

Billie hurried back into the kitchen and sat down at the table with her coffee and a cold Pop-Tart. She scanned the newspaper and learned that a study determined women are genetically predisposed to handle stress better than men because they are wired differently. No shit. The entire front page of the Charleston county section was about old Judge Norris finally getting a whole state highway named after him. The article went through his resume point by point beginning when Harold Norris was a good ol' boy state senator and ended with his retirement from the South Carolina Supreme Court five years ago.

The judge looked old in the photo, Strom Thurmond old. Even though he wasn't as old as Strom, he was still pushing ninety-five. His son, Bob Norris, longtime US senator, had spearheaded the honor because he couldn't stand to think of his daddy dying without a bridge or a highway or some major structure named after him to recognize over seventy years of public service. The fact that Bob's bid for reelection was just six days away didn't hurt either. What would Billie do when the judge's people found out Sadie Byrd was back in town? She skimmed Dear Abby. As usual, it was chock full of nuts. How could anyone not know the answer before they ask a question like, "should I un-invite my new boyfriend to a dinner party because the hostess is upset that he's an ex-con?" The man couldn't outrun his past any more than Billie could or Miss Sadie could. Forget the old woman's determination to unburden her soul, Billie could ignore that open arrest warrant with Sadie Byrd's name on it all she wanted, but Bob Norris would go over her head.

CAPRICORN. Jesus was a Capricorn, so was Billie. "It would be good to have someone wise by your side during trying times. Remember, you can't do everything all by yourself." No shit. Better to make like Meryl Streep and leave.

She raked the crumbs off the table and thought about cleaning up the dishes. Instead, she wedged the coffee cup into the mess in the sink and set the plate on the counter. There was no sound coming from the nursery, which meant Amber had gotten lucky and Little Man was out. She cracked the door to Miss Sadie's room again to see that she was still sound asleep. The clock in the hall read 7:15, Mama would be up.

There were three pairs of clean jeans on Billie's dresser. She hadn't noticed them the night before, but gave Amber points for doing the laundry and actually folding it. She slipped on a pair of worn Levis and a GOT PORK T-shirt from the Stanton Pig Parlor and grabbed her car keys. She scribbled a note and taped it on the bedroom side of the doorknob so Miss Sadie couldn't miss it; *Be back soon. Left to check on Mama. Make yourself at home.*

The 1958 Ford truck her daddy left her looked like it had been driven right off the showroom floor, except for three small dents her ex, Paul, swore he hadn't put there for spite the last time he left. Daddy had shown her how to change a tire on that truck and how to change the oil, skills Mama was sure would push Billie even farther away from laying down her tomboy ways and accepting a girly womanhood. Daddy's acceptance of Billie didn't have anything to do with the way she turned out, but it had felt good he knew that was the way Billie was made. And it was okay.

Daddy was long since gone; he'd died when Billie was in college, majoring in barhopping and criminal justice. When they put him in hospice, she'd taken the semester off and didn't leave his bedside because she didn't want to miss him. But she missed him. God, she missed him. Every time she turned the key that made the ancient truck purr, every time she wanted to lay down the self she'd become by default because she was the one who stuck. The one who was stuck.

Mama's house was close by. Billie was already emotionally weary and knew she'd be even more so after her visit. Rather than surrender to fatigue, she should probably jump start her metabolism and run the short distance or at the very least walk. But if Daddy was there, sitting beside her, reminding her to go easy on the clutch, he'd say riding in style was more sensible than lazy.

Inez Hawkins waved as Billie pulled into the driveway. Inez was the go-to gal whenever Mama ousted the sitters, which she did often and with gusto. Inez started out as a neighbor, but after her husband died, she started cleaning houses and had been Mama's housekeeper since Billie and her brother John were in grade school. After a few years, Inez worked exclusively for Mama and became more like a sister than hired help. She was a little older than Mama but sharp, and it pained her to see Mama in the throws of Alzheimer's.

"Hey," Inez called, making her way to the truck. Billie wrapped her arms around the old woman who always smelled like bacon and fresh baked biscuits. "You come get you some breakfast before you waste away to nothing."

"Thanks, Inez. I already ate."

Inez looked at Billie like she was a liar. "Look at you, thin, like a sparrow. You young folk, y'all don't take care of yourselves. Y'all just think the old ways is going to kill you. Nobody in my family ever died from a good breakfast every morning, I can tell you that."

Billie ushered Inez toward the porch as she complained about how no scientists had ever proven that lard had killed anybody. "Besides, you can't make biscuits without lard," she fussed as Billie opened the front door. "Excuse me, but they say to put olive oil in everything, maybe Crisco. Crisco my ass. The South was built on buckets of L-A-R-D, and we are all still standing, thank you very much."

"Yes ma'am." Billie knew better than to disagree.

Two places were set at the kitchen table. Mama sat at hers, staring into space. Inez put another plate on the table and poured Billie a cup of coffee. Billie sat down so that Mama could see her eye to eye, which seemed to coax a good day out of her every now and then.

"Hey, Mama."

Mama tilted her head and looked at Billie like she was trying to place her.

"Aida, Billie come to see you this morning. Ain't that nice?" Inez said as she sat down. "Billie, you know that nurse lady quit your mama again," she said under her breath as she shoveled some eggs into Mama's mouth and smiled at her like the two of them were in a breakfast food commercial.

"I know, Inez."

"I say good riddance; the fool woman couldn't change a diaper. I've been changing diapers since before I was born and just because they're bigger, don't make it no different. At least this one didn't try to rob your mama blind like them others." She took a spoon full of grits and held them to Mama's lips, waiting patiently until they opened, then praised Mama like she'd just won a big prize. "I'll stay till you get somebody. You know I don't mind."

"Thanks, Inez. I've just had a lot going on and—"

"Who are you?" Mama's sounded like she had a mouthful of marbles.

Alzheimer's was cruel, but not half as bad as hope that refused to die. As smart as Billie was, as honest as she was with herself that Mama's illness was progressing to a bitter end, Billie still got sucked in by the before moments. Those seconds before Mama didn't know Billie's face, those seconds waiting, hoping that today Mama would remember herself, reverse course, and come back to Billie.

"It's me, Mama, Billie," the words caught in her throat. "Your youngest. How are you doing this morning?"

"I had snakes in my bed last night. Everywhere. Copperheads, rattlesnakes, too."

"Ain't no more snakes," Inez said. "Aida. I seen to that. Remember?"

Mama nodded blankly.

"I had a dream about a snake last night too," Inez said under her breath to Billie.

Just the word snake sent Mama into a panic because her older brother used to kill them and coil them in her bed so that when she pulled back the covers, she'd scream. But there was no reaction to the word, just the hollow sound of Mama breathing.

"Good or bad?" Billie asked.

"Oh, it was good alright," Inez began and then lowered her voice. "A great big copperhead was just a rubbing himself across the cornerstone of this very house. I watched him writhe around with your mama and she wasn't afraid one bit cause she knew what it meant."

Billie didn't want to get sucked into Inez's optimism; it hurt too much. Still she couldn't deny that tiny part of her brain that was throwing a party over the minuscule possibility that a snake dream might mean a cure for her mother. "So what does it mean?" Inez paused for effect, like she was holding the keys to save the world or at the very least, Billie's world. "It means there's a healing coming, and to this house too. That big fat copperhead, all poisonous shedding his skin means protection from sickness, like the Alzheimer's. It means there's a cure out there for your mama, and I'm going to stay here while you go out and hunt for it."

Yeah, Billie thought, I'll put that on the list, right after I find a cure for lovesick teenage moms. Better to change the subject. "Inez, do you remember Sadie Byrd?"

Mama jumped when Inez slammed her fork down and looked at Billie like she was crazy for asking such a question. She reached across the small dinette table and fed Mama another spoonful of grits.

"Folks don't talk about such things, especially *Crazy Sadie*. Selling her own flesh and blood like she did. Good God."

"I don't think she was ever crazy Inez, but who wouldn't be after all she went through?"

"I don't care what you got wrong with you, there ain't no excuse for what she did, letting that husband of hers breed her like an old sow."

"I'm working on a case that involves her."

"Good," Inez bit out. "Hope you put that woman under the jailhouse."

"Folks stayed out of other folks' business back then. Nobody called the law for a lot of things that were wrong. But my case isn't about that."

"Well, it ought to be. I heard they tried to put her away after Judge Norris's little girl died, but she ran away. I know for a fact she was a baby seller; wouldn't put it past her to be a murderer, too."

"I've seen a lot of women like Sadie Byrd over the years."

"Baby sellers?"

"No, Inez. Battered women."

"I never once saw a mark on that woman. Just a big old belly that was there one day and the next day it wasn't and with no baby to show for it. Her? Battered? That's a bunch of hooey."

"A man doesn't always have to raise a hand to a woman to beat her. I believe Mrs. Byrd didn't have a say in what happened to her back then. She was a victim."

"Victim my ass. I say use the backbone God gave every single one of us. That's what I say."

It would be nice if it were that easy. Billie picked at a biscuit that was out of this world, especially with the honey butter Inez had made. She tried to chat with Mama, but their one-sided conversations were always an affirmation that Mama would never come back to her.

Billie looked at her watch. Miss Sadie would be getting up soon. "I've got to get going." She kissed Mama on the cheek. "I'll make a couple of calls about a nurse, Inez, and, maybe, you know—a place—"

"You hush this minute! When your mama was taking care of your daddy, and him so sick in that hospice, I'll never forget her looking me straight in the eyes and saying she never wanted to go to a home. Those homes are worse than that old ramshackled place that baby seller lived in, and you know what that place was like."

Billie shook her head like she didn't, but that was a lie.

The whole thing had been Jimmy Malden's idea. She didn't like it but didn't say anything because the Wild Boys had just started letting her hang out with them. Besides, Pee Wee Jackson said it would be an adventure, maybe their best one yet.

They met at the Esso station that morning. It was cold, but like most Lowcountry children, all of them were still barefooted, except Billie. Mama had forced her to wear the stupid-looking saddle oxfords that were really corrective shoes in disguise. Mama didn't care that they were ugly and were one size too big so Billie wouldn't grow out of them in five minutes.

The shoes had rubbed nickel-sized blisters on the backs of her heels, and Billie hated those shoes almost as much as she hated hearing Mama and Daddy arguing over how much they cost.

Jimmy Malden was still the leader of the Wild Boys, but even then Billie's daring threatened him. He made a big deal about her wearing the black-and-white shoes and stomped on her left shoe to make sure the white part Mama had polished that morning wasn't white anymore. "Stupid girl," he'd said. She raked her left foot over the other shiny two-toned shoe and gave him the finger. There'd be hell to pay when Mama saw them, but it was worth it to see the other boys rolling around on the ground laughing.

Nobody gave Jimmy Malden the finger. He pushed his chest into Billie's breathing hard, his forehead pressed against hers as he growled at her. "Fucking girl."

The world stopped. While the Wild Boys were guilty of a multitude of sins, including an occasional damn or shit, nobody had ever uttered the f-word. Billie felt her nose sting and her eyes fill with tears. If they saw her cry, she was dead. She reared her head back and spat in Jimmy's face and then pushed him into next week. "Fucking boy," she said, and started off toward the shack. "Come on, boys."

Her heart beat fast and her head buzzed with adrenaline when they actually followed her. She might go to hell for swearing back at Jimmy, but she felt powerful stomping down the path, until she reached the shack.

It was made out of scraps of wood with a flat roof made out of an old metal sign she'd remembered seeing on the side of a barn near the highway on the way to Charleston. Tin can lids dotted the side of the house and glimmered in the sunlight, holding adjoining boards together. Binkie Wilson was the first to notice the smell; he pinched his nose, laughing so hard he could barely point to the turds around the house. "They ain't got no sense," he howled. "Shitting where they live."

"Can't go far from the house at night. Might get bit by a copperhead," Jim Burns said quietly, like he was talking to himself.

Power swirled around Billie like dirty water sucked hard down the drain. Her face was flush. Her nose stung hard, threatening to release unshed tears. She narrowed her eyes, hoping the boys would mistake her weakness for meanness. Everybody, even Jimmy, sucked in their breath when Billie pushed against the plywood door.

She stepped into the one room shack; the others followed, nobody saying a word.

"Look, y'all." Slick Johnson broke the silence, laughing out loud. They got no floor. It's dirt." He picked up a handful of sand and let it sift through the air.

Billie kicked an empty tin. Even on the dirt floor it seemed to make a deafening sound.

"Jesus, Billie," Slick Johnson said. "You gonna wake the dead."

"There's nobody here," she said, poking around in a small basket on a wobbly old table in the center of the room. A thimble, thread, a lock of hair. Wade Hopkins picked up some reddish brown–colored strips of cloth and put them on his head so that they hung down his back and the sides of his face like long hair. Jimmy picked up a wad and did the same.

"Those are her rags." Billie tried to give Jimmy a smug look, but her insides were screaming—Stop. Don't do this. Leave. "As in on the rag."

Wade threw the rags in the dirt and looked like he was going to puke. Jimmy did the same, only he looked like he was going to kill Billie.

In the bottom of the basket was an old photograph of a stone-faced woman and a little girl, maybe five or six years old with straight blonde hair much like Billie's. Their clothes were old-timey and fancy, the little girl smiling and holding a ball up like she was offering it to the photographer. Someone had written in fancy cursive writing on the back of the photo—me and Mama before Daddy passed.

"What you got there?" Jimmy snatched the photo away from Billie and pushed her down hard. "A pretty picture?"

"Give it back, Jimmy," she spat.

Jimmy's grin was sickening. "Sit on her if you have to, Slick. Don't let her up."

Two boys sat on top of Billie. "Give it back. Give it back." She hated the desperation in her voice, but there was something in Jimmy's eyes that was wild and dark and frightening.

God and everybody feared Dewy Byrd, but Billie wished hard that he would burst through the door and shoo them all away. And if that couldn't happen, she prayed Miss Sadie was still on her bench in the park with her tattered baby doll, and that she wouldn't walk in on them.

Jimmy took out his pecker.

It wasn't the first time Billie had seen one; the boys peed whenever they had a mind to, except when other girls were about. Jimmy threw the picture on the dirt floor.

"No," she screamed and turned her head away. At Jimmy's command, Slick Johnson wrenched her face toward the photo. Her cheek pressed hard into the fine dirt floor. She refused to watch Jimmy and strained to look at the newspaper layered thick on the walls to keep the cold out, the rags that were stuffed into knot holes in the wall to do the same.

The lamps scattered about the one-room shack gave off the faint scent of kerosene that was all but overpowered by the smell of earth and rancid fat. She wanted to puke as spatterings of piss dotted her face.

After Jimmy had peed a river on the ruined photo, he waved his pecker in triumph before tucking it back in his pants. "You're no Wild Boy," he said, and left Sadie Byrd's shack with the other boys trailing behind him.

"*Billie Sue Warren.*" The vinegar in Inez's voice brought Billie back to the present. "I'm telling you right now on a stack of Bibles, as long as I can draw breath, your mama will stay right here."

Billie shook her head. "She needs to go a memory care place, Inez."

Billie saw the old woman's bottom lip quiver and then stiffen with resolve. "She *ain't* going."

"We'll talk about this later," Billie said to Inez, then kissed the top of her mother's head. "Bye Mama."

"Good woman," Mama's reply was whispery and garbled, but plain as day. "Sadie Byrd."

CHAPTER FOUR

The old AM radio in the truck only picked up two stations clearly, an all sports station out of Charleston and a little country station somewhere between Charleston and Kiawah Island that began most mornings with a on-air swap meet.

A welder, who sounded half-drunk, called in offering his wife's Kitchen Aid mixer he bought at Sears two Christmases ago. According to him, he paid over $300 for it but was willing to let it go to the highest bidder. Better yet, he would swap it for a bumper for the '67 Mustang he and his brother were restoring.

When the morning guy at the radio station asked the man if his wife knew he was selling the mixer, he said nobody ever used it, that it just sat on the counter with the cover on it that matched their kitchen wallpaper. Hell, if he could get that bumper, and it was in real good shape, he would be happy to throw in the cover for free.

Billie was back home and never knew if the guy got any takers on the mixer. Better to occupy her thoughts with mindless stuff like a swap meet on the radio than dwell on Mama's statement about Sadie Byrd.

Many times over the past eighteen months, Billie had been sucked in by Mama's moments of semi-clarity; it was a cruel game, and Alzheimer's always had the upper hand. When those moments came, Mama usually came halfway out of the fog to remind her brother not to plant the sweet potato shoots too deep, or to ask Billie how her day at school went.

What was it about Sadie Byrd that brought Mama into the here and now? Even if was only for a few seconds.

She shook the thought out of her head and turned her attention to the knee-high grass in the backyard that was bent low in the spot Tyson had parked his sleek black Trans Am. The car screamed "redneck" to any woman with good sense, which was another mystery. Things with Amber might have been different if Tyson Cantrell got around on a ten-speed bike or a scooter. Unless he was hitchhiking, for some reason a penniless, homeless Brad Pitt look-alike would always get the girls, even the smart ones.

Billie parked the truck beside the lawnmower sitting in the corner of the carport. It would take forever and a day to cut grass that high, and it was already hot, unusually hot for the end of October. Better take a Weed Whacker to the mess, and then rake up the thatch.

Billie's agreement with Amber had always been that Billie would take care of the yard, Amber would keep the house picked up, and the two of them would clean on Mondays, Billie's day off. But for the past six months, Amber had taken care of the baby and watched soap operas, when she wasn't living her own. Jumping in and picking up the slack was wearing on Billie. She was stretched as thin as a piece of cellophane and dreaded the breaking point that was sure to come.

Something had to give, but did she have the gumption to climb onto her own soapbox today? No. It was just easier to shut up and do the work herself. Save the lecture for later when she really needed Amber to do something. Billie had learned that little trick from Mama—put your pissing and moaning in your pocket.

Never know when it may come in handy.

Miss Sadie opened the screen door dressed in Mama's powder blue housecoat with the big iridescent buttons.

"How's your mama?" she asked, wiping her hands on a ratty old dishrag.

"She has good days and bad days. This one wasn't so bad."

Billie walked into the kitchen to see the dishes that had been piled in the sink the night before were clean and neatly stacked in the dish drain. Little Man's bottles, most likely sterilized, were turned upside down, drying on a paper towel. A cup of black coffee and two pieces of dry toast were on the kitchen table.

"Miss Sadie, you didn't have to do this."

"It was nothing."

"Trust me, it was something. Sit down and eat your breakfast, please. Can I get you something more than toast?"

"No. I straightened up the kitchen, waiting for my coffee to cool. Can't drink it hot and don't like ice coffee."

"Please, sit and eat." Billie poured herself a half-cup of the thick brew, filling it up the rest of the way with milk, before she sat down at the table.

The full weight of the present and past was suffocating, making Billie wish she could put Miss Sadie to bed the way Amber had put Little Man back in his crib. But that wasn't going to happen. Sadie Byrd had come all this way to report a murder, and that was exactly what she was going to do.

Fifteen minutes passed—Billie's threshold for waiting for anything. But instead of sitting down and starting her story, Miss Sadie picked her cup and plate up off of the table and emptied the coffee grounds into the trashcan. *Good. A kindred procrastinator.*

Miss Sadie toddled back over to the table, sat down, and smiled at Billie.

"You got a pretty grandson," she said. "Saw him before your daughter went in her room. She said to tell you she's getting ready to go out. I said out where? And she said to just tell you out because she's not talking to you. I sure am sorry for that."

"Don't be. It doesn't have anything to do with you." Billie smiled. "I was so sorry about your son."

"I was real sorry too; Cecil was so good to me. I'm glad I got to keep him."

Billie wanted to ask about the other children. How many had there been in all? After what Delores said, there was no point in asking the old woman about Cecil Byrd or her daughter, Donna. But there were things Billie had always been curious about. Had any of her children contacted her over the years? Whatever happened to her husband, Dewey Byrd? Did she ever try to get away from him?

"You know, Cecil took me to get my hair done every Friday, even after I got the blow dry cut and could do it myself. He bought for me all the time too, nice things, never second hand. Sometimes they were full price and not even on sale."

She looked up at Billie to see her reaction. Billie smiled. "He sounds like a very nice man. I know you must have been proud of him."

"Yes, and Donna was as bad as Cecil was good. She got it honest from her daddy, and that's all I'll say about that man."

Billie took a sip of the coffee that still had a bite to it, despite all the milk she had added. Even after the internal pity party she'd just thrown for herself, she was still a cop. "Do you feel like talking about why you came here last night?"

Miss Sadie looked confused. "I came here because you brought me."

"No ma'am. I mean the reason you came from Columbia to the Stanton police station."

Miss Sadie hung her head. "It sure was hard losing my babies." She kept her head down; her hands folded in her lap. "Hard. Real hard. They were all pretty, you know. Dewy said that's why they fetched such a high price—because they were pretty. Whenever I would cry and beg him not to get me in the family way, he would say sweet things like that."

Energy seemed to leave the old woman as her secrets began to seep out into the light of day. For as long as Billie could remember, she'd wanted to know those secrets. When Billie was a kid and even into her early twenties, she thought that knowing them might somehow justify the horrible thing she had done to the old woman that day in the park and in her dreams. But that morning, as Miss Sadie sat at Billie Warren's kitchen table, drinking coffee, Billie found herself not wanting to know the story as much as she didn't want to know that Mama's mind would never be right again.

"Look, you don't have to talk about this now if you don't want to."

Miss Sadie clutched one of the oversized blue buttons and pulled the housecoat tight around her. "What happened has been inside of me for so long, it seems to have a mind of its own. But if I can't say what happened and make it right, I won't see the face of Jesus. Won't ever see my boy again."

The baby laughed in the nursery, charming his mama while she primped. Miss Sadie heard the baby; there was a little spark in her sad eyes.

"If anybody's going to see Jesus, it will be you," Billie said. "Maybe you just need a little more time, and I really need to cut the grass before it gets any hotter. Tell you what, I'll put Mama's shower seat in the tub, rinse out your clothes, and throw them in the dryer. A bath will do you a world of good. You'll see."

"I always knew you were one of the good ones."

The words struck Billie in a funny way. She could almost hear her brother John back when his main goal in life was to make her cry.

You don't look anything like Mama and Daddy. They didn't want to hurt your feelings, but I'll tell you, you little shit. Crazy Sadie is your real mama.

Billie shook the memory out of her head. "I have to cut the grass now."

"You be careful out there. I can't remember an October as hot as this."

Billie nodded blankly. Studying Sadie Byrd's face, she couldn't find anything in it that resembled her own. But the eyes were the same. Piercing blue eyes.

CHAPTER FIVE

Billie set the good towels out in the bathroom and started the shower before leaving Miss Sadie to her bath. Her clothes from the night before were folded on top of a mountain of dirty laundry in Amber's room. A navy mid-calve A-line skirt with a matching cable knit sweater by Liz Claiborne, and a white silky blouse, also by Liz. A pair of thick support stockings was neatly stuffed into Miss Sadie's burgundy Aigner flats.

She rinsed the blouse and stockings out in the laundry room sink and tossed the skirt and sweater into the washer before she went out to cut the small front yard whether it needed it or not.

Amber had dubbed the grass mullet grass because Billie always kept the front short so the neighbors wouldn't complain and let the back grow too tall.

The mower buzzed easily across the front lawn. By the time she blew off the driveway, the washer had stopped. Amber was in the kitchen making brunch for herself, still not speaking. Little Man was flat on his back, playing with the overhead gym that on good days kept him entertained for hours.

Billie poured herself a glass of tea and looked at her grandson, who had grabbed the elusive gold plastic ring that dangled in front of him. "Good boy," she said. Little Man turned his head toward the sound of her voice and squealed with excitement when he caught sight of her. "Sorry, buddy, can't play right now."

She checked the labels on Miss Sadie's garments. Tumble dry. Low. There was another tag she'd missed earlier, sewn awkwardly into the collar of the blouse with Miss Sadie's name and phone number. Maybe Cecil had done that in case his mother went to the Piggly Wiggly for milk and ended up in West Virginia, but Miss Sadie seemed reasonably sharp for her age. Maybe Cecil had anticipated what Billie couldn't even bear to think about. She pushed the thought away and hauled the mower into the backyard.

She yanked the pull cord, sending a cloud of thick oily smoke into the air. The mower didn't make it two feet before it choked down in the tall grass. There was no choice except to get the weed eater and whack the Bahia until the mower could handle what was left.

About an hour into the job, Billie noticed a watery glass of sweet tea sitting on the deck and hoped it was a peace offering from Amber. Billie chugged it down, then wiped her eyes with the T-shirt she shed when she began the backyard. She looked good in her cutoffs and sports bra, tanned, lean. She wasn't the kind of woman to trot around town like that, but she was the kind of woman who liked to sweat, to work hard.

The October sun felt more like the hottest day in July and was giving her all she could take as she bagged up the last of the grass. Miss Sadie was standing at the kitchen window, looking out at her, smiling. Billie flashed a thin smile back as she threw the bags into the wheelbarrow to cart out to the curb. There was nothing left to do except put the mower and the weed eater away and go inside to hear Sadie Byrd's story.

"You work too hard," Miss Sadie said as Billie pushed through the door.

Before she could reply, Amber made her grand entrance into the kitchen dressed in jeans and a new halter-top.

"Where are you headed?" Billie asked.

Amber shot Billie a look. With the grace of a seasoned stripper in skin tight low cut jeans, she bent slowly at the waist to scoop Little Man's favorite rattle off the floor and made sure that if her hot pink halter didn't scream she was going to bed Tyson Cantrell, her matching lace thong did.

"Amber?"

She plopped Little Man onto her hip. He crawled around to her middle like a human shield and laid his head against her shoulder. "I'm going to Walmart for diapers; I'll be back whenever."

This was the part of their conversations where Billie usually told Amber what to do. *Stay away from Tyson. Fill out your SAT application. Get a job.* Amber waited for a beat or two and seemed a little addled that Billie didn't hold up to her part of the unspoken bargain they'd struck, to snipe at each other until one of them ended the standoff with a painful jab.

"Whatever," Amber hissed on her way out the door.

Billie watched her storm toward her car, the baby bouncing wildly on her hip. When she turned around, there were two plates on the small kitchen dinette and two glasses of tea. On top of cleaning up the kitchen, Miss Sadie had foraged around in the refrigerator while Billie slaved in the backyard and made chicken salad out of leftover rotisserie chicken.

After everything that had happened that morning, topped off with a healthy dose of teenage drama, the last thing Billie wanted was to hear Miss Sadie's story. So she said she was too dirty to sit at the table. It was true, but stalling couldn't last forever.

The shower felt good as the water washed away the fine gray sand caked on her body. She scrubbed and scrubbed, then scrubbed some more like there was such a thing as a clean slate then bowed her head in surrender. The water streamed down her body, but would never wash her clean. The pressure in her chest pulsed in time with the stinging in her face, especially her nose, around her eyes.

The last time she needed the release that only comes from sloppy, uncontrollable sobbing, she had just let Cole go. She needed that same release now, but what was point? Tears never changed anything. By the time Billie was dressed and at the table, Miss Sadie had eaten and looked better than she had earlier.

Billie wasn't hungry, but, with Miss Sadie watching her, she ate the sandwich anyway. "Thank you. That was delicious."

"You're welcome." Miss Sadie took Billie's empty plate and put it in the sink. "Your grandson is so sweet."

"Yes ma'am, he is. His mother is a different story"

"She seems nice enough."

"Don't get me wrong; Amber's a good girl, and I love her to bits. It's just that she still wants to act like a teenager, but, with the baby, she doesn't have that luxury."

"A baby changes everything." Miss Sadie ran some water in the dishpan.

"Yes ma'am." Billie started to get up from the table. "You made lunch. I'll straighten up the kitchen."

"Sit down and rest now. I was worried about you out there in that hot sun, working like a man."

A few minutes later, Miss Sadie put the last dish in the drain to dry and sat down at the table. "I think I can do this now."

Billie knew there wouldn't be any need for a notebook; she would remember every word Sadie Byrd said. But procedure said to write down the report, document the story. Did procedure apply if you're off the clock? Billie reminded herself that she was still a cop and tipped her chair back on two legs until she could just reach the note pad she kept by the phone.

"You're going to topple over, Billie Warren."

Billie snagged a pen along with the pad as she set the chair down on all fours. She tore an old grocery list off and wadded the paper into a ball. The next page was a list of people who had called at some point. Amber wrote down their names, the times they called, but no date. The last message was in all caps—COLE 11:15 THURSDAY NIGHT, which Thursday night was anybody's guess.

"You know there's a warrant for your arrest?" Billie asked, and Miss Sadie nodded. "Why did you come back to Stanton?"

"To make things right. If I don't, I'll never see my boy again."

"Tell me about the murder."

"I need to start at the beginning. If I don't, you won't believe me any more than the law would have believed me so long ago."

"Then start at the beginning."

She nodded and swallowed hard. "We were living in a lean-to Dew made from things he found at the dump. It was covered with a tarpaulin a man gave us because he felt sorry for us. We didn't have any money. Dew sharecropped a little, wouldn't let me work. He didn't do much working either, at least not enough to make crop rent so we could live in a real house.

"A woman saw us in town one day. She said her name was Gert Nightingale, like that nurse that helped people. She saw I was in the family way and said she wanted to help us, bought us some food, even bought us each a pair of shoes. She said it was a crying shame to bring a tiny baby into the world, living like we did. I didn't like her, but I was glad for the shoes and the food. She went on about how young I was, how I had my whole life ahead of me. Dew didn't seem to hear a word she said until she said she could give us cash money for the baby.

"'How much?' Dew pipes up." Miss Sadie stopped and shook her head. "I told that woman I'd spit in her eye before I'd give my baby away. At first she looked like she was going to backhand me for sassing her, then the edges of her face got as soft as her voice. I can hear her in my head as good as she was standing here now, cooing, 'Sadie, just look at yourself. Half starved, didn't even own a pair of shoes except for the ones I put on your feet. Is this the kind of life you want for your baby?'"

Miss Sadie looked up for a reaction. Billie put her best cop face on and was grateful Miss Sadie couldn't hear the voices inside Billie's head. Her and Amber arguing over Amber having an abortion, the huge blow out over giving Little Man up for adoption. The fact that Billie had begged Amber to do away with Little Man or give him up sickened her. But hadn't she had that same argument with herself just after she and Paul had married and she realized what a huge mistake she'd made? Billie shook the thought out of her head and continued. "I know this is hard."

Miss Sadie swiped at her eyes with a crumpled tissue. "Dew saw how that woman planted the seed that I couldn't be a good mama, living like we did, and he worked it. Deep down, I knew I didn't have a choice; he would make me give up my baby.

"I remember the exact minute I decided I would do it. It was pouring down rain and cold and us with nothing but that makeshift tent. I was so big, having to make water all the time. Dew wouldn't let me go in the pot; he made me go away from the lean-to. I was squatting with the rain pouring down, my teeth bumping together. I was so wet and cold. I felt my baby stir. I stared at that mess of brush and boards Dew called home. Right then and there I decided that woman was right, my baby deserved better."

Billie nodded but couldn't look up from her notes. "So, you sold your baby."

"I told Dew I didn't want the money and didn't want any trouble with the law. He said there was nothing to worry about. He called that lady who bought us the shoes. Collect. She said a lawyer named Mac Dalton would do it all legal and give my baby to a rich lady who couldn't have any. 'We can have another baby when the time is right,' he'd said. I gave my baby girl up so she could have a better life. But the second they paid Dewy Byrd three hundred dollars for my firstborn, that was the beginning."

Billie knew the answer, before she asked. "Did you ever try to get away from him? Try to ask for help?"

"No. I was too afraid of Dew, and after he sold my first baby and then the next—there was no point. I heard what folks in town said about me, sometimes to my face. I was too ashamed to ask for help. Looking back, I believe there were those who would've helped me, but most of them wouldn't even look my way. Your mama was different, always good to me."

There were a lot of things Billie could believe about Miss Sadie's story, but that was not one of them. She'd never seen her mother with Sadie Byrd, never even heard Mama speak of her unless it was to dispel some rumor Billie or John had heard. But after what Mama had said this morning? Maybe Miss Sadie was sick like Mama. Maybe the whole thing about knowing who killed Caroline Norris was made up. But somebody had killed the little girl forty years ago. The question was who.

"What was your connection to Caroline Norris?" Billie asked.

"She was the spitting image of me. She was mine."

"How many of your babies stayed in Stanton?"

"Dew said none, but I know that wasn't so. That little Lawson baby looked exactly like Dew, and those Webber girls were mine too, I'm sure of it."

Billie scribbled Joey Lawson's and the Webber twins' names on the page but didn't have the heart to tell Miss Sadie that even today, almost forty years after his death, Joey Lawson was a cautionary tale. Just days before his third birthday he'd drowned in barely two inches of water when his mother left him in the bathtub to answer the phone.

The Webber girls' story was equally as tragic. They'd graduated top of their class and were courted by colleges all over the country until they'd said yes to Duke University. They were the pride and joy of Stanton until they partied too hard the night they graduated from high school and plowed their daddy's new Cadillac into a tree.

"Those twins had small hands and big feet. They had my eyes." Bitterness cut into the sadness in Miss Sadie's voice. "It tore my heart in two when folks around here would show off my babies like the stork brought them. They never heard the whispers, folks saying, 'bet that's one of Crazy Sadie's babies,' but I did."

"People are stupid and cruel." Billie included herself in that estimate.

"What was worse, sometimes it seemed that every baby I saw was mine."

There was a long silence. Miss Sadie drew in several deep breaths. Her head hung low. She was trembling. Billie was, too.

"Caroline was mine, but even if she wasn't, I would have helped her, especially after I saw what he was doing to her."

The old woman's words tailed off into a pitiful whine before she broke down. After all she had been through, it didn't seem right to Billie to soothe her just to make the crying stop. But Billie was losing her objectivity fast. Every sad word from Miss Sadie ratcheted Billie's chest a little tighter until she could barely breathe; her heart pounded in her ears like a washing machine off kilter. She steadied her hand and wrote down a bunch of gibberish, to buy time, to separate herself from Miss Sadie's story. But the story was like a baby coming fast and hard whether the world was ready for it or not.

"I was walking through the woods on the way from town when I found that precious little girl crying so hard she could barely dress herself. She made pitiful little sounds, trying to hold the crying inside. But she couldn't stop anymore than she could stop what that man was doing to her."

"You saw the man who assaulted her?"

"Not that day. He was gone, and she was alone. She never had to say exactly what was done to her. I knew just by looking at her. I asked her to let me help her, but she said that if she told, all the Norrises would go straight to hell, and it would be her fault." Miss Sadie wrung her trembling hands and then raised her eyes to meet Billie's. "She asked me to help her die."

"Did you?"

Billie's words stung Miss Sadie hard; she shook her head and squeezed her eyes shut. "Kill a child? I told her I could never do that. But she wouldn't take no for an answer. She put her hands on my shoulders, pressed her forehead against mine and begged me to help her die. 'We can go away' I told her, and I meant it. 'Just you and me and the baby.'"

"You were pregnant?"

Miss Sadie nodded, "With Donna." Her lips sputtered, trying to choke back the sob as she held her hands way out beyond her belly. She'd been big at the time of the murder, probably near term.

"And you and Caroline were going to leave?"

She wrapped her arms around herself and rocked back and forth slowly. "Dew always strung me along, telling me, 'You straighten up and fly right, and you can keep the next one.' But he never let me keep my babies. I knew it wouldn't be any different with that one. I figured if me and Caroline could run away, I'd save her and keep my baby, too.

"When I said we could run away, she stopped crying. I know enough about what hope looks like to know I saw it in her eyes. I wanted to go right then, but she said we couldn't since it was almost suppertime. She said if she wasn't there, we wouldn't get far. 'If we're going to get away from him for good, we need money or it'll never work.'"

"Did she say who that was?"

Miss Sadie shook her head. "No and I didn't ask. She just said for me to meet her in that very spot the next day before the sun went down, that she'd be back with her things and enough money for us to go far away forever. I didn't believe a word I said to her about us running away; I was just trying to keep her alive. But then I got hopeful. With her having money, it might just work. Without it, as big as I was, we wouldn't have gotten far.

"I told her if we walked to the main highway somebody was bound to pick us up. We were going to ask them to drop us off in the next town where we could get on a bus."

"Where were you going?" Billie asked.

"We didn't care. We were just trying to get away."

"Okay, you made contact with Caroline, you had a plan to save her. Can you talk about the murder now? Where did it happen?"

"In those woods. Near Clauson's Creek." She pointed to the glass patio door that overlooked Billie's backyard that was flanked by pastureland and a five-thousand-acre hunting preserve. The Norris family had owned the land since before there were such things as plantations. Amber grew up playing in those woods; Billie had too.

She tried to steady her hand as she scratched some notes about Miss Sadie's demeanor, body trembling, eyes downcast, voice quivering.

"Caroline met me around six o'clock, just like she said she would, with a little piece of grip. She was dressed up pretty in a little yellow frock, smocked across the top with pink roses, and white patent leather shoes with lacy socks. She looked so pretty. As happy as I was that we were running away, it made me sad to know I'd never be able to give her anything like that.

"Then we heard footsteps coming hard toward us through the woods; he was calling her name. She threw the suitcase in the bushes. 'I'm going to run,' she whispered, 'When he gives up looking for me, I'll come back for you.' I said, 'No, Caroline, we'll fight him together.' She was so brave but so afraid. She grabbed my shoulders like she did the day before and pressed her forehead against mine so that all I could see was her blue eyes, my eyes. 'You can't run with the baby. Hide. Now. It's our only hope.'"

"Where did you hide?"

"She pushed me toward the grip and took off. I hid in a thicket of mostly blackberry bushes. I was all scratched up, heart beating so hard I could feel it pounding in my brain. All at once, my legs went wet. The labor started, but my head hurt so bad, everything went blurry." Miss Sadie wiped her nose with a ragged tissue and continued. "But I felt him hurry past me, so close, I could have reached out and touched him."

"Did you get a good look at his face?"

She shook her head. "Not with my head pounding. Not until later.

"He called her name all sing-songy. Like they were playing a game. I could hear him talking but couldn't make out what he was saying. He never raised his voice, but, when he found her, she did. She sassed him. I prayed she'd just hush and think on us getting away instead of what he was going to do to her. But I reckon she'd had all she was going to take.

"I heard him slap her hard, maybe across the face. The way she whimpered, I knew he'd taken the fight out of her. She was still crying. His belt buckle jangled. She cried harder. Begged him no, please no. Then he was making animal sounds.

"I didn't think about staying hidden or getting away. I just wanted to save her. He must have been too worked up to hear me struggling. When I got to my knees, he screamed. Cursed her for biting him and hit her. With every blow he delivered to Caroline, the pain in my head got worse, and I knew he wasn't trying to take the fight out of her, he was going to kill her.

"Another contraction laid into me. I tried to scream but nothing came out." Miss Sadie shuddered and wrapped her arms around her middle. "The pain from the baby mixed with the pain in my head made me pass out. When I came to, Caroline was dressed in that pretty little dress again, and the judge was carrying her out of the woods like he was going to put her to bed and tell her a story, except he was covered in her blood."

"He never saw you?"

Miss Sadie shook her head.

Billie remembered she was in church the day Judge Norris offered a hundred thousand dollar reward for information leading to the capture of the murderer. The preacher held the judge up as an example of a man willing to give up his kingdom for justice. Could the judge really have been arrogant enough to kill Caroline and put on such a performance?

"What did you do then?" Billie asked.

"My labor was so bad, I barely made it home to have the baby. Dew was cleaning Donna up when I told him about what I saw. He said it wasn't right what was done, but it wasn't right for me to fret over the girl. Then he did something he'd never done, he put my baby in my arms, and then he left out in a hurry.

"She was still in my arms when he came back just after midnight with a wad of cash money. He said we had to run because the law thought he killed that sweet little girl and that I helped. I told him I didn't do anything wrong, that Caroline was going to be buried here and I wasn't going anywhere.

"Then he said it like the snake in the garden. He said, 'If you go, without a fuss, I swear you can keep this one.' I don't remember leaving Stanton or who drove us out of town. It was like Dew snatched me and the baby up roots and all and the next thing I knew we were in a different place."

"Columbia?" Miss Sadie nodded, but her answer puzzled Billie. If Billie was on the run from Stanton, she wouldn't stop at a hundred miles.

"The hole in my heart from that day was so big, but my baby needed me. Dew must have felt real bad about what happened with Caroline because after I got in the family way with Cecil, he let me keep him, too.

"I don't know anything else." She looked up from the tissues in her lap and cupped her hand over Billie's. "Can you tell me what happened after I left Stanton? *Was* Caroline buried good and proper?"

Billie was only nine when Caroline Norris was buried; before that, she didn't really believe a kid could actually die. She'd heard the rumors about how badly the little girl had been beaten. She'd asked her mother if they were true. Mama gave her standard answer for such things: "Don't believe everything you hear." But Daddy was on the Stanton police force back then. She overheard Mama ask the same question of him and then saw her bury her face on his shoulder when he told her the rumors weren't half as bad as the truth.

"Please. Tell me," Miss Sadie said softly, "I want to know."

Billie looked into Miss Sadie's sad blue eyes. She wanted to tell her about the reward, that if the judge killed his daughter, he'd offered a hundred thousand dollars for his own head. But the truth was too cruel.

CHAPTER SIX

Billie found herself split down the middle again, like she had been so many times lately. Anybody else would have listened to Sadie Byrd's story, patted her on the back, and told her not to worry about a murder that happened forty years ago. If Jimmy Malden were chief, he probably would have taken money out of his own pocket and sent her back to Columbia to die, believing justice would be served. And what would anybody else do with a case that would demolish the reputation of the nearly dead and almost sainted Judge Harold Norris? Nothing. Jack Shit.

Maybe it had something to do with Billie being a woman or a mother. Maybe it had something to do with her always feeling like she was responsible for Mama, for Amber and the baby. For those sad little children with the saucer-sized brown eyes in third world countries who panhandle on the television at three o'clock in the morning. Billie Warren was responsible all right, too damn responsible. *Kramer vs. Kramer*? Who was she kidding? She was never Meryl Streep. She had always been Dustin fucking Hoffman and there was nothing she could do about it.

"I should have saved her." Miss Sadie's breath was quick and shallow. Her skin was ashen and cold to the touch. "I should have saved her."

"No." Billie shook her head. "No. What happened to Caroline wasn't your fault."

"There were times raising Donna that I wished I had died saving that sweet soul to make up for the one in my house that was so lost. Donna was God's wrath on me for letting Caroline die. I deserved what I got, and whatever I got coming to me, but Caroline didn't deserve to die like that."

"You came a long way to file a police report about a terrible crime, and you did that. Right now, I'm worried about your health. Do you take any medicines? Something for your heart?"

She shook her head. "Don't like pills."

Billie got up from the table and rifled through a cabinet in the kitchen until she found a blood pressure cuff. "I used this when Amber was pregnant and her blood pressure was high."

Miss Sadie already had the sleeve of her blouse pushed up. The cuff swallowed her frail arm. Billie pressed the button on the machine that hissed and buzzed as the small compressor inside filled the cuff with air. The machine didn't give a reading at all the first two tries, but on the third try the red digits on the tiny monitor flashed in warning.

"It's kind of high." Really high. Billie tried not to sound nervous. "Are you sure you don't take any medicine?"

"Just an aspirin every day, maybe a little Epsom Salt once in a while when I have trouble going to the bathroom. How bad is it?"

"One hundred forty over ninety-nine."

"It's never been that high before."

"Take a couple of aspirin and lie down while I get ready for work. I'll check your pressure again before I leave, if it's not better, I'll have to take you to an urgent care in Mt. Pleasant."

She helped Miss Sadie up from the table and guided her down the hall toward Amber's bedroom. "I'll be okay after I take a little nap, you'll see. I don't need a doctor; don't particularly like them."

"Get some rest." Billie spread the patchwork quilt Mama had made Amber for her thirteenth birthday over Miss Sadie. Miss Sadie closed her eyes and was asleep before Billie closed the door.

The kitchen clock read 2:15; she had to be at work by 3:00. There had been a handful of times in her life when Billie felt like she really needed a drink, and this was one of them. She hoped a shot of Grey Goose would settle her nerves. Hell, since old Judge Norris was accused of being the perp, maybe two.

She moved packages of boneless skinless chicken breasts and way too many Lean Cuisines around until she found the bottle tucked away in the back. There seemed to be less of it than the last time she dug the Goose out of the freezer, a lot less. She poured the thick, potent liquid into a Mickey Mouse shot glass and threw back two drinks. It didn't take long to feel light headed, a baby buzz. Mission accomplished. She heard a car drive up, stuffed the Goose back into the freezer, and peeked out the dining room window. Abby. Shit.

Abby was her best friend and, aside from Amber, the most high maintenance woman Billie knew, but she was also the kind of friend who would walk through fire for you. Fresh out of college, she'd scored big with her first book, *How to Find the Man of Your Dreams: And Get Him to the Altar*. She was broke when she'd written the book hoping to make a little money until she turned twenty-five and her trust fund kicked in.

Twenty years and eleven unpublished manuscripts later, Abby was three times divorced, still living off the money her rich daddy left her, and her out-of-print international best seller sold for seventeen cents on Amazon.

"You don't call. Hell, you don't even write." Abby opened the freezer, snagged the Goose by the neck, and poured herself a drink in the shot glass on the counter. "And I had to catch you at home before you went to work just to say 'hey.' What kind of friend are you anyway?"

"The worn out shitty kind." Billie watched her knock back the drink. "Are you driving?"

"What? Are you going to bust me? Boy you are a shitty friend. Not to mention that cops are supposed to have the best pot and you never have any. Now, tell me again why I'm still speaking to you."

"I'm just too damn busy these days, even for you. Besides, you don't do drugs."

"Maybe I should start. Seems like all the really great writers did. Maybe I'm just not messed up enough. By the way, if you're leaving early to check up on Amber, I can save you the trouble. She's sucking face in the Dairy Queen parking lot with Tyson. Little Man's passed out in the back seat. Damn, he's a cute baby. Looks just like his daddy."

Billie growled and started down the hall, stripping down to her underwear on the way to her bedroom.

"And another thing, I work out six days a week, and I don't look half as good as you. What the hell am I doing wrong?"

"Dairy Queen?" she laughed over her shoulder.

"Skinny bitch."

Billie would love to pull through the drive-thru and order everything on the Dairy Queen menu, but none of it ever tasted as good as it did when she was twenty-something, and not even close to as good as it looked in those glossy storefront pictures. She closed the bathroom door and put her uniform on.

"So, what's new, Billie Sue?"

Tyson slinked out of Amber's bed last night. Sadie Byrd walked out of the ether to name Judge Norris as his own daughter's killer. "Not much. How about you?" She pushed open the bathroom door, still tucking her shirt into her pants.

"Well, I'm writing fiction now. Turns out, real life is just too damn scary. I met a cute agent in a hotel bar; we got shit faced. He said he loved my work."

Billie gave Abby a look before she strapped on her gun. "But you have an agent."

"Had. I divorced her. I *really* like this one."

Billie put a dab of product in her palm and rubbed her hands together before she worked it through her short blond hair. She needed to get rid of Abby before Miss Sadie toddled out of Amber's bedroom. "Abby, do you love me?"

"You know I can't resist a cop with a big shiny gun."

"If you'll go by and check on Mama now, I promise I'll stop in for a drink after work tonight."

"Are you kidding? I get some of my best dialogue listening to Inez go on about *the world today.*" Abby took her car keys out of her jeans pocket and gave Billie a peck on the cheek. "Remember, you promised. See you tonight."

Billie watched Abby pull out of the driveway and then made a beeline down the hall to Miss Sadie's room. The old woman fought to keep her eyes open while Billie checked her blood pressure. One-twenty over eighty. Most likely better than Billie's.

"I'm sorry, Miss Sadie, but I have to go to work now. Amber will be in and out, just make yourself at home. I'll take you home to Columbia tomorrow."

The old woman nodded and pulled the quilt up to her chin. "Don't worry about me. I'll be all right," she said, fighting to keep her eyes open.

"My phone numbers are on the bedside table. If you need anything, call me. Okay?"

Billie went into the kitchen and scribbled a note to Amber to keep an eye on Miss Sadie and then headed out for work.

———————◆◆◆———————

Delores glanced up from the new *People* magazine. "Did she tell you?"

"God, yes, but you shouldn't have questioned her."

"All I said was 'how you doing, shug?' and she started talking. Almost peed my pants. Old Judge Norris, a murdering child molester? She *is* a crazy old bat."

"You really think she's crazy?"

"I'm sorry, evidently you and Miss Byrd must be competing for that title." Delores laughed so hard, she snorted. "Come on Billie. She *heard* a man rape and kill Caroline Norris, but didn't see his face. Then she passed out and who knows how much later she saw the judge carrying that little girl's body off?

"Sure, when she was telling her story, I was so caught up in the drama of the whole thing and thought yeah, the old judge could have done that. But after I thought about it, I considered the source. We're talking about Judge Harold freaking Norris versus the town loony."

"Former town loony," Billie added.

"And I didn't say nothing last night, but you and I both know there's an open murder warrant for Sadie Lawrence Byrd."

"I know, Delores, But I'm not convinced she had anything to do with that little girl's death."

"Didn't your daddy work that case with the old chief Malden? You of all people ought to know how crazy that notion is."

Maybe it was Billie's nine-year-old perspective, but it seemed nobody had worked the case. It was like the most horrible thing that could ever happen did, and a bunch of grown-ups just talked about finding the culprits. And when folks heard the Byrds had skipped town, they felt safe and felt their children were safe. The fact that there had never been another murder in the town since Judge Norris's daughter's cemented the notion that Dewy and Sadie Byrd were guilty as sin.

To Billie, it seemed like people wanted their lives to go back to the way they were so badly, they just forgot about Caroline Norris. But not Mama. She asked Daddy all the time and his answer was always the same, "The State Law Enforcement Division is on the case, they'll get whoever did it. Justice will come, I promise."

But they never charged anybody. Sadie Byrd and her husband moved to Columbia where the State Law Enforcement Division is based. Dewy Byrd died there. Miss Sadie raised her children right under their noses and nothing happened.

"Daddy didn't work the case. The state took it over."

"Nothing new there."

"But it just doesn't wash. With the judge involved, the case should have been a priority." Billie thumbed through the mail on the desk and opened a complaint against a neighbor's barking dog. "So, you don't believe any of what she said is possible?"

"I don't think it much matters if I believe her. The question is, do you, and if you do, what are you going to do about it?"

"I don't know, Delores."

"Honey, this is big, real big. Most folks think the judge is right up there with God and Jesus. Besides, Miss Sadie's so old and frail, she'd never hold up through a circus trial."

Billie stretched her small slender frame and yawned. It was just after 3:00 and time to head out. "Serious shit wears me out. Wish I could take a nap."

"I thought that was what you cops do out there on patrol," Delores snorted. "You be careful now."

Delores always said that, but as Billie started up the cruiser and pulled out of the parking lot, the words didn't sit well. Stanton wasn't a dangerous place. The only danger she ever faced was from domestic disputes and she knew when those flared up. Saturday nights were always interesting. Couples fighting over money usually acted up the first and last part of the month. Assholes like Melvin Gifford were less predictable.

Penny Gifford. *Shit.* She punched in the number of the county jail; a woman with a redneck twang answered the phone.

"Can't give out any information on the prisoner; you'll have to come by during visiting hours like the rest of the world."

Billie blew out a breath. "Put Jake Ross on the phone."

"Look now," the woman stammered. "I'm just saying what they tell me to. You want to talk to the boss man? All right then."

"Penny's fine," Jake said. "Checked on her myself a few minutes ago. Ol' Melvin must have missed having somebody to knock around. He came up here trying to bail her out so she could make him breakfast. We told him to go to Hardee's and get a biscuit, that she was going to be here for a while."

"Asshole."

"Penny knew you'd call, said to tell you not to worry; she's okay."

"If she needs anything, just call me or Delores."

"I'll do it," Jake said. "Between you and me, I wish she hadn't missed her mark. With all that's been done to her, she'd have gotten off easy."

"Me, too, Jake," Billie said and ended the call.

She continued driving until she came to the pasture the judge had cleared for cattle forty years ago. She pulled the patrol car onto the shoulder, got out, and walked over to the fence that overlooked the crime scene. The land on this part of the Norris property was stripped bare of trees, roots and all, and didn't resemble the thick woods Billie remembered as a child. While the cattle were long gone, somebody still tended to the pasture so that it looked like a picture out of a coffee table book.

Billie tried not to think about how strikingly beautiful the place was. It was a crime scene wiped clean. Something horrible had happened here. Caroline Norris. Pretty. Blonde. Dead.

Now that Billie knew Sadie Byrd's story, she understood why Miss Sadie wandered the park with that battered old baby doll. If living with Dewey Byrd hadn't pushed her over the edge when she lived in Stanton, hearing her little girl beaten to death had. And what about the judge? It was no secret the roots of the good ol' boy hierarchy ran deeper than kudzu in the state of South Carolina when Caroline Norris died. Today wasn't much different.

A high profile case like Caroline's wouldn't have stopped at bringing in the State Law Enforcement Division; the judge had enough pull to even have the feds weigh in, but the case went nowhere. Why?

Billie drew in a deep breath and let it out slowly. She could ask some questions, stir things up just enough to make it look like justice. Maybe that would be enough to buy Miss Sadie a little peace. But where would Billie find her own?

CHAPTER SEVEN

Billie would've been happy to cruise the town until dinnertime, rolling Miss Sadie's situation around in her mind. But after Patti Dawson's minivan passed a stopped school bus Billie had no choice but to pull her over. Patti claimed she had forgotten her preteenage daughter, Danielle, had an orthodontist appointment and she was trying to make up for lost time. If she hadn't nearly hit the little Bledsoe girl, Billie might have let Patti slide, even though folks ignoring a bright yellow school bus with flashing strobe lights and a big protruding STOP sign was one of her pet peeves.

"You *know* me," Patti began, like most everybody did when they were trying to get out of a ticket. She looked at her watch and then checked the appointment card in her hand. "God damn it; now we're gonna be late."

"Mama!"

"Well, I'm sorry Danielle."

"You're a Sunday school teacher."

Billie decided to cut Patti some slack and not take the time to run the plates. She filled out the ticket as quick as she could, because poor Danielle was clearly horrified over her mother's behavior. Billie handed her the pad and showed her where to sign the ticket.

"I want you to know, the orthodontist is going to charge me $45 for missing this appointment." Patti was steaming as she scratched her name on the pad. "Holy, Lord Jesus, this is going to cost me $300 *and six points?*"

Billie signed the ticket and tore off the top copy. "Go to court next month on the sixteenth. The magistrate will probably knock it down to three points, but you'll still have to pay the fine. You're pretty lucky that little Bledsoe girl is so fast. You didn't miss her by much."

Patti gave Billie her most Christian go-to-hell look and snatched the ticket out of her hand.

"I'm not going to pay this," Patti sniffed. "To hell with you; I'll call Uncle Harold."

Patti jammed her finger into the button and rolled up the electric window. She took off without signaling to get back on to the road and exceeded the 25 MPH speed limit. Add all of that to the annoyance that came from Patti threatening to call Judge Norris and Billie had had all the justification she needed to stop her again. But then she thought about Danielle, sitting there in the passenger seat with her AWANNA vest on, full of pins like a Girl Scouts' sash full of badges. Only Danielle's rewards were for memorizing scripture and serving the Lord.

Billie wished she had a dollar for every time she heard somebody in Stanton say they were going to call Judge Norris to fix a ticket. Chief Malden hated to get those calls from the judge. They'd always put him in a bad mood for the rest of the day. Billie didn't like them either. Now that the judge was so old, a woman his son, Bob, hired to take care of the judge's affairs made them.

Deidre Lawson was a smart, pretty woman in her thirties. Word around town was that Deidre had been Bob's chief of staff in Washington or, as Abby loved to say, "the chief of Bob's staff." Bob's wife, Nikki, had found out about the affair and said she didn't want a divorce, but she demanded Bob fire Deidre. Knowing that Nikki Norris adored being a senator's wife more than anything in the whole world, Bob sent Deidre to Stanton, and Nikki stayed in Washington.

The whole town was abuzz when Deidre arrived. It was like Monica Lewinski had come to Stanton. But Deidre was smart. She dyed her long, dark hair blonde, cut it short, and stopped snapping to attention every time some Tom, Dick, or Harriet called for the judge to get them out of trouble. If Patti called the judge, Deidre Lawson would probably tell her to just suck it up and pay the fine.

Billie found herself wishing that the judge himself would call so she could question him about the murder. Sure his mind was probably as sharp as Jell-O, but even if she nailed his balls to the wall for the murder of Caroline Norris, nobody was going to send a ninety-five-year-old man to jail, especially one in poor health. Especially Judge Harold Norris.

No doubt there'd be a high price to pay for calling the judge's stellar reputation into question. His senator son would make sure Billie lost her job. Bob Norris would use his influence in South Carolina and beyond to make sure Billie would never be a cop again. At her core that was who she was, and if she couldn't be a cop, who was she?

Delores's booming voice came through the radio. "In progress, a 10–56—"

Billie's heart pounded hard in her ears. She touched the gun on her belt to confirm it was still there. She would kill Tyson Cantrell if he'd dumped Amber again and would be glad she'd done it.

"That's a 10–56A." Delores's voice crackled. "Harry Bennett's at it again."

A 10–56 is police code for a suicide. When you add the "A," it's an attempt, or, in Harry's case, a mild threat.

Billie let out a huge sigh of relief. She wiped away tears mingled with sweat and drove straight to the quarry.

Like Billie, Harry stood there on the edge in so many ways. Also like Billie, he had a gun. But she knew him well enough to know the tension she felt in her belly was unnecessary. Her breath was long and steady, the stink from the hundred-foot-deep quarry stung her nose. When she was little, she thought the huge mud puddle was a pretty place. Sometimes it was, especially when the surface of the thick brown water reflected off a clear blue sky making the stink hole look the prettiest shade of jade. Today it was an ominous black-brown and looked every bit as bottomless as the locals swore it was.

Against the wide expanse of the quarry, Harry looked fragile, and with the exception of his shiny bald head, childlike. His back was to her. He stared down at the water, the front of his thighs pressed against the guardrail. A gun dangled from the crook of his index finger like something as harmless as a six-pack. She walked his way slowly, not eyeing the gun but completely aware of it as she took her place beside him.

His breathing was ragged and caught periodically in his throat like he'd been crying all day. She waited for him to say something, and when he didn't, she put her hand on his shoulder.

"Give me the gun, Harry." He gave a little shrug and extended his hand. It was small, nails bitten down to the quick. As he offered the butt of the loaded forty-five to Billie, his stubby fingers trembled slightly, then lingered like he might change his mind.

"Come on, Harry, that's not how it goes."

A year ago Billie could set both her calendar and her watch by Harry Bennett's pity party that commenced every Thursday at 5:45 at the deserted quarry.

"Sorry." The little man gave her a sheepish look, turned loose of the gun, and shoved his hands deep into the pockets of his well-worn khakis.

One of the advantages of policing a cracker-box-sized town is knowing people. And knowing Harry Bennett had almost made his weekly suicide charade seem harmless. Just when Billie thought about not answering Harry's calls, they'd stopped. It was good timing; Amber had just been admitted to the psych ward with a belly full of pills and a broken heart.

Whenever Billie saw Harry around town, he looked better. And it gave her hope her daughter would get better too. Still, it chilled her to the bone when she thought of that first time she'd answered the call to the quarry. Harry had stood on the edge of the forty-foot drop, his whole being so broken, so dejected Billie almost overlooked the gun in his hand. With the exception of the mark on his temple where he'd pressed the barrel, he looked docile enough and seemed glad to see her.

But it wasn't the barely visible mark on Harry's pale soft skin that kept Billie answering Harry Bennett's calls for weeks on end, it was that vacant, sad look that said Harry's little drama could go either way.

Billie let out a ragged breath, unloaded the gun, and ran through the lines they'd rehearsed since Harry's lover left town with some Irish gypsies. Fresh out of sympathy, her words came out flat and unconvincing. She was tired of playing Dr. Phil. There were people in Stanton with bigger problems than Harry Bennett, like Billie, for instance. She pushed down the words that bubbled up inside of her. *Knock off the jilted lover act, Harry. And don't call the police station again unless you're really going to pull the trigger!*

"Come on, Harry, it's been a long time."

"A year today."

Who could blame Harry for getting in touch with his inner drama queen on the anniversary of his equally homely lover running off with a gorgeous Irish gypsy?

"I thought you were done with this."

His chin quivered. He shrugged and smiled a cartoon smile that was meant to hold back tears. "I thought I was, too."

"Anniversaries like this are hard."

He looked at her and then looked toward the abyss. "You knew."

"I didn't know Jake was tied up with that guy, Harry. Nobody did."

The gypsy clan had come through early that spring and ripped off a long list of elderly folks who needed work done on their houses. Billie had kept her eye on one of them in particular. Not the leader of the clan who could sell working tits to a boar hog; she'd watched the boy who was surreally gorgeous and too young for Billie. But what the hell, she wasn't blind or dead, just forty-eight to his nineteen.

But who knew the gypsy god's door swung both ways? Just five days before Harry's lover split town, Billie had tapped on the window of a late model Chevy Malibu out by the quarry. Through the fogged up windows, she could see the outline of that beautiful boy on top of some skank. Anybody would have gawked at his godlike body.

It took the woman belting in the key of O to remind Billie she was a cop. When she rapped her nightstick on the windshield, the gypsy looked up. Dark shaggy hair fell across dangerous emerald eyes that were fixed on hers. He raised up and hovered far enough over the woman to show Billie he was well-skilled in more than just thieving and carpentry. A thin smile crossed his beautiful face as he came into the whimpering puddle beneath him.

Harry Bennett never had a prayer.

"Nobody saw it coming, Harry. But that doesn't matter. You're better now. I've seen it." He raised his eyebrows and shrugged. "You know, I ought to keep this gun, but you'd just go down to Gun-Mart and get another one."

"Think of me as job security." He smiled as she handed him the unloaded gun.

"Go on home now." Billie wiped the tears away from his cheeks. "Take a sick day tomorrow. Get dressed up, go to Charleston, and have some fun. You'll never get over a man like this."

Harry nodded his head and wiped his nose with the back of his left hand, his right arm was folded across his body with the gun dangling from his stubby index finger. "I just thought I'd be over him by now."

"It's not over till you say it is."

He nodded and hugged her like he didn't want to let go. She felt the cold barrel of the forty-five pressed against the small of her back. He pulled away, sniffled, and cracked the tiniest smile before slinging the pistol into the bottomless quarry. Billie felt a gush of relief the second the gun struck the surface of the murky brown water. Harry took a shaky step back from the edge and with a full grin, let out a deep sigh. "Men are shit."

"That's the spirit."

Harry hugged her again, then got into his Chevrolet relic, and Billie followed him back toward town. The police radio squealed and crackled again.

"Chief?"

"I spent a little more time with Harry than usual, Delores. Everything okay?"

"Come on back to the station."

"You've got that tone in your voice that makes the bottom fall out of my stomach. Something's up, and it's not good."

"Just come by and get you some crock pot chili before you go out on evening patrol," Delores said, like she's old enough to be Billie's mother. "Besides, we got to talk about you traipsing out to the quarry. I know good and well that Harry Bennett's the only openly gay man in town, but he's been pining for way too long. And it's costing the tax payers big money."

"Jesus. What's got your back up?"

"We got a letter saying city employees gonna get health benefits cut again. They try to make it sound all nicey nice, but it sounds plenty bad to me. If folks like Harry Bennett didn't need a baby sitter, I figure I'd still have a $15 co-pay and a decent drug plan. And another thing, I ain't Jesus."

"If the folks of Stanton didn't need baby sitting, Delores, we wouldn't have a job. Besides, it's Harry. What do you want me to do?"

"Take the damn gun and get me my $15 co-pay. Hell, give me the gun, and I'll shoot him myself."

"Delores."

"Don't start in with that touchy feely crap. Just get your ass in here. I got Oprah on the DVR, and it's a doozy."

"No lie, Harry tossed the gun in the quarry."

"That's progress, but that ain't going to get me my $15 co-pay back."

Delores was right, but Harry tossing the gun into the quarry was the start of something good. Billie signed off and pushed the button on the little boom box she kept in the front seat of the squad car. The first few cords of "The End of the Innocence" began to play, or as Amber liked to call it, the anthem of the entire nation of women over forty. Billie sang along with Don Henley like she'd lived the words rather than just knew them.

But the same sweet lyrics that had once seduced her into keeping her ex-husband Paul around longer than she should have and, later on, have a fling with a Don Henley look-alike half her age, had a different meaning now. Mama's Old Timers' disease Billie had joked about for years was now full-blown Alzheimer's. Amber was a mom, making grown-up decisions, albeit the wrong grown-up decisions. And Miss Sadie's return to Stanton would require more from Billie than a simple apology.

Billie pulled into the spot marked Chief Malden. It used to gall her that the city never whitewashed over the name of her predecessor, but it made sense. Gerald Malden was the law in Stanton for thirty years until he went missing during a cross-country trip with his wife in the tiniest motor home Winnebago made. That was eight years ago, when folks used to poke fun at Billie for being the only female police chief in the state of South Carolina. Even then she was too smart to let anybody think she had her back up over what some fool said, much less a little aluminum sign perched on an old tire rim.

After a while the teasing stopped. Still, it never occurred to anybody to put Billie Warren's name on that sign. Maybe nobody thought she'd stick around long enough for something as official as a proper sign. But if Billie Warren was good at anything, it was sticking.

She wiped her feet on the mat outside the door of the police station and then on a second mat Delores had put just inside the door because Martha Stewart said on her TV show one day that two mats are better than one.

"What ya know good, Miss Delores?"

Gretchen Wilson's "Redneck Woman" was blaring from Delores's iPhone docked on a portable speaker. She acknowledged Billie with a nod as a little bit of mayonnaise and chili dribbled down her first chin. It was sliding down her second chin when she set the hot dog down, and reached for Billie's messages before grabbing a napkin. "Wipe your feet."

"I did. Twice." Billie gave Delores a nod. "That the only song on that thing?"

"It made it to the top of the charts back in 2004, and it's been number one in my heart ever since. You got a problem with that?"

"No ma'am." Billie smiled at the bleached blond groupie's habit of punctuating every statement she felt strongly about by digging her fists into her expansive hips. "I'm guessing you wanted me to come in because I have messages."

"Park your butt and eat some supper. I don't want you running off on an empty stomach."

Delores nestled two pink pieces of paper into her mile-long cleavage.

"You think I won't go get it?" Billie tossed her Lean Cuisine lasagna in the microwave and set the timer. "No telling what I might find in there, maybe Chief Malden."

"Well, it ain't like he's never been there before." Delores's whole body jiggled when she laughed. She parted her gigantic bosoms and gazed into the abyss. "Let's see what we got in here. My paycheck, one of them miniature horses like they got down at the Pet and Purr. Oh, yeah, and them two messages you ain't getting till you eat."

Billie smirked as the timer on the microwave signaled dinner was ready. "Honestly, I don't know why I keep you around."

"That's what Chief Malden said, and look what happened to him."

Billie peeled the slimy film from the plastic Lean Cuisine tray and sat down with the *County Herald* sports page.

Delores passed the front page across the table, but Billie shook her head.

"Too depressing," she said.

"You need to read that big article on Judge Norris."

"Hell, no. I skimmed it this morning, don't need to read it again, thank you very much."

Billie had four and a half bites of lasagna then scraped the black plastic tray with her fork. It would have been nice if it had actually tasted as good as the picture on the flimsy box looked, but in truth, it was just a stingy serving of pasta, with a little something in the middle that was supposed to taste like ricotta cheese, and a lot of bitter tomato sauce. She fished the box out of the trashcan next to the supper table and glanced over the nutrition information. Less than 300 calories. No wonder.

"Don't you start counting calories," Delores fussed.

Billie tossed the box back in the trash and rinsed off her hands. When she turned around, Delores had set a bowl of coffee and a huge slice of coffeecake at Billie's place. It was the thick kind, not the little skimpy Betty Crocker type out of the box. As usual, she'd been overly generous with the topping: brown sugar, cinnamon, and roasted pecans. The dish had endeared Delores to every cop who'd worked there for the past ten years.

"Good girl," Delores said, as Billie tore into the cake.

Delores parted her bosom again and pulled out the messages. "Eat," Delores demanded, "if nothing else, maybe the good will even out the bad."

The first message said Mama had a really good day except she snapped out of Neverland just long enough to accuse Inez of taking her wedding ring. She pitched such a huge fit that saintly Inez felt Billie should know, and there was no way on God's green earth anybody was putting Mama in a home. Shoot, Mama didn't even have a wedding ring. She lost it at the beach a few years after Billie's father passed away and never got another one.

"Taking care of your mama is wearing on you and Inez," Delores said.

"She needs to be in a home. I can't take care of her. Inez can't take care of her much longer."

"That Nelson gal is looking for work," Delores said. She poured Billie another cup of coffee. "I think she used to work at a nursing home in Mt. Pleasant when she first got out of high school. She's young, might be desperate."

Billie looked at the second message and speared another chunk of cake. There was an awful lot of bad to cancel out.

Deidre Lawson had called and left a message for Billie to call her back. She didn't say it was urgent, and the good news was that if Billie didn't call before 5:00 p.m. Deidre would be out of pocket for a couple of days. It was 6:45. Crisis averted. If Billie wasn't looking for trouble, why did she drive out to what Miss Sadie said was the scene of the crime? "I drove out to Clauson's Creek."

Delores narrowed her eyes. "You got plenty on your plate, Billie Warren. It's sweet and gooey. Don't screw it up."

Delores had a heart as big as her giant bosoms, but how could she look into Miss Sadie's eyes, hear her story, and not believe her? And if Delores couldn't see the truth in Sadie Byrd, how could Billie expect the county prosecutor, Robert Bland, to believe her? Robert would listen to Billie. He might even talk to Miss Sadie, but that's as far as it would go.

And for good reason, halfway through Robert's junior year of college, his daddy died. Robert worked two jobs to keep his head above water and help his mother and little brother back home in Stanton. His grades began to suffer, and his LSAT scores were not good. Robert asked Judge Norris to help him out, and when Robert told the story years later, he always pointed out that he was expecting a letter of recommendation or a phone call. But the judge didn't just make a call. He drove up to the University of South Carolina and had lunch with the dean himself. The next thing Robert Bland knew, he was on his way to becoming a lawyer.

Ask and ye shall receive. That's how things worked with Judge Harold Norris. It would be hard to find many people in the Lowcountry who weren't beholden to the judge in some way. Even Billie was grateful he threw his support behind her when the city was trying to decide between her and Jimmy Malden for the police chief's position.

Now that she thought about it, Jimmy Malden was the only person she could think of who didn't owe the judge. There was no way to make something stick against the judge, not just her. She could talk to Jimmy about Miss Sadie's statement. He might laugh his ass off. No, check that, he would definitely laugh his ass off. But maybe he was a good enough cop to want to see if there was something to it.

CHAPTER EIGHT

The rest of Billie's shift was uneventful. She rambled through town three more times, riding by Mama's with each pass to see if Abby was still there. She was. Just after ten-thirty, she pulled over one of the Webster twins for speeding. She called him Tad when she asked for his license and registration. He was crying but managed to remind her that he was Tim.

The poor guy was a mess, trying hard to hold back the tears, and then he would break down and blubber for a few seconds. His girlfriend, Haley Sanders, was almost hugging the passenger door, crying too, but the look on her face told Billie it wasn't because her boyfriend got pulled.

"Y'all doing all right?" Both of the teens nodded. Billie shone her flashlight into the front seat and then the back. "How about you, Haley? You okay?"

The girl nodded again.

"Well, Tim, you were going forty-seven in a twenty-five-mile zone. You in a hurry to get somewhere?"

He raked his sleeve across his eyes and nodded as he fished the license out of his wallet. "Haley was supposed to be home by ten. We lost track of time. I guess I lost track of how fast I was going, too. I'm real sorry. It won't happen again." He sputtered the last words and then jutted out his jaw like that might keep him from crying. "I just can't get a ticket, Ms. Warren. My daddy said one more and I'm done driving until after graduation next year. Please."

"Where did you get all those tickets from?"

He shook his head and tried to slow his rapid-fire breath. "I work at Best Buy in North Charleston on the weekends and got two in one day . . ." He swallowed the last word and paused to keep from bawling again, "on I-26, just last month."

Billie wanted to ask him if Best Buy was hiring so she could send Amber over there first thing in the morning. Instead, she looked at her watch to fill out the ticket. It was almost eleven.

"I'm going to let you off with a warning this time, Tim. But you'd better slow down or you're going to be walking to Best Buy."

The boy let out a huge sigh and a nervous little laugh as he signed the warning. "Yes, ma'am. Thank you, oh God, thank you so much."

"Now go on and get Haley home before her daddy calls the station house and reports her missing."

Patti Dawson could have taken a lesson from the boy on how to proceed after getting a ticket. He put his blinker on, then looked back over his shoulder to see if the way was clear before he crept onto the highway.

Billie got back in the car and called home. Amber answered the phone, said she had gotten home around nine. Miss Sadie gave Little Man his bath and had officially graduated from "that old woman" to amazing.

"I went for a job interview today at that tax place that makes people dress like the Statue of Liberty and stand beside the road holding a sign nobody reads. They're looking for a receptionist."

Billie forced back the urge to ask a hundred questions. "Good for you."

"I told them I'm not dressing up, but I'd answer the phone and file stuff." Billie could hear Miss Sadie cooing to the baby in the background. "Oh, and Tyson watched the baby for me after he got out of class."

"How did the interview go?"

"Did you know they work from eight in the morning until ten mid-January through April 15? That's a really long day."

"They probably don't expect the receptionist to be there the whole time."

"Yeah, he said they did, Tuesday through Saturday. I told him I had a little baby, and that just wouldn't work for me."

"You know you could have taken that job while they work normal hours, just to get your feet wet, and then find something else before tax season got cranked up."

"Not after the look on that man's face after I told him about Little Man."

Great . "Is Miss Sadie ready for bed?"

"I guess so; she's got Grandma's nightgown on."

"Let me talk to her."

Billie spoke to Miss Sadie briefly and told her she'd be home late.

"You're a good one, you are," Miss Sadie said. "And don't worry about me. I'm fine."

"Good. Get some rest. I've got the day off, I'll take you home tomorrow."

"So—" Miss Sadie paused. "That's all there is to it?"

"Yes ma'am. I've got your statement and will be in touch with you."

"You've been awful good to me, but I'll be glad to get home."

"Alright then, I'm going by my friend's house when I get off work, but you can call me on my cell if you need me."

Delores was too engrossed in the beaten-up Sandra Browne novel she was reading to look up when Billie entered the station house.

If there was a grown-up version of the Reading Is Fundamental program, Delores would be the poster child. She read mysteries and romance like it was her job and kept the local used bookstore in business, recommending books to Stanton's thrill seekers and romance junkies. And for that, the owner let her fill up a grocery sack with all the paperbacks she could carry once a month for free. If she came back for more, which she often did, he charged her five dollars for another sack of books.

"Your hair is on fire." Billie picked up the log to sign out and laughed when Delores gave her the finger. "Isn't Sandra Browne the author with the nipple fixation?"

"Go ahead and make fun," Delores said, her eyes still glued to the book. "But it takes a really creative soul to write your basic bodice ripping suspense novel so that the fornicating doesn't get old by the nineteenth time."

"So how far did she get this time? What's the record now?"

"One time Sandra got all the way to page 28 without one single solitary nipple, thank you very much. Besides, there ain't nothing wrong with a little nipple. Shoot, it might be what they call one of those literary devices."

Billie laughed. "You going home?"

"Yeah, I'm beat." She dog-eared her page and put it in the sack with the rest of the smut. "Abby called and said to send you straight over to her place after work. Maybe if you stop by Cole's you can get you a little bodice ripping and fornicating. You sure look like you could use some."

"Thanks, Delores, I needed a boost."

"That ain't all that needs boosting," Delores laughed as the screen door slammed behind her.

"See you tomorrow," Billie called after her.

"If somebody went to ripping Delores's bodice, they'd get two black eyes. Never seen a woman shaped quite like her with those short skinny little legs and huge bosoms. Looks like a bowling pin stood on the wrong end," Pete Sanders said as he came out of the bathroom drying his hands with a napkin from the break room. "You're out of paper towels again. I'm going to Sam's Club tomorrow. Want me to get some?"

"Yeah, Pete, that would be great."

Pete sat down at the desk and leaned his chair back against the wall to simulate the recliner he spent most of his time in at home. He wasn't a Stanton policeman, just a retired cop from up north who needed to get out of the house and liked to man the phone that almost never rang in the middle of the night. When it did, and he deemed it serious enough to warrant attention, he forwarded the call to Billie or the sheriff's office.

"Night Pete."

"Billie? This is none of my business, but Delores told me about that woman who came in here last night, accusing the judge of rape and murder. I know I was still a flat foot up north when all that happened, but it looks like somebody let this thing lie for a long time. Maybe you ought to do the same."

Billie turned the Toyota onto the highway toward the secondary road that led to the Row. A blanket of cool evening air covered the warm marsh, giving rise to the dreamy looking fog that rose off the water. The salty Lowcountry smell the tourists found unpleasant was comforting. Billie could almost step outside of herself, or the self she had become since that dam broke and one insurmountable problem had followed the next.

It was almost funny, how she was drowning and nobody had a clue because she was Billie Warren. Tough. A Wild Boy. And why would anyone think otherwise?

When trouble came calling, she always drew in a deep breath and let it out slowly, controlled, and dug deep to deal with whatever came her way. Her mother. Amber. Her ex-husband. Her brother John, who refused to do his part with Mama. But Billie had dug so deep for so long, she was pushing through to the other side of the world.

She pulled into the driveway in front of Abby's cute little

house and smiled at the icicle lights still up from last Christmas that Abby had turned on for her. Getting out of the car, Billie felt a little better. She and Abby would have a couple of drinks, laugh a lot. Abby already had the music turned up loud enough to hear Harry Connick Jr. crooning. Billie didn't recognize the song, but who didn't love Harry Connick? Those images from the movie *Hope Floats* of him in tight jeans, a cowboy hat, that N'awlins drawl laced with a smile.

Billie knocked twice, then pushed the door open.

"Hey," Abby squealed and took a sip of her martini.

"Looks like you started without me." Billie took her gun belt off and draped it across a chair in the living room. She plopped down on the overstuffed couch that overlooked the marsh and gladly accepted the apple martini Abby handed her. "These are like candy."

"No," Abby said, fishing the cherry out of the bottom of her empty glass and popping it into her mouth. "These are better than candy."

"Thanks for making me come over," Billie said. "I really need this."

"I'll say." Abby mixed herself another martini and shook it wildly in time to the dizzying big band music. "That ought to do it." She poured herself another drink, dropped a maraschino cherry in the bottom of the glass, took a sip, and closed her eyes in approval. "Oooh, I wonder who that could be." Abby walked toward the front door even though a doorbell or knocking couldn't be heard over the music.

Abby flashed Billie a devilish smile and threw open her front door. "Oh, look Billie, it's Cole. Now, my two favorite people are here. This is going to be so much fun."

Cole smiled at Billie. She took another long sip of her drink. *Not interested.* He completely ignored her man repellent and sat down beside her on the couch.

"Hey, Cole." She gave him a sisterly peck before giving Abby the stink eye. Abby looked like she was going to pee her pants over the prospect of Billie and Cole on the same couch. She made some stupid excuse about needing to refill the ice bucket that was already overflowing and disappeared into the kitchen.

"Hey, Billie." He kissed her cheek, lingering just long enough for her to feel his breath on her skin and weaken her resolve. She closed her eyes and ran through all the reasons she'd said no to him; the main reason—it was for his own good. But he smelled good, so good, like citrus and musk, something earthy and almost sweet that she couldn't name. Before she knew it, she was fisting his shirt in her hand.

She let go of the shirt like it was white hot, downed the rest of her drink, and moved away from him. Even with the loss of contact, her body still hummed. She wrote it off to the martini and scooted until she and the armrest were one. The tail end of "There's No Business Like Show Business" played. Show tunes and martinis were good. Safe. Who could get sucked into romance with that combination? And where was Abby?

"I left a message on your cell last night."

Billie swirled her glass like it was still full but didn't look at him. "I'm sorry, things just got crazy this morning and—"

"Left a message a couple of days ago—at the house."

"If it's not for Amber, she doesn't write it down." God, she was lying to him? Of course she was. If she told him that she loved him, missed him, he'd scoop her up and take her home with him now. And then five minutes or five days later, when the bottom fell out of her life again, she'd be right back where she started. Saving the world, her world, with nothing left to give him.

He didn't move closer, didn't have to with those long arms, just reached out and pushed her blond scruff behind her ear. "I miss you, Billie."

Abby came back from the kitchen with an old fashioned glass, half full of Knob Creek for Cole. Billie gave her a look to let her know that she didn't appreciate Abby's less than covert efforts to play Cupid. Abby turned her head so that Cole couldn't see and mouthed, "You need to get laid." Then she stretched out on her crystal blue chaise like a fat cat, delighted with her latest catch.

"Billie, did you know Cole has a big show coming up in Chicago? He's done so many incredible new pieces; God, it's going to be fabulous."

"That's great, Cole; I hope it goes well for you. Excuse me." Billie gave Abby another look before she opened the French doors and went out onto the veranda. "I've been cooped up in a car all night. I need some air."

She was sad to see the moon had slipped away behind thick clouds. Still there was enough light to see the marsh that seemed to go on forever. She felt a hand on her shoulder. "My coming out here wasn't an invitation."

Cole didn't say a word, just massaged her shoulders until his thumbs found the sweet spot at the base of her neck. He laughed when someone moaned; her entire body blushed when she realized it was her. "You know, people this tense die young, and I'd pictured you living forever, Billie Warren." Her muscles betrayed her; she purred as she gave in to his touch. "You sure you don't have time for me?"

It was an invitation, an enticement. She arched her back toward him. What was she thinking? "No."

His thumbs pressed deeper, making the muscle that was piano-wire-tight relax. "Make time." He whispered.

She pushed his hands away and turned from him. "I don't even have time to die, Cole."

He pulled her close, her back to his front, and rested his chin on the top of her head. "Sometimes you just have to say screw it, screw everything and tend to your own needs."

"God, you're such a man." She made a half-hearted struggle to get out of his arms and then stopped. "It's not that easy," she whispered.

The moon wasn't full but was big and bright, showing off over the river. Inside, Abby changed the music to something bluesy and sexy and turned the volume up so that it competed with the night sounds. This was the best part about being with Cole, just being. If she missed anything it was whatever it was that they had that didn't require words or music or even sex to feel part of a whole. They just were.

He kissed the top of her head. "Come to Chicago with me."

"You know I can't do that."

"It's forty-eight hours."

"Forty-eight hours I don't have, Cole."

"After that, when you jump back into your life, you'll be better for it. We'll be better for it. What do you say, Billie?"

She pulled away from him; he reached for her again and winced when she let out the sarcastic little laugh that always allowed her to move seamlessly from one catastrophe to the next.

"The same thing I said two minutes ago, Cole. It's not that easy."

"You're wrong, Billie. And the worst part of it is you know you're wrong."

"I'm not going to stand here and offer some explanation because it doesn't matter. Right now my life is what it is, and there's not a damn thing I can do except see it through to the end. It's the way I'm built."

"Bullshit. You're scared. Scared of needing me, scared of loving me back. Why is that?"

"I don't *need* you to wait for me, Cole Sullivan." Her eyes darted away from him, a liar's telltale.

He turned to leave and was halfway across the yard before he turned and stalked back. The look on his face reminded her of the time she'd found him alone in his studio with a four-hundred-pound block of burl wood, swearing at the muse he was sure had left him for good. He stopped at the foot of the stairs and kneaded the banister hard with his right hand before he looked up at her.

"I can't help but wait for you, Billie Warren. It's the way I'm built."

CHAPTER NINE

"Don't think for one second I'm as easy to ditch as Cole." Abby was still sitting in her fat cat chair and was positively radiant from drinking too many martinis. "Freshen up our drinks, and I'll get the tiaras."

Years ago, Abby read *Queen for a Day, Every Day* when it was all the rage. It wasn't her all-time favorite book, but she did agree with the queen's commandment that all women should have at least one tiara. Being a woman of extremes, Abby had three; her favorite was the one she picked up on her last trip to Mardi Gras. The other two were basic state pageant winner models.

Billie poured a second martini and dropped two cherries in the bottom of her glass. She took a sip and sifted through some CDs while Abby went into her bedroom to get the tiaras. Billie settled on the Queen of Soul, put the CD in the deck, and pushed play. The whine of a steel guitar signaled the beginning of "Respect" followed by uncontrollable head bobbing.

Billie took her place on the couch again and laughed when Abby came strutting out of her room in time to the music with her state pageant tiara on. The special Mardi Gras crown was in her right hand and two white feather boas were draped over her shoulder.

"I took one look at your face today, *girl*," Abby's words were choppy, in perfect time with the music. "And I said to myself. I said, 'self, we're gonna need us some great big feather boas tonight.'"

Aretha cut loose, *R. E. S. P. E. C. T. Find out what it means to me* . . . Abby bobby pinned Billie's tiara on tight and swore at her for having short hair, which always was a challenge for tiara wearers. Then she draped a boa around Billie's shoulders and kissed her on top of her bobby pin pierced head. "There."

Billie took a sip of her drink and resumed her head bobbing, at one point almost sending the sacred crown flying across the room. Abby squealed and nearly lost her own as she plopped down in the fat cat chair. "I've just got to get some good head-bobbing tiaras for us to wear. Aretha should come up with her own line of them; she'd make a blessed fortune. She could make them with Velcro, like those headbands they stick on bald-headed baby girls."

"You've got that Miss Texas hair that never moves," Billie said, "I've got your basic Meg Ryan scruff."

"Meg Ryan can never wear a tiara and bob her head, poor thing."

Billie held onto her crown and finished out the song. She finished her second martini but wasn't feeling buzzed. Martinis were sneaky; usually the third one knocked her for a loop.

"Your glass is empty, you silly bitch!" Abby attempted to get out of her chair. After three tries, she collapsed in laughter. "Officer. Officer. I can't get up. Would you please fetch that martini shaker for li'l ole Miss Texas?"

Billie tossed the end of her boa over her shoulder and obliged.

"And now you," Abby said after Billie poured her another drink.

"I'm driving."

"Oh, Billie, please stay. We haven't had a slumber party in a really long time, and I got out the tiaras and everything."

"Can't. I have to get home."

Miss Texas made her best pouty face that always made her look like a four-year-old. Billie shrugged and kissed her on top of her head.

"Well, okay, you don't have to drink, or sleep over," Abby whined. "Just sit down and talk to me."

Billie unpinned the tiara, set it on the coffee table, and replaced the boa on her shoulder with her gun belt before she dug into her pocket for her keys.

"One stinking problem. Is that too much to ask?" Abby was officially tanked and slurring her words. "I'll put your troubles in the tiara box; they can't survive in there. Only genuine rhinestones can live and breathe in a tiara box."

"You're so good to me." Billie sat on the edge of the chaise. "I love you."

"Come on, Billie. Give."

She hung her head. "Mama's not going to live much longer. The doctor says her Alzheimer's is progressing faster. He didn't say she's going to die tomorrow, but sometimes she has trouble swallowing." When she looked up at Abby, she could feel herself tearing up. God, she hated crying. It made her feel weak, and she couldn't afford that. "Inez said she had a good day, but some days, she can't even hold her head up." She swiped at her wet face with her shirtsleeve. "I thought I got over her not knowing who I am a long time ago, but I didn't. Not even close. How am I going to survive her dying?"

"Oh, and I thought you were going to give me the skinny on Cole," Abby sniffled and wiped her eyes with the boa. "Promise me you'll call your brother, make him help you."

Billie spread a chenille throw over Abby. "Go to sleep now."

"The asshole didn't lift a finger when your daddy was sick. Don't do this by yourself again."

Billie took the martini glass out of Abby's hand and put it more than arm's distance away on the end of the coffee table. "I love you, Miss Texas."

She eased out the front door and unplugged the Christmas lights. The tiny buzz from the pair of martinis had been chased away by sadness. As she got into her car and headed toward the highway, she thought about what Abby had said. Maybe she would call John tomorrow. He'd been too busy to visit or return phone calls since he made partner last year. If he and Nan weren't warming the bleachers at their kids' Saturday soccer games, he ought to be home. Maybe he would drop the high and mighty Atlanta lawyer act long enough to talk about Mama.

Billie sped past the marsh like it wasn't beautiful and hoped there was forgiveness for such a sin. She pulled onto the highway toward Stanton but took a brief detour before heading home. In her mind, she knew she would have another sit down with Amber about Tyson, and if Amber was dead set on them being together, she would have one with Tyson, too. God, they were both so young, too young to be playing house.

And Mama was going to die—until tonight, Billie couldn't bring herself to say the words out loud. Mama had always called Billie her heart, and John, too, when he was around. But the truth was that when Mama passed, a piece of Billie's heart would be gone forever.

She pulled off the highway alongside the pretty field where Caroline Norris's blood was spilled and turned on the high beams. Was this the place Judge Norris raped and murdered his daughter? Sadie's daughter?

Sadie Byrd had never really been crazy like the stupid song had said. She had been emotionally bludgeoned by a man who kept her pregnant and then took her precious babies to market. But had Miss Sadie told the truth about what happened in this pretty place so long ago? Delores was a good judge of character, better than Billie sometimes, and she didn't believe Miss Sadie for one second.

Billie pulled back onto the highway. It only took about ten minutes to get home. She eased into the kitchen and went down the hall to the nursery. Little Man was sound asleep, lying on his back with his mouth open. Billie gave him a kiss on the forehead and then kissed her own baby goodnight. She picked Amber's *Teen People* magazine up off the floor and set it on the dresser before she left the room.

The hall light invaded the room; Miss Sadie didn't stir. Billie spread another blanket over the old woman and stepped out of the room without making a sound.

For most of her adult life, Billie had relied on her gut rather than her heart to tell her the right thing to do. It was rare that the two enemies ever came together, but when they did, they usually screamed at her in a voice she couldn't deny. Tonight was one of those nights; Mama would be gone soon, and Sadie Byrd was telling the truth.

CHAPTER TEN

The sun was making a lame attempt to crawl its way up the horizon when Billie awoke the next morning. Patches of light filtered through a gray haze. It was just before dawn, the time all good soccer parents were getting ready to walk out the door. The truly dedicated ones, like her brother John and his wife Nan had been up for at least an hour to make sure duffel bags that were bigger than their children were packed and ready to go.

All those families piling into oversized SUVs with all that equipment always made Billie glad that Amber had been into Facebook and shopping. Still, there was a lot to be said for parents who had parked themselves on metal bleacher seats so often, they had permanent lines etched across their butts.

She grabbed her cell phone off her bedside table and dialed John's number. The phone rang once.

"Hello!"

"Dana? I thought this was your dad's number."

"My dad gave me his old cell phone. Why? Who is this?"

"It's Billie. Can I speak to your dad?"

"Can you call him back on the house phone? I'm expecting a really important call before I leave for my game."

"Boyfriend?"

"Shhhhh. Daddy hates him, but then he hates every guy I've brought home. Promise you won't tell him. Okay?"

"Promise. Good luck at the game."

Billie took a deep breath and called John's home phone number. It rang six times and the answering machine picked up. John's voice interrupted his youngest daughter Maggie's cutsie recorded greeting.

"Hey, John, it's Billie."

"Damn machine. There's four other people in this house and not one of them can answer a phone."

"So, how are you, big brother?"

"With three teenage daughters? How the hell do you think I am? They all have cell phones and this one still rings off the hook. Hormones raging. Nobody ever has anything to wear. And all three of them, even Nan, have PMS at the same time every month."

"I have a legal question for you."

"Thank God. I understand the law, but I've long since given up on understanding women. I've got thirty minutes before I have to leave for the game. At some point, during that time, I have to shower and take a crap, so spill."

"You're my brother, so I'll just drop the disclaimer."

"Billie, I live in Atlanta. For Pete's sake, I'm not going to *tell anybody*."

"Okay. Remember Sadie Byrd?"

"Crazy Sadie?"

"Yeah. Two days ago, she came into the station to report a murder."

"No shit. Who'd she do?"

"She didn't kill anybody, John. Remember Caroline Norris?"

"Yeah, sure. I was a freshman in high school; her brother, Bob, was a senior when she died."

"Well, Sadie Byrd says Judge Norris raped and murdered his daughter. And the worst part is, I believe her."

"Holy shit, Billie. You don't want to mess with the Norrises."

"If I take this to the solicitor's office, I'll be laughed out of the county. State Law Enforcement Division won't do anything."

"When has SLED done anything worth mentioning anyway?"

"That's not fair. I know some folks with SLED; they're good people."

"But you're talking about charging Judge Norris with murder, the soon-to-be-dead and nearly canonized Judge Harold Norris."

"Yes."

"Look, I'm not a criminal attorney . . ."

"I thought we were doing away with disclaimers."

"Force of habit. I get hit up for free legal advice all the time."

"So what do you think?"

"Listen Billie, after forty years, you and I both know that dog won't hunt. Even if you brought charges against the judge, you couldn't get twelve people in the whole state to convict a hundred-year-old judge. Especially him."

"He's not a hundred years old."

"Didn't Sadie Byrd and her husband skip town right after the murder?"

"They did. Her husband died years ago, but the warrant on her is still open."

"The papers made a big deal about those warrants, but it seemed like nobody did much to follow up on them. Don't remember much more than that; I was just a high school flunky back then."

"You were never a flunky at anything, but that's pretty much how it went down. Judge Harmon signed the warrants."

"Great, another sainted judge, not on the same level as Judge Norris, but still. Don't hold your breath if you're expecting to see some sort of Lifetime Channel justice in this scenario. It's not happening. Look it was good talking to you, but I've got to go lay some pipe . . ."

"You're still disgusting."

"Give me a break. Nan doesn't let me talk dirty around here. Call me if you need anything. Okay?"

Billie waited for a moment. "John—you didn't ask about Mama."

"I'm sorry, I'm putting you on the same level as Nan. You all just seem to handle everything among yourselves, and I have to tell you, I'm glad for it."

"Mama's not going to live much longer, John."

There was a long silence at the other end. John didn't say a word; his breath was long and steady.

'I'm sorry for that. I'll be glad to pay for nurses 'round the clock, whatever you need to take the pressure off you and Inez."

"Mama's had nurses living at the house for over a year now, John. The last one just quit. Inez is staying there now until I can get somebody else, but that's not the issue. Some days, Mama's okay and some days she has trouble swallowing and can't hold her head up. She's going to get worse John, and she's going to need nurses, but she needs you too."

"God damn it, Billie. Ask me for free legal advice or money—big money, but don't ask me for that. I can't. Nan will come help out. Katherine's a senior this year, and she can drive the girls to school and practice when she goes to the soccer complex. That'll work. It'll have to; I just can't do it, Billie. I can't see Mama like that, being fed, having somebody wipe her ass like a baby. She's my mother."

"She hasn't been able to wipe herself for two years, John. Besides, she's my mother, too." She'd decided she'd dished out enough guilt for one phone call. Too much and it loses its effect. "Anyway, thanks for the free legal advice. I have to go."

"Nan'll call you today and set something up."

Billie hung up the phone. If John sucked at responsibility, Billie sucked even more at doling it out. But he was right about one thing, trying to help Sadie Byrd was a no-win situation.

It was 7:30 when Billie walked into the kitchen. A box of Bojangles biscuits was on the table with a jar of jelly and a plate of scrambled eggs. Just off the kitchen, in the den, Tyson was watching the tail end of a show on the Game Show Network. Miss Sadie and the baby were sitting on the couch playing pat-a-cake.

"Hey, y'all," Billie said.

"Morning, Mom. Tyson brought biscuits, and I made eggs for you."

"Looks good, Amber."

"Thanks. Help yourself; we've already eaten."

Billie could feel Tyson looking at her, waiting for her to acknowledge him. Amber was giving him a look and shaking her head slightly.

"Not now," Amber hissed just loud enough for Billie to hear.

The announcer said that *The Price Is Right* would be back after the commercial break. Amber seemed to know Miss Sadie liked the show. "Is the television loud enough for you, Miss Sadie?"

"Oh, it's fine, child. That Bob Barker is such a good-looking man."

Tyson scooped Little Man up in the air, making him giggle and then nestled him between himself and Amber. "Da da da da."

"See, I told you he could say it," Amber gushed. "Tyson, who's this? Come on, now. Show your Da Da you can say his name."

Little Man let out an earsplitting squeal and chomped down proudly on his left hand, sucking on it for all he was worth.

"Say Da Da, Little T. Come on, buddy," Tyson cooed. "Say my name."

For the first time since Billie met Tyson Cantrell, he looked more like a goofy, awestruck dad than the poster boy for Abercrombie & Fitch. She reminded herself that she didn't much like him, speared some eggs, and turned her attention to the last bit of breakfast.

She rinsed off her plate and put it in the dish rack before she poured herself another cup of coffee. She was tired, real tired, and sized the day up as, at the very least, an eight-cup day. When she turned around from the sink, Amber and Tyson were standing there, with the baby between them like a shield, looking at her like it was time to talk.

"What's up?" Billie said, as her entire being screamed *Nooooo*.

"I know you've never liked me," Tyson began.

"It's not that I don't like you, Tyson; it's the fact that you dumped my pregnant daughter for a string of bimbos. You broke Amber's heart, and it nearly killed her. That's what I don't like about you."

"Mama—" Amber snapped.

"She's right," Tyson interrupted, "Look, Ms. Warren, I'll admit that I did some really stupid things. I wasn't ready to be a dad."

"And you're suddenly ready now?" Billie laughed, but she had to give him credit for looking her square in the eyes. "Hell, Tyson, nobody's ready to be a parent, but by God, there are those that hang in there and don't leave."

"Mama."

"Da da da da da," Little Man screamed on cue. "Da da."

"I love Amber and Little T more than anything. It just took me a while to figure that out."

Almost a damn year, Billie thought. You left my daughter to cry and grieve while you were out screwing God knows how many Abercrombie & Fitch girls. And then there was the day she saw you with one of them at Walmart, and the stupid bitch you were with laughed at Amber because she was as big as a house with your baby.

"Mama . . . I'm pregnant."

Billie's heart leaped into her throat and pulsed wildly. "I can't do this. Honest to God, Amber, I can't nurse you through another drama."

"But it's okay, Mrs. Warren. Me and Amber are together now."

Billie barely heard his words over the memory of the constant crying and then Amber's dark time when she was hospitalized two weeks after the baby was born. And how Billie herself had cried her eyes out taking care of the little guy, because she was so afraid she was going to lose Amber.

"It's okay," Billie heard Tyson say. "It's forever." She cringed at the words.

Before Amber had come home from the hospital, Billie had worked to get rid of anything that would remind Amber of Tyson. She remembered throwing out stuffed animals, cheesy pictures, and a Spanish notebook that had Amber and Tyson FOREVAH! written all over it.

"No. You're only nineteen," Billie rasped. "You're too young for one baby, much less two."

"We're getting married," Amber gushed, holding out her left hand to reveal a sliver of a gold band with a microscopic diamond. "Why can't you just be happy for us?"

When Billie first turned around to see the happy couple there in the kitchen, she'd felt like she did whenever she laid on her back and let Little Man tap dance across her chest. The pressure had increased now—lots of pressure, then more pressure. Pain streaked through her chest and riveted up her back and neck settling on the left side of her head. *Breathe*, she told herself as Amber and Tyson laid out their plan. She heard bits and pieces as the pain intensified, something about Tyson staying in school. Oh, God, did they say they were going to live here? *Breathe!*

"Mama?"

Billie barely heard Amber as the room went black. She could feel the bump rising on the side of her head after she fell hard on the tile floor. Suddenly, the excruciating pain was replaced by a marvelous sense of peace, of floating, resting. Her fists that had been clinched earlier were limp and open. She felt insulated from the outer world. She wanted to smile, to laugh out loud but didn't dare disturb the cocoon she'd fallen into. It was a special place filled with peace, sweet bountiful peace.

CHAPTER ELEVEN

Her thoughts were hazy but certain as the sharp scent of ammonia rocketed through Billie's head. She wanted to stay in the cocoon and made a lame attempt to swat at the smelling salts that seemed to be chasing her out of her stupor. For the first time in—well, she couldn't remember how long—she felt safe, insulated, completely relaxed. But whoever was waving those damn salts under her nose refused to stop until Billie shoved the hand away from her face.

A boy paramedic who looked all of twelve grinned at Billie. "See there," he said, "I told you she was fine."

"Mama," Amber said, leaning over Billie with Little Man on her hip, "are you okay? Please, be okay."

When Billie nodded, the motion sent a lightning bolt crashing into the side of her head, the room darkened and then came back into a hazy focus.

"She's going to be fine." Tyson put his arm around Amber and looked down at Billie as the paramedics worked on her. "Amber called Doc Hanson about twenty minutes ago. He was getting ready to tee off with his wife. I think that's them pulling into the driveway now."

Doc Hanson was retired, and he and Martha had been Mama's backdoor neighbors for fifty years. Doc was famous for wearing the "flashiest"—code word for tackiest—golf apparel money could buy. And Martha was famous for beating the hell out of him and most every other retiree at the Olde Marsh Country Club.

The sight of Doc's screaming chameleon plaid shorts and hot melon–colored shirt sliced through the final strings that had tethered Billie to her dreamy stupor. She propped herself up on her elbows and considered sitting up, but only for a second or two.

"You lay back down this instant, young lady." Doc rummaged through the paramedic's medical bag like it was his own. "This isn't the first time I've seen a knot on your head, and I'm sure it won't be the last."

Her mind was still hazy as Doc took her through the same drill he had put her through when she fell out of Billy Donnigan's tree house. She answered the easy questions—she knew her name, she knew the day of the week, not the date. "I always have to look at a calendar."

"Any chest pains?"

"No."

"You're sure about that? Amber said you put your hand over your heart. Maybe there were chest pains and you're too damn stubborn to admit it. You were always a hardhead."

"Some tightness, maybe. I don't know—OUCH."

Dock stopped poking on her. "Sorry. Looks like you and the floor went at it and the floor won. I'm going to call that workaholic son of mine and have him admit you for observation. Possible concussion, that's a little concern. Chest pains, now that's a big one, especially with your family history."

"I'll call Jeff now." Martha pulled her cell phone out of her pocket, and in a matter of seconds, she was fussing at the receptionist to put her son on the phone this instant. "Hey, honey. Sorry to interrupt. Your father wants to speak to you."

"Busy?" Doc made some notes from his exam and gave them to the paramedic. "I'm at Billie Warren's house. Looks like she passed out, maybe from chest pains. Her blood pressure's not good. Has a big bump on the side of her head like that one she laid on yours when you locked her cat in Miss Simpson's basement," Doc laughed and listened to his smart-aleck son for a while. "The med techs think they ought to take her on to the hospital; I think it's a good idea, Jeff, unless you want her to come by the office first."

Doc ended the call, and the paramedics loaded Billie on the gurney against her will.

"Mama, just go and get checked out," Amber was crying now.

"All right. Just stop making such a big deal about this. I'm fine."

Doc was wrapping up his conversation with the med tech when he noticed Miss Sadie standing in the hallway. "Well, as I live and breathe—Sadie Byrd." Doc was pleasantly dumbstruck. "You—you—look wonderful; doesn't she Martha? My Lord, it's been, what, almost forty years now? How are you?"

"I'm good, but I'm worried about Billie. Is she going to be okay?"

"She'll be fine. She's going to the hospital to get checked out—aren't you, Billie?"

Billie grimaced and smiled ever so slightly at Tyson who propped the storm door open for the paramedics. He looked concerned. He really was a good guy—no, wait a minute—he had gotten Amber pregnant again.

Amber had stopped crying and was scrambling around for her purse and the diaper bag to follow the ambulance to the hospital. Tyson took the keys out of her hand. "I'll drive," he said. She wheeled and looked at him wildly, strands of blond hair stuck to her tear-stained face. "There's no way you're driving with our babies as upset as you are, Amber." He stood his ground.

Billie liked that. Doc, Miss Martha, and Sadie followed the gurney out the door. Sadie took Billie's hand before the techs hoisted her up into the truck. "Are you going to be okay?"

"Yes—sure I am. This is just for Amber's peace of mind."

She let go of Billie's hand. "And mine; I always did worry about you."

"Billie, Jeff will drop by to see you before he goes to lunch," Doc said. "The ER doc will take a look at you, too. When they see the knot on that hard head of yours, they'll keep you overnight if they have any sense at all, Jeff included."

The doors to the ambulance closed before Billie could protest. She was a little more lucid than she had been since she came to, but still tired. The added weight of the new burdens, piggybacked with the old ones, had born down hard on her, knocked her to her knees, and then out cold. She struggled with the edge of the fleece blanket that was tucked around her like a fuzzy straight jacket. She pulled it up to her chin and closed her eyes to search for the remnants of the cocoon.

———————◆◆◆———————

"Honest to God, I didn't do it." Billie winced when Jeff touched the side of her head; she opened her eyes slowly. "But as many times as I got into it with you, it's not like I didn't want to. Lucky I was faster than you."

"You were never faster than me." Billie attempted to smile.

"Sure I was. You just have this really bad bump on the side of your head and don't remember. It's called amnesia, and I can promise you'll never remember things the way they really were. For instance, I was incredibly good looking, and an amazing athlete, and—"

"I kicked your ass whenever you asked for it."

"Hey, you've got amnesia, remember?" Jeff took Billie's blood pressure again. "You want to tell me what happened?"

"I felt like someone was standing on my chest. At first it was a little person; before I hit the floor, it morphed into a baby elephant. Hell, maybe a full-grown one. I don't know. I have a lot on me, Jeff—then Amber told me she was pregnant again. And I just checked out."

"Ahh, the topper. That'll do it." Jeff sat down on the bed and smiled. "Looks like you've had yourself one heck of an anxiety attack and a mild concussion to go along with it."

"I thought anxiety attacks just kept people from leaving their homes."

"You're thinking about agoraphobia, sometimes patients can get that with anxiety attacks. When they come on suddenly like yours and very intense, they can make you lose consciousness, even mimic the symptoms of a severe heart attack. Looks like you're the lucky recipient of all of those symptoms except being a prisoner in your own home."

"Thank God."

Jeff smiled and rubbed the bridge of his nose for a second or two like he had his own headache. "Trust me, with a three-year-old and a set of twins who are thirteen months apart, I can relate. Throw in two teenagers from the first marriage-go-round and you—hell, you should get off the gurney and let me lie down."

Billie had always liked Jeff. When her brother John went away to college, they became close, and for a long time Jeff was more of a brother to her than John was. She hadn't seen him much since he remarried and moved closer to Charleston where his wife owned a fancy teahouse.

"Are you going to let me go home?"

"Yeah, but as your friend, I strongly advise that you take some time off. There's sort of an unwritten guarantee with anxiety attacks; once you have the first one, you'll keep on having them unless you acknowledge the problem and do something about it. And doing something about it usually just means taking time to regroup. However, in your case it means getting some help for your mom and just letting go of the rest."

"Great. And what's your advice, as my doctor?"

"No driving, no work for at least forty-eight hours. That means no police calls forwarded to your house. Just take it easy. If your headache gets worse or if you have any vomiting, call me at home." He wrote a phone number on the back of his business card. "That's my cell number, too."

"Hey, it's Saturday. What are you doing in the office on the weekend?"

"Mouths to feed, alimony to pay. Braces. College for Brandon next year—$61,000 a year for Furman. His other choice, Duke. Honest to God, Billie, when he laid that on me, I was afraid to ask how much that would cost."

"You're right. You should lie down."

Jeff helped her sit up. She waited until her brain stopped sloshing around in her head before she tried to stand. An orderly arrived with a wheel chair and helped Billie into the seat.

"Nice ride. What are those, thirty-six-inch rims?" Jeff gave her a kiss on the cheek. "Take care of yourself. Call me if you have any questions."

The orderly shook his head like Jeff was some flirty doctor and then pushed the wheelchair out of the ER and down the hall toward the waiting room. As they turned the corner, Billie saw Amber holding the baby; Tyson had his arms around both of them. Cole was standing as close as possible to the entrance. Given the fact that the only thing he hated more than doctors was anything remotely resembling a hospital, it was a labor of love he was there. Doc and Martha had put their golf game on hold and were chatting up Miss Sadie while Abby held court in an effort to take everybody's mind off the fact that the mighty Billie Warren had fallen.

Cole was the first to see Billie coming down the hall. He was a step ahead of the others, the color drained from his beautiful face. Before he could get to her, Amber scrambled past him with Little Man bouncing on her hip and burst into tears.

"I'm okay. *Shhh*. It was just an anxiety attack. I'm okay."

"I'm sorry," Amber sobbed. "I'm so sorry."

"It's okay. We'll work it out. You know that."

Amber nodded and wiped her eyes with the back of her hand. "Uncle John called and said that Aunt Nan will probably be at the house when we get there. She's going to help out for a while. Inez wanted to come, but Tyson told her to stay with Grandma."

Cole put his hand on Billie's shoulder and let out a deep sigh. "You scared the hell out of me." His voice was hoarse.

She touched his hand. "I'm sorry."

"I want a hug, too," Abby scrunched in and then took a look at the bump on the side of Billie's head. "What did the doctor say? No tiaras for a week? Wow. Look at the size of that thing. Maybe two weeks."

"I'm so glad you're okay," Miss Sadie said. "Praise the Lord."

With all of the commotion over Billie, the other folks at the hospital must have thought she'd been raised from the dead. Tyson surprised Billie with a peck on the cheek and took charge, suggesting everybody clear out so that she could go home and get some rest. "Amber, why don't you ride in the back with the baby and let your mom sit in the front so she can lay the seat back."

As they walked out to the car, Amber looked at Tyson like he had just recited a sonnet. The orderly helped Billie into the car and she fumbled with the seatbelt for a few seconds until Tyson helped her find the clip. He smiled his Justin Timber-lake smile, proud that he was not only playing the part of a responsible adult today, he was sure he was going to win some kind of award for it.

Abby stuck her head in the window and kissed her on the cheek. "They had to fight me and Cole for the honor of taking you home. We lost. But Cole and I will stop by the minute you feel up to having company. I love you, Billie Sue."

Billie thought about the look on the orderly's face when Jeff had done the same and smiled to herself. "It's okay," she had told him on the way out of the ER. "The doctor's just sucking up to me because I used to kick his ass when we were kids."

"It's true." Jeff had said. "As a matter of fact, her mother raised her to kick the world's ass."

Billie closed her eyes and smiled again. That was just about the nicest thing she could ever remember anybody saying about her.

CHAPTER TWELVE

A silver Mercedes station wagon was parked on the street in front of Billie's house. Nan. As Tyson pulled into the driveway behind Billie's car, a round, preppy-looking woman with a neat blond bob bounded out of the house toward the car.

"Who are you?" Billie said.

"Oh, my God," Nan looked at Amber, "You said she was okay."

"I don't have amnesia, I just didn't recognize you with your new look, but then I haven't seen you since last Christmas. You look amazing."

Nan tossed her head and let out her signature laugh as she and Tyson helped Billie out of the car. "John went to the bar convention at St. Simons Island one week and the girls and I played Extreme Makeover. You like?"

Billie moved in for a closer look. "Oh, my God, you had your eyes done."

Nan nodded and batted her baby blues. "Well, the girls didn't do *that*. But John bought a damn Harley for his fiftieth birthday. Can you believe that? So I got my eyes done. And a breast reduction," she whispered the last part barely loud enough for Billie to hear.

Tyson opened the front door and he and Nan guided Billie to the overstuffed couch where Nan had pulled candles and jewel-colored satin pillows from Amber's bedroom and arranged them to make the outdated couch look like something from the Home and Garden Channel. A TV tray was full of essential oils and lotions, nail polish, and every pedicure product and tool known to womankind. The large ruby and gold glass bowl Amber bought at Pier One's After Christmas Sale last year was set up as a foot tub, already full of steamy peppermint-scented water.

"Tyson," Nan said, putting her arm around his middle. "Now you know that I love you, but I've got the hen party set up here, and the truth is—you'll have to leave."

Tyson smiled and gave her a peck on the cheek. "Amber, do you want me to take Little T?"

"Oh, I don't mind keeping him," Miss Sadie said.

"Come on, Miss Sadie, we could all use a little pampering," Amber said.

"Miss Sadie, I'm Nan, Billie's brother's wife, and that Amber's a smart girl. Have a seat. Take your shoes off and soak your feet. I'll be with you in a bit."

Nan began spreading an avocado-oatmeal mixture over Billie's face with a pastry brush. "You'll love this masque. I got the recipe from a gal who used to work for Elizabeth Arden in New York before she went *au naturel*. Mixes everything up in her kitchen and makes a blessed fortune. And it's marvelous."

Amber sighed after Tyson whispered something in her ear and then touched his lips to hers. Little Man grabbed her hair and leaned forward like a Tarzan baby, hoping to swing from daddy back to mama, but Amber unlatched him and kissed his little bald head. "Bye boys," she said and let out a decadent giggle as she closed the front door.

"Delores heard you were going to be out of commission for a while and dropped some books by for you, a whole grocery bag full of bodice rippers." Nan placed slivers of cucumber over Billie's eyes. "She said to tell you she'll be around soon to make sure you're behaving yourself and that she's already lined up somebody to fill in for you next week."

"I have Sunday and Monday off. I should be okay by then," Billie said.

"Mama," Amber began. "Maybe you ought to take off more than just a couple of days."

"Lord, Amber, I'd go nuts."

"Well, I can tell you from personal experience that you'll go nuts if you don't." Nan grabbed a little wooden stick and surveyed Billie's hands. "My God, when's the last time you had a manicure?"

Billie lifted up one of the cucumber slices and looked at Nan.

"Don't you give me that look, Billie Warren, you'll mess your face up."

"Aunt Nan, if it's okay with you, I can start Miss Sadie's pedicure," Amber said.

"Okay. This may take a while; your mama's nails are a disgrace."

"She works like a man, that one does," Miss Sadie yawned. "You ought to have seen her out there yesterday cutting the grass in the heat of the day."

Nan dabbed peach oil on each of Billie's cuticles and massaged it in. Billie could feel a tension between the two of them that would only subside after Nan spoke her mind. But instead of beginning the unburdening process, Nan announced that she had picked a pretty nude-colored polish that sparkled when the light hit it the right way and then started applying the polish while she no doubt rehearsed her "you need to take better care of yourself" speech in her head.

That was one thing Nan was really good at. Whenever she reached her *stresshold*, as she liked to call it, she always scheduled a mandatory full day at the spa. For a long time, she was big on retail therapy. But after her oldest started middle school, she found great solace in pampering herself through hard times. The end result was a meticulously dressed woman who towered above adversity with perfect hair and flawless skin.

"Is this the Sadie John told me about?" Nan whispered as she removed the cucumber slices.

Billie looked to see Miss Sadie had already fallen asleep with her head resting against the side of the wingback chair, mouth gaped open, snoring softly. Billie closed her eyes in affirmation.

"What in the world is she doing here?" Nan asked.

"It's a long story."

"Mama?" Amber whispered as she spread a chenille throw across Miss Sadie's lap. "Is this the Sadie . . ."

Billie sat up to give Amber a look, but the pain made her think the better of it, and she lay back down.

"Crazy Sadie?" Amber hissed. "In the same house with my baby?"

"Oh, to hear John tell it, she was never really crazy," Nan whispered. "Besides, I know I'd be if what was done to her was done to me."

"When I was a kid, everybody called her that. She was in the park all the time. She cried a lot, but mostly she just watched us play." Billie tried to sound nonchalant, but her insides churned at the memory of the day Jimmy Malden dared her to steal Miss Sadie's doll.

The only reason Billie went back to the hollow tree in the park was to kick Jimmy's ass for pissing on that photograph. When she got there, she saw a group of girls playing jacks on the sidewalk. They wore dresses and culottes and ribbons in their hair, and they dusted off their behinds every time they stood up. Their high-pitched giggles sounded like a flock of sick birds as they darted from safe sidewalk games like hopscotch and jacks to the swings.

They didn't even swing, just sat there with their arms wrapped around the chains talking about stupid stuff. Billie had never belonged to their brood, and never wanted to belong, but, watching them, she knew if she couldn't become a Wild Boy, she would be alone. No kid in her right mind wanted that; still, she'd be damned before she'd beg Jimmy Malden to let her join the pack of boys that roamed the streets of Stanton in search of high adventure. So Billie would either have to beat Jimmy up and take his place as leader or, worse, kowtow to him and hope he'd let be a Wild Boy. She'd rather die.

But if she started something she couldn't finish, Jimmy Malden would find a steamy fresh pile of dog shit and make her eat it.

She watched Jimmy drawing the boys in with one of his stories that were always the same, Jimmy doing something disgusting like pissing in his daddy's beer when he was too drunk to notice or beating the crap out of anybody he thought deserved it. Even though they'd heard the same stories a thousand times, the Wild Boys couldn't get enough of Jimmy Malden.

He was a head taller than Billie and thick through the chest. His arms were too long for his body and were the reason some of the kids called him Ape, but never to his face. If things didn't go the way she hoped they would, he could hurt her all right. And if the rest of the boys piled on? Billie shuddered at the thought.

"Hey, Billie," Skip Johnson called, making all the boys look her way. He motioned her over. She pushed her flat chest out and walked coolly toward them, fists clenched, fingernails digging into the palms of her hands. Wait, her brother, John, had told her how to fight, and the first rule was to assess her surroundings. Great, she was out numbered fourteen to one. She tucked her thumb inside her fingers. No, that wasn't right. She readjusted her hands so her thumb was on the outside and lengthened her stride. She needed to remember how to set her feet when she got to Jimmy, parallel to her shoulders, her dominant foot one half step back. Knees slightly bent.

Her first instinct was to hit Jimmy hard in the stomach, but John had said always go for the weak spot—the temple or the jaw. If she hit *him just right, he'd go down hard. Her heartbeat pounded in her ears. She felt the blood from her thighs racing toward her heart. "High and hard," she whispered. The fight was just a few paces away. "Pull back. Guard my face. Set my feet and hit him again."*

Billie walked right up to him positioning herself between Jimmy and the boys. "Hey, butt face," Jimmy said.

Billie set her feet, mostly to keep her knees from knocking, but she'd refused to show Jimmy Malden she was afraid. Before she could put up her dukes, Olen Patterson piped up. "Hey, Billie, Jimmy's gonna let you join up for real."

"All you got to do—is steal Crazy Sadie's doll," Jimmy growled, "but you won't do it. You ain't got the guts."

"I got the guts." She was breathing hard. Terrified, fighting back the tears. "To kick your ass."

"Whoa now," Skip sandwiched himself in between them. "We like you Billie. You're one of us. Ain't no need for anybody to get their ass kicked." Skip was facing Billie; she could see he was afraid for her. "Just do what Jimmy says and you're one of us. Forever. Like blood brothers. Ain't that right, Jimmy?"

"She don't have it in her to be one of us." Jimmy's head was bent, his forehead pressed against hers, eyes narrowed in a death stare.

"Don't be so sure." Billie bit out.

"You hit me and I'll beat the ever loving shit out of you." His breath was stinky and hot, and she wanted to cry. God, she wanted to cry, but she didn't dare. "You hit me and you'll never be one of us."

She knew he was right, but seeing Sadie Byrd every day in the park, watching the kids play, Billie was almost as afraid of her as she was of tearing into Jimmy Malden. But stealing the doll was better than getting beaten up. She turned on her heel and headed toward the bushes on the other side of the park that butted up to the bench where Crazy Sadie always sat. Billie waited a long time on the other side of the hedge for her to set the doll down. When that didn't happen, Skip helped Billie out.

He came tearing across the playground and skidded out right in front of the bench, clutching his leg, pretending to cry. The woman put the tattered doll on the bench and tended to Skip who hooted and hollered like he was dying. Billie knew it was wrong, but what choice did she have? Besides it wasn't like she was stealing a real baby. It was just a doll, and if Jimmy didn't wreck the thing, Billie could put it back after the boys went home for supper.

She snatched the doll and stuffed it under her shirt and headed back to the other side of the playground where the Wild Boys watched the scene play out. When Skip saw Billie leave, he miraculously recovered and ran back over to their den, which amounted to a hole in the thick red tip hedge.

They all watched Sadie Byrd toddle back to her bench. She was frantic, looking for her doll. She started to cry, to scream. "My baby. Where's my baby?" She collapsed on the ground. Billie had never heard a sound like that, not from a human. It was more like a wounded animal, a horribly wounded animal.

Billie prayed Sadie Byrd was too grief stricken to hear the Wild Boys laughing, to see them spill out of the bushes, rolling around on the ground. But even at nine, she had the very real sense that she had done something horrible, something she'd never forgive herself for. Something she would never forget.

Nan applied the rest of the goo onto Billie's face. "I can't even imagine how hard it must have been for her, pregnant all the time and never being able to keep her babies. No wonder she was drawn to the park to watch the children play; she must have believed that some of the kids there were hers. Did she ever approach any of the children?"

"No, she told me her husband convinced her it would kill her babies to know who their real mother was," Billie said. "She believed a lot of her children were adopted out to families in Stanton. Every day, she watched us play in the park, but never said a word to any of us that I know of."

"Bless her heart," Nan said.

Sadie's story was sad enough without Billie adding the latest chapter. She had come back to Stanton to report the murder of a little girl. There would be no trial, no public reckoning for the crime. No justice.

Nan swiped her eyes with the back of her sleeve. "Poor thing."

"Why didn't you tell me?" Amber's tone had softened considerably.

"I don't know," Billie said. "For one thing, I didn't want you to flip out."

"Thanks, Mom. So, why did she come back to Stanton?"

"Does it matter why she came back? Besides, you know I can't discuss work stuff with you."

"Well," Nan said quietly, "we can never undo what's been done, but we can order an extra measure of pampering for Miss Sadie Byrd."

Nan was right. Miss Sadie was due something for all she had been through. Billie owed her. Hell, the whole town owed her for letting Dewey Byrd get away with the things he did to her.

Nan took a steamy hot hand towel out of a cooler beside her and began taking the avocado oatmeal goo off Billie's face and neck. She let out a deep sigh and shook her head. Billie looked at Nan and then at Amber who had finished Miss Sadie's pedicure and was looking at her own sad nails. "Look at that poor old woman, completely worn out. Didn't stir one bit while Amber worked on her feet."

Billie didn't say anything.

"What do you think Miss Sadie wants?" Nan asked.

Billie shrugged. "She came here to find a little peace, but I'm afraid she came a long way for nothing."

"There's got to be something we can do for her."

"What, Nan?"

"There's just got to be."

"We can't always make things better. Life's not fair. If anybody knows that, it's Sadie Byrd. Good women like her get screwed over every day. It's a sad thing, but there's not a damn thing I can do about it. The worst part of this whole thing is she doesn't have any family. After she settles her son's estate, I don't know what she'll do."

"Mama, we can't just send her home alone."

"I know it doesn't seem right, Amber, but—"

"That's because it's not right," Nan said flatly.

Billie was quiet while Nan emptied the bowl in the kitchen sink and refilled it for Billie's pedicure. She was tired from all the talking and pretending like her head wasn't trying to explode, but her nails looked nice. She rubbed her fingertips across her face; it felt deliciously soft. Nan was really good at this pampering stuff.

"Good God, Billie, don't you ever do your feet?" Nan slipped Billie's feet into the water.

If Nan had been in Billie's shoes forty years ago—well truth be told, Nan would never have been in Billie's shoes. She would never have been mixed up with the Wild Boys, and never in a million years would she have stolen Sadie Byrd's doll.

Nan would have kicked any Wild Boy who got in her way right in the nuts and then sat herself down beside Miss Sadie on that park bench. Then she would have tried to make sense of everything and make things better, like she always did.

"Maybe there is one thing that I can do for her," Billie said.

"Good," Nan said, "because this one is killing me."

"A couple of times, she's asked me if I knew where her babies were."

"Well, do you?"

"No, but I can take a few days off, help her settle her son's estate. Maybe see what I can find out about the adoptions."

"See there." Nan grinned, "I knew there was something."

Amber propped a pillow behind Billie's head, then she sat down on the couch, and nuzzled her way up under Billie's arm, something she hadn't done in a very long time. Billie's eyes were heavy now. She fought hard to stay awake—to talk to Nan. It was so good to see her, and she wanted to stay awake just to feel her own baby snuggled up against her.

"Mom, I can help. I'm good at finding stuff on the Internet," Amber said.

"Thanks honey; that would be nice." Billie's words were slow and groggy. "You really look good; how far along are you? Are you feeling okay?"

"I'm fine, Mama. I'm seven weeks. You go to sleep now."

"Amber?" Billie whispered. "Why didn't you tell me?"

"Hush, Mama. Get some rest now."

"I don't know about—you having another baby—but I hope it's a girl. Yeah, a sweet baby girl."

CHAPTER THIRTEEN

For the first hour or so, it was nice to be waited on hand and foot. But two days of being pampered to death had nearly killed Billie. Her headache was long gone, her vision had cleared, and her skin looked radiant. She was expecting Jeff to come by on his way into the hospital for rounds and was surprised when she answered the door to find Cole on her front porch.

"I thought I'd lost you," he said, and the look on his face told her he wasn't just talking about the anxiety attack.

She assured him she was fine, still refusing to talk about the two of them. He touched her head lightly where the goose egg had been. His fingers trailed down the side of her face. She turned away.

"I'm not giving up, Billie."

"Why not Cole?" She looked at him. "It would be easier for you, for me."

"All this stuff that's happening to you won't last forever. It can't."

"How do you know that?"

"I just do. I love you."

"Then stop."

"Do you think it's that easy, that I could just stop if I wanted to?" He raked his hand through his hair. "Love doesn't work that way, Billie, and you know this because you love me too. You say we can't be together because you've got nothing left inside you to give, but I'm not asking for anything from you. I just want to be there for you, to love you through this, but you won't let me. What are you so afraid of, Billie?"

Of him. She was afraid of him. Of loving him. Of losing him. She'd barely survived the loss of her father, almost losing Amber, but there was no way in hell she'd survive losing Cole. Was her fear rational? Probably not, but with the immanent loss of her mother gutting her on a daily basis, she couldn't risk opening her already broken heart to this man.

A car door slammed. She was grateful for the distraction and pulled the curtains back and glanced out the living room window to see Jeff coming up the walkway.

"That's Jeff."

"Give me something, Billie. Anything." She turned her head toward the door waiting for the knock and sagged with relief when Jeff rapped twice.

"You should go." Her voice didn't come out at all like she meant it to and was barely above a whisper.

He tipped her chin up until she had no choice but to look into his eyes. "You're betting that if you keep sending me away, I'll give up. Go away for good." Well, yes, but she couldn't get the word out, couldn't even nod. The doorbell chimed. Cole touched his lips to hers, lingering just enough to weaken her significantly. "It's a bad bet, Billie. A really bad bet."

The ache in her chest from just watching him leave said Cole was wrong.

———————◆◆◆———————

Jeff said it was his first house call and joked around a bit before he announced the knot on her head had gone down enough to give her the green light to slip back into her old life slowly. The last thing Billie wanted was to slip back into her old life, but she didn't have a choice.

After Jeff left, she heard Miss Sadie up and rumbling around her bedroom. Billie knocked softly and opened the door. "Morning."

"Morning. I stripped the bed linens and put my towels with them. You were awful good to let me stay."

"Thanks, but you didn't have to do that. Bet you're excited to be going home."

"It'll be good and bad with Cecil not there. But I'm ready to go." Amber screamed. "What in the world?"

Billie sprinted to the nursery and threw open the door to find Amber on the floor with her laptop and a bunch of printouts scattered about.

"Look, Mama!" Amber was staring at her laptop screen. "Seventeen hits on this message board alone."

Billie took a deep breath to slow her skyrocketing heartbeat. "Jesus, Amber, you scared the shit out of me."

"Sorry, I'm a little wired. I've been up all night going over the adoption boards. Just in the southeast, there are thousands of people looking for their birth mothers."

Miss Sadie poked her head in the door. "Is everything all right?"

"Oh, Miss Sadie, I put the birth dates you gave me on a bunch of the adoption reunion sites to see if anyone was looking for you." She turned the screen around toward Miss Sadie. "We got seventeen hits."

Miss Sadie looked confused but excited. "But I'm only looking for my twelve."

"That's okay," Amber said, "The way the message board works is, you put your information on there and people who are looking for their birth mother contact you to see if you're a match. Sometimes an angel makes the contacts."

"An angel?" Miss Sadie sat down beside Amber.

"They're called search angels; they're people who help adoptees find their birth parents," Billie said, sitting down on the futon beside Amber.

"Way to go, Mom."

"A lady contacted the station a couple of years ago looking for information on a runaway who was arrested back in the 70s. The woman said she was an angel, kind of like a private detective for folks who are looking for their birth parents."

"And because of the Internet, a lot more parents are looking for the adult children they gave up for adoption." Amber scrolled down the page at a dizzying pace. "But mostly, the boards are full of adoptees looking for their birth mothers."

"All these years, I've wanted to know them," Miss Sadie's voice was thick with emotion. "It never occurred to me that some of them might be looking for me."

"Mom said all your adoptions were private, and before 1983 when the adoption laws in South Carolina changed. That makes information harder to find—Oh, my God." Amber put the computer in Miss Sadie's lap. "We got a hit on one of the black market boards."

"It says, URGENT—Born February 6, 1961. Boy. I am a Dalton baby, adopted through Mac Dalton with falsified birth records. I am in desperate need of medical information." Miss Sadie adjusted her glasses. "Do you think he's mine?"

"I don't know. The sex and the birthdate are a match. The response just says, call as soon as possible." Amber grabbed her cell phone, punched in the number, and handed the phone to Miss Sadie."

"But I don't know what to say."

"Tell them you think you're the person they're looking for," Amber said.

"Hello?" The voice at the other end said. "Hello?"

"But what if I'm not the person they're looking for?" Miss Sadie handed the phone to Billie.

"Hi," Billie said. "I'm calling for my friend. She got a post from a young man who was looking for medical information."

"That was from me." There was a long pause before the woman on the other end of the call continued. "My son waited for someone to answer that message for a long time."

"If the birth information you have is correct, my friend may be the woman you're looking for. Is there a good time she could meet you and your son?"

"David searched for his birth mother for three years before he died."

Billie looked at Miss Sadie's hopeful face and shook her head. "I'm sorry for your loss. If you don't mind me asking, why did you reply to the post?"

"I'd like to meet your friend as soon as possible, and if she is David's mother, I want to hug her neck." Billie took down the woman's address and agreed to meet her in a couple of hours.

"He passed away, didn't he?" Miss Sadie asked quietly.

Billie nodded. "His name was David and his mother, his adoptive mother, wants to meet you. You feel up to that?"

"Yes, I want to meet her too." Miss Sadie nodded sadly. "He was born before Donna; they were thirteen months apart."

"I'm so sorry." Amber rubbed Miss Sadie's arm and gave her a warm smile. "Tyson's helping too. We'll keep looking until we find the others."

"Amber." Billie hated for her to make promises she might not be able to keep, but Billie was proud of her for trying and enlisting more help. "Try Dalton babies, Mac Dalton, illegal adoptions, and see what comes up."

Amber nodded and tapped away on the keyboard. "There's a State Newspaper article from almost five years ago. Holy crap." She scanned the article and passed the laptop to Billie.

"'Maggie Dalton has been looking for her birth mother for twenty years while trying to make amends for the family business. Her adoptive father, the late Mac Dalton, was a former president of the South Carolina Bar Association, a stalwart supporter of Christian charities and the Red Cross, and was a baby seller,'" Billie read and then scanned the rest of the article. "There's an address and a contact number."

"Dialing it now." Amber scratched down the address on a sheet of notebook paper and handed it to Billie.

She shoved the paper into the pocket of her jeans and listened to the long message with instructions for adoptees calling in. "Ms. Dalton, my name is Billie Warren, my friend, Sadie Byrd, was the birth mother of several babies we believe were sold by your father. We'd like to meet with you as soon as possible." Billie left her contact information and ended the call.

———————◆◆◆———————

"Are you sure this is the place?" Miss Sadie stared at the massive home.

When the woman on the phone gave the address, Billie expected what anybody would if they were going to 32 South Battery, but not this. The South Carolina Historical Register plaque said that the house was built in 1782 by Colonel John Ashe, a shipping magnate and militia leader during the Revolutionary War. Billie looked across the street at Battery Park and the stunning view of Charleston Harbor, then back at the directions.

"This is the place." Billie opened her car door but Miss Sadie stayed put. "What's wrong?"

"Dew did right by him," she said sadly. "Look at where he grew up." She motioned to the house and beautiful White Point Gardens in the park across the street. "I bet he played on those old cannons and the statues in the park when he was little. Maybe had his first kiss there in the gardens by that gazebo." She shook her head. "I feel like a fool coming to a place such as this."

"I have to admit the house is pretty intimidating," Billie said. "But this man looked for his birth mother for three years, and his mom kept up the search. Don't you owe it to yourself to know if he was your son?"

"But how can I be sure?"

"I don't know, but if we walk away now, you'll never know."

Miss Sadie rang the bell that chimed an elaborate tune. A housekeeper answered the door and showed the two women into a sitting room just off the foyer. The room was stunning—dark honey–colored heart of pine floors, cream-colored walls that matched the semi-modern furniture, a gleaming Steinway beside the floor-to-ceiling windows overlooking a garden that put the famous one in the park across the street to shame.

"I want to leave," Miss Sadie said. "Now."

"Please. Stay." A woman pushed a walker into the room. She was dressed in expensive looking slacks and a silk blouse that complemented the décor of the room. She was beautiful and could have passed for early sixties, but her body gave her away. "I'm so grateful you came."

"Mrs. Herron, I'm Billie Warren, and this is Sadie Byrd."

"Call me Polly." She extended her hand to Miss Sadie. "Please, sit. May I call you Sadie?"

"Yes, ma'am." Miss Sadie sat down on the edge of the white satin brocade couch, between the woman and Billie.

"You have a beautiful home," Billie said.

"Thank you. People say that all the time, but with my husband Graham and David gone, it just seems big and empty." The woman smiled at Miss Sadie and then reached for her hand. "It's so good to finally meet you, Sadie Byrd. My son looked for you for a very long time."

"Do you think I'm his birth mother?"

"I don't know. After we were presented with the gravity of

David's diagnosis, I searched the face of every woman I passed on the street, hoping to find his mother." She studied Miss Sadie's face. "Such a strong resemblance."

"I know your loss," Miss Sadie swallowed hard and looked away from Polly. "I buried my boy last week."

"I'm so sorry. I'd like to tell you that you get over it; but I'd be lying. It's ironic to have battled death for years with Graham and then with David. Fought it tooth and nail. Now, I find solace knowing I'm near the end of my life and will see them again when I pass." Polly sifted through a half dozen thick leather bound photo albums until she pulled one of them onto her lap. "Would you like to see some pictures?"

Miss Sadie nodded.

"All of these albums are David's; he was our only child. He was two days old in this picture." The woman turned the pages slowly; Miss Sadie stopped her when she got to an eight-by-ten picture of a little blond-haired, blue-eyed boy dressed in a fancy jon jon suit. She ran her fingers across the boy's face. "You recognize him, don't you?"

"Cecil." Her voice quivered. "He looks so much like my boy, he takes my breath away."

"Then your son was beautiful." Polly turned the page.

Miss Sadie touched one of the photos of the boy in a Halloween costume. He was dressed as a frog and had a silly smile on his face. A stunningly beautiful Polly was looking at him adoringly. "We didn't have money for pictures, but that's the way I remember Cecil at that age."

The woman flipped the pages stopping at a picture of a lanky older boy in a tuxedo at a grand piano. "David studied music—piano—and was quite good, but he loved teaching best. He taught music theory here at The College of Charleston; his students adored him."

"What happened to him?" Billie asked.

"David was thirty-eight when he was diagnosed with chronic

myelogenous, an insidious form of leukemia. They said he wouldn't live more than five years without a bone marrow transplant from a blood relative. They were right."

"I wish I could have helped him," Miss Sadie said.

"When we began our search for David's birth parents, I wanted to cut Mac Dalton in two for the phony birth certificate that said my husband and I were David's blood parents. When David was little, that lie made me feel safe, and we were so close, it was easy to pretend I gave birth to him. After he got sick, I paid the highest price for the luxury of pretending."

"You contacted Mac Dalton?" Billie asked.

She shook her head and looked away toward the piano. "Mac had already died. There were so many hands in his till after his death, the estate stayed in probate until a lot of powerful people made sure everything was neat and tidy." She waived her hand dismissively. "Even with our considerable resources, no one would help us."

"I contacted Maggie Dalton this morning," Billie said, "but haven't heard back from her."

"Since Mac's death, Maggie has tried to sort things out, set them right. But it's just her, trying to find answers for hundreds of babies Mac Dalton adopted out—most with no papers of any kind. By the time the estate turned the records over to Maggie, David had already passed away.

"I still wanted to find his birth mother, but Maggie had living adoptees who took precedence over my need to know her identity." Polly closed the album.

"That's why you answered the post," Billie said.

"After working the boards for three years because David's life depended on it, I can't stop." Polly squeezed Miss Sadie's hand. "Mrs. Byrd, you're the only person to ever answer any of David's posts."

"Billie's daughter found it on the Internet for me, but I'm glad she did."

"I invited you here to ask you for a DNA sample to know for sure whether you were David's birth mother, but, seeing the resemblance in your face, your eyes, that doesn't seem necessary anymore. You're his mother. I'm sure of it."

"I'm so sorry about your boy, but if it's okay with you, I'd like to take that test."

Polly nodded. With shaking hands, she pulled a long plastic vial out of the basket attached to her walker and handed it to Billie. "Would you mind?"

Billie had never done the test before. Her job rarely required the use of forensics, and when it did, the county always took care of it. But she had watched enough cop shows to know what to do. She swabbed the inside of Miss Sadie's cheek, returned the Q-tip to the container, and handed it back to Polly.

The room grew awkwardly quiet.

"We'd better go," Billie said.

"It was so good to meet you," Miss Sadie said, "Meant a lot to me to see those pictures of your boy."

"Thank you for coming." Polly hugged Miss Sadie before she and Billie stepped out into the blustery wind. "I hope you are David's mother, too."

Across the street from the historic mansion, White Point Gardens was stunningly beautiful. Crisp amber-colored leaves fell like confetti from ancient live oaks. Masses of snapdragons, pansies, and other fall-loving flowers framed the huge gazebo in the middle of the historic park that had witnessed pirate hangings and Revolutionary War skirmishes. On the other side of the park, the Charleston Harbor rocked angry and blue. White caps slapped the top of the sea wall.

Billie helped Miss Sadie into the car and took it all in, hoping such a sight would chase away the sadness that came from the meeting with Polly Herron. Polly's struggle with death reminded Billie of when her father got sick, of the futility of her own struggle with her mother.

Somewhere in the distance a ship's horn sounded twice to signal a change of course. Across the bay, toward Sullivan's Island, storm clouds were moving fast.

CHAPTER FOURTEEN

It was hard to ride through the picturesque streets of the Holy City and say David Herron wasn't better off growing up with the trappings of Charleston finery. Polly Herron and her husband had given him everything a child needs to thrive—security, opportunity, love.

Billie shook her head and glanced at the gas gauge; it was low. She was hungry, too, but she didn't think she could stomach anything after wrestling with the questions she couldn't get out of her mind. How many other well-to-do couples behind those fancy iron gates had bought Dalton babies? And how had so many people kept such a huge secret?

Then again, the whole town of Stanton knew what was happening to Sadie Byrd and did nothing. Did they just not care or were they trying to protect their own children?

Billie thought about Amber and Little Man. Would she twist the law to protect them? Would she break it? If she knew she'd lose them forever, she would do anything to save them. No wonder the Dalton's family business had stayed hidden for decades; hundreds of adoptive parents willing to do anything to protect their children, even if it meant keeping them away from their rightful mothers.

"Billie?" Miss Sadie said. "Would it be okay if you took me home tomorrow?"

Miss Sadie looked emotionally and physically beat. "Sure," Billie said. "We can be back at my house in less than an hour."

"Orangeburg isn't far from here. If you don't mind, I'd like to stop by Mac Dalton's old place, see if his daughter will talk to us?"

"You look so tired. Her place is on the way to Columbia; we could stop by tomorrow."

"This won't wait," Miss Sadie said and closed her eyes.

The scenery on the street transitioned from one grandiose home to another, to retail shops and restaurants, to a less shiny part of Charleston. Billie pulled into a Gas and Go before she got onto the interstate. It was dirty and shabby compared to the trendy shops on King Street. While Billie filled up the car, she checked the caller ID on her cell phone that she'd silenced before the meeting at Polly's house. No word from Maggie Dalton. But Abby had called seven times, which either meant she'd actually sold one of her novels or she'd bought a cute pair of shoes she wanted Billie to see.

"I'm going to call Maggie Dalton and make sure she has time to see us."

"Don't." Miss Sadie said. "I don't want her to know we're coming."

"Why?"

"Seems like she's happy to help the children her daddy sold; I'm worried she won't be as glad to see one of their mothers."

In less than fifty minutes, Billie and Miss Sadie were in Orangeburg, standing in front of another mansion, only this one looked big and gaudy among the tiny Augusta brick houses that lined both sides of the street. The porch was wider than Billie's three-bedroom two-bath home back in Stanton, and the glossy wood planks made it look like a dance floor. Billie knocked on the tall ornately carved oak door. When there was no answer, Miss Sadie peered in the windows. "It's empty." Billie peeked through the floor-length windows at a huge room, maybe a living room with polished wooden floors.

"This is the address," Billie said, "but the house looks vacant."

As Billie helped Miss Sadie down the steps, an elderly neighbor waved from a mass of camellias she was pruning. "Are you all looking for Maggie?"

"Yes, ma'am," Billie said.

"Well, you're not the first folks to show up and peer into that empty old place. Maggie hasn't set foot in there since her father died; she lives in the carriage house around back. I believe she's home; I've been out here all day; haven't seen her leave."

"Thanks," Billie said.

Miss Sadie nodded at the woman. "You have a pretty place."

"I was born in this house and lived here all my life. I just couldn't believe it when it all came out about what Mac did. I'd heard talk but nobody ever really thought such a thing went on in our little town. I think everybody believed he was adopting those children out good and proper." The woman nodded at Billie. "You must be a Dalton baby."

"No, ma'am."

She looked at Billie like she didn't believe her. "Well, if that's why you are here, don't judge Maggie for what her daddy did; she's a good girl. Spends every waking minute trying to undo his sins; has all kinds of people coming and going, all of them wanting answers." The woman looked Miss Sadie over. "Pardon me for saying, but you're old like me, too old to be one of his."

"Guess I came for some answers, too," Miss Sadie said.

The woman didn't try to hide her astonishment. "Why, you're looking for your children, aren't you?"

"Yes," Miss Sadie nodded sadly and started walking toward the fancy little carriage house in the right hand corner of the property. Billie followed, the palm of her hand cupping Miss Sadie's elbow, supporting her across the large smooth stepping-stones.

"Well, I'll be," the woman called after them. "You're the only real mama that I know of that's ever come looking. I sure hope you find what you're looking for."

The tiny white cottage looked like something out of a fairy-tale with its gleaming gingerbread in all the right places. The windows and front door were arched, and a circlet of tall yellow and pink snapdragons brushed the bottoms of window boxes full of friendly pansies.

Miss Sadie stepped in front of Billie and rapped the palm of her hand hard on the lemon yellow front door. A youngish, redheaded woman threw open the door. She was on the phone with someone and seemed to be trying to get a word in edgewise with the person on the other end of the call. She shrugged apologetically at Miss Sadie and Billie and waved them into the tiny house.

It was a cozy place with bright floral furniture that might have looked nice if it weren't cluttered with laundry baskets full of files and law books. In one corner of the tiny three-room house, two waist-high stacks of files were marked with a DONE sign. Maggie held the phone away from her ear and massaged it for a moment before returning to the call.

"I understand your dilemma, sir, really I do, but again, my focus is on the Dalton babies. The answers you're looking for are there, you just have to look harder and be patient." *This may take a while*, she mouthed. "But I want you to know that you're lucky your adoption went through the Mayfield Home in Camden. They kept more records and more accurate records than my father did. Stay with it. Something will turn up."

Maggie ended the call. Introductions were made as she cleared off the floral chintz settee. "My house is so small, seems like all I ever do is move stuff around. Please, sit."

"You have a beautiful place," Billie said, "especially the garden."

"Thanks. People who don't know me are too polite to ask why I live out back. This is the house Mama and Daddy bought when he first got out of law school. They built the big house after he got into the adoption business."

"You were raised there?" Miss Sadie asked nodding toward the back of the mansion that was almost all windows. "You were lucky to have such a nice home."

"It was an interesting place to grow up. The wing to the left there was the nursery, complete with full-time nurses. My friends and I used to play dolls with real babies, dress them up, feed them. They were never here for more than a few days. I didn't know that what was happening was intrinsically wrong, but somehow I knew not to get too attached to them," Maggie said. "I'm sorry I didn't return your call. It's been a busy morning, but I'm glad you're here. How can I help?"

"Your daddy—" Miss Sadie blurted out, "sold my babies and I want to find them."

Maggie Dalton's face softened considerably. "I'm so sorry for the children you lost. I've never had a birth mother come looking for her children."

"That's hard to believe. Why wouldn't someone want to know their own child?" Miss Sadie asked.

"A lot of the babies who were adopted through my father's office came from unwed mothers who went on to get married and have kids of their own. Most of them never told anyone about the child they gave up, so when an adult child finds their birth parent, it can bring up a lot of pain from the past and cause a lot of pain and confusion in the present."

"I always hoped if I found them we'd all be happy," Miss Sadie said, absently. "You're saying if I found them it could hurt them?"

"Yes, but I have reams of cases that prove those meetings can be equally as joyful. A lot depends on the present-day families of the adult child and the birth mother. How everyone views the new relationship."

"We have no idea what's involved in the search, but we'd still like to try," Billie said. "My daughter sent you an e-mail with the birth dates of Miss Sadie's children."

"I haven't had a chance to check the data base." Maggie scooped up her laptop and pecked away on the keyboard. "I had a company digitize my father's records so I can access them easily. He practiced law for sixty-two years. There were so many documents, they are still at it." She pursed her lips together while she scanned the screen and then looked at Miss Sadie. "I'm sorry. There's nothing here with those birth dates."

Tears streamed down the old woman's face. Billie reached for her hand, but Miss Sadie yanked it away. "It's okay," Billie said.

"No, it's not okay. What was done to me will never be okay." Miss Sadie's voice trembled with anger.

Maggie closed her laptop. "You're right, Mrs. Byrd, what my father did to you and hundreds of women like you will never be okay."

"When everything inside me said it wasn't right what my husband was doing to me, I still loved my babies. All I have ever wanted in this life was to see with my own eyes that they're okay." Miss Sadie swiped at her nose with a wad of tissue. "Even as old as I am, that need never goes away."

"That wanting you have? I have that same wanting to know my birth mother. To see her face, to know her story, for her to know mine. Every time I help someone find their birth mother, it makes my heart ache that much more to see her."

"If you can't tell me where my children went, tell me why nobody ever tried to put a stop to this." Miss Sadie waved her hand at the mountains of file folders.

"Because back then, what my father did wasn't illegal." Maggie winced at the truth and looked out the window toward the magnificent garden sandwiched between the mansion and the carriage house. "Not in most states, and, at the time, not in the state of South Carolina."

"How could something that wrong not be illegal?" Billie asked.

"Mainstream adoption didn't even become popular until the 1940s," Maggie began. "It was so new, there weren't any laws on the books to regulate adoptions, much less laws to control the black market."

"Why didn't somebody make a law? Put a stop to it?" Miss Sadie asked.

"Times were different for women than they are now," Billie offered. She was glad Amber had had the option of keeping her baby without the shame and the backlash unwed mothers experienced when Billie was Amber's age.

"You're right. Nurses, clergymen, and doctors were complicit because, at the time, society told them it was the right thing to do," Maggie said. "But people like my father were in this ugly business for the money. He and the Mayfield Home in Camden handled the lion's share of adoptions in South Carolina for almost thirty years.

"The majority of the babies came from maternity homes all over the state. People who ran the homes made a good living because they got paid on both ends. Families of the pregnant girls paid room and board to hide their pregnant daughters until they gave birth. If families couldn't pay, new mothers stayed behind like an indentured servant until their debt was worked off. The homes also collected a fee when the baby was sold.

"Births were split down the middle with half of the newborns sent here and the other half sent to the Mayfield Home. At least my father used whatever means were available at the time to screen the families. The Mayfield Home sold babies to anybody who was willing to pay the asking price. Since older children went for less, my father dealt only in infants and left the toddlers to the Mayfield Home.

"With no regulations, homes had free reign to do anything they wanted. There are records of some adoption agencies starving children to keep them small so they would fetch a higher price. Many died of malnutrition."

"They starved little children?" Miss Sadie was trembling hard. "They let them die?"

"Sadly, yes. There was a woman named Georgia Tann in Memphis who did those things, but she's also responsible for popularizing adoption. Even with all the horrible things she did, people like me owe her a huge debt because she made adoption almost fashionable. Before she came along, unwanted children were used as farmhands or worse. They were examined like livestock; their teeth were checked; the small and the weak were never chosen. And if you were a redhead, you were considered defective."

"I've been a cop for twenty-seven years, and I've never heard of any of this until now," Billie said.

"Ever heard of the 'niños robados?'" Maggie asked. "It's Spanish for stolen children, over 300,000 to be exact, sold by the Spanish government under Franco and after he died, by the Catholic Church to couples in the UK for over fifty years. Adoption activists have been trying to get a formal investigation since 1975, but neither government will agree to even talk about it."

"How do you hide something that has a million accomplices?" Billie asked.

"Poor unwed mothers would have their children only to wake up and be told by a nurse or a doctor, maybe a nun, that their babies were dead. Most of the mothers were so grief stricken they didn't ask to see the corpses, and the ones who did were shown stillborn babies that were kept frozen for show. The same basic scenario happened thousands of times here in the states."

Billie shook her head. "Who's going to question a doctor or a nun?"

"With enough complicit people, anything is possible. Even here in the United States. Even in South Carolina. Unless you were in the market for a baby, you wouldn't have known about any of this," Maggie said. "My father sold upward of four hundred babies. Many of those, he stole by tricking poor women into signing away their parental rights."

"But I never signed anything," Miss Sadie said. "Dew said your daddy would make things legal but I never saw any papers."

"You didn't have to sign anything," Maggie said. "My father was powerful enough to fill in the blanks for the documents to say whatever he wanted them to, and he had the support of enough people in high places to make all of it stick."

"I get that the right people make anything happen, but how does a whole hospital full of professionals let this happen over and over again?" Billie asked.

"Some were paid to look the other way. Some thought they were doing society a favor, but for the most part, the system was lax," Maggie said. "Most women gave birth at the maternity home where they were housed. If there were complications, one of my father's assistants or someone from one of the homes would go to the hospital and check the birth mother in under the adoptive mother's name. Back then hospitals didn't check your ID ten times over before they admitted you. They just assumed you were who you said you were.

"The mother gave birth, the adoptive parents walked away with the baby and authentic-looking birth documents."

"It's still hard to believe that everybody looked the other way," Billie said.

Maggie rubbed the bridge of her nose and sighed. "Truth is, I've tried to figure this thing out for the past fifteen years, and the best answer I've come up with is, black market adoption thrived everywhere, including South Carolina, because a lot of powerful people were tied up in it. As a matter of fact one of them lives in your neck of the woods."

"Judge Norris." Billie said.

"If my father ran into a legal snag, one of his cronies was always there to fix it, and the judge was at the top of the list."

Billie shook her head. "It's hard to believe that all of this happened back then."

"You say 'back then,' but in 1984, *Time* magazine called South Carolina 'the baby supermarket of the South,'" Maggie said. "Which wasn't fair because black market adoption was in every state in the Union. Babies were big business until the mid-eighties when state laws changed. Things are better now; adoptions are more open. The birth mother isn't a throw away in the process. She has more rights, more say. But the sad truth is, if you have enough money, you can go to almost any town in this country today and buy a baby."

"I'm sorry for coming in here so spiteful and angry," Miss Sadie said, "I know you're hurting, too."

Maggie attempted a smile and shrugged. "Wish I could have been more help."

"You have our contact information," Billie said. "We'd appreciate a call if you run across anything."

"Of course. But I want to be honest with you; since Miss Sadie didn't sign any documents—"

"Do you have papers from when you were born?" Miss Sadie asked.

"No." Maggie shook her head and swallowed hard. "I found out I was adopted when I was a freshman in college. My mother told me before she died. After she passed, I waited what seemed like a respectable amount of time and told my father I wanted to contact my birth mother. He stalled for years and went to his grave swearing he didn't know who she was.

"I hated him then, for keeping her from me. After the moving company cleaned out his office and delivered these files, I realized he really didn't know who she was."

"We appreciate you taking time to meet with us," Billie said.

"My father called the women who trawled for babies for him wranglers. As far as I know, only one is still alive. She lives in the Upstate now and won't have anything to do with me, but she might help you. Her name is Gert Sampson."

"Gert Nightingale?" Miss Sadie gasped.

"Gert may have told women in your situation that her last name was Nightingale, but she was no angel of mercy. After my father got sick, he told me if I still wanted to find my mother, Gert would remember who she was. He told me about the other women who worked for him coercing expectant mothers into giving up their babies. They did it because they thought it was the Christian thing to do and wouldn't take a dime. Gert treated it like a game and was in it for the money."

"Do you think she will help us?" Miss Sadie asked.

"I don't know. She says she knows who my mother is, but she refuses to tell me."

"Why wouldn't she tell you now, especially after your father sent you to her for answers?" Billie asked.

"Because I'm trying to find the birth mothers she scammed, and that threatens her." Maggie scribbled down an address on a notecard. "If you offer her enough money, and don't mention my name, she might help you."

CHAPTER FIFTEEN

Sitting in Maggie Dalton's driveway, Billie had two choices, and she didn't like either of them. She could call Delores for information on Gert Sampson and get fussed at for playing detective off the clock. Or she could call Jimmy Malden, who would make her share in great detail why she wanted the information.

Jimmy had made a name for himself five years ago when he "solved" a cold case involving the disappearance of a soldier's new wife. It wasn't like Jimmy did any great detective work to pull off what the papers had called a "coup." He just happened to be drinking in the right bar one county over five years to the day Ted Winston's sister-in-law disappeared.

When he sat down beside Ted at the bar, Jimmy had no idea Ted was carrying around ten year's worth of guilt in a five-year sack, until the six-foot-six, four-hundred-pound drunk broke down and confessed to rolling over on his brother's wife and smothering her to death.

It was such a juicy story, especially since Ted's brother, Al, had been deployed in the Gulf at the time his wife, Rita, disappeared.

Nobody looked at Ted for the crime, but rumor had it, Jimmy made sure the TV guys were crawling all over the Francis Marion Swamp the day the excavation crew dug her up.

A few weeks after Jimmy starred on the six o'clock news, he was bumped up to sergeant thanks to dumb luck and buying Ted Winston three beers. Since then, Jimmy had been poking around cold cases, just itching to make captain. Better to call Delores and take her medicine.

"Where are you?" Delores huffed, "I went by your house to make sure you were still recuperating good and proper and guess what? You're not there. Nobody was, and when I got Amber on her cell, she tells me about this wild goose chase you have no business being on in your condition."

"You're not my mother, Delores."

"Oh, well don't you sound like a grown-up? Honestly, I should have sent a sack full of bungee cords to keep you strapped to that couch instead a sack full of books."

"Look, I get that you're mad—"

"I just don't think you get how mad I am. You're family to me, Billie. Hell, you're better than family because I actually like you. But you don't take care of yourself. You—"

Billie shrugged at Miss Sadie and held the cell phone away from her ear until Delores's anger died down enough for Billie to get a word in edgewise.

"Feel better now?"

"Honest to God, Billie Warren," Delores's voice cracked a little, "I don't know what I'm going to do with you."

"I promise you, I'm never going to do anything that will put me on that godforsaken couch again. I got the all clear from the doc. If you don't believe me, call Jeff's office and ask him yourself."

"You think I won't do it. Don't you?"

"I'm not calling to taunt you, Delores. I'm calling because I need some background information on a woman named Gert Sampson, aka Gert Nightingale, who may have other aliases. Last known address is in the Upstate." When Delores harrumphed, Billie decided to play the sympathy card. "I need this for Miss Sadie."

There was dead silence. She could hear Delores's rapid, angry breath. If Billie wanted the information, she was going to have to call Jimmy Malden to get it.

"I'll call Doctor Jeff and if he tells me you're right as rain, I'll think about it."

"Thanks, Delores, and I'm sorry if I upset you." Billie continued with her apology until she realized Delores had already ended the call.

"She seems like a nice friend," Miss Sadie said, "but I believe she's mad with you."

"Delores always says she can get glad as quick as she can get mad. She'll call Jeff, for sure and then—" Billie's cell phone chirped. Delores. "What'd you find out?"

"She still goes by Gert Sampson. Eighty-six, did fifteen years at Women's Correctional for trafficking pot, was released at seventy-one because she was near death. Apparently, she made a miraculous recovery and lives, like you said, in the Upstate. No phone. No cell phone that can be traced back to her, but that doesn't mean she doesn't have one."

"Is it a Traveler's Rest address?"

"Yeah, sounds like a real nice place. Forty-six Trash Pile Road. There's not hide nor hair of a death certificate, so I reckon she's still kicking. What do you want with her anyway?"

"She might be able to help track down some of Miss Sadie's children."

"She don't sound like the helpful type; did three years extra for snatching some poor inmate baldheaded . Literally. But I am the helpful type, and I'm telling you, sooner or later the Norrises are going to get wind of you helping that poor woman, and it won't end pretty."

"Thanks for running that down for me, Delores."

"You're still gonna birddog this thing as far as it'll go?"

"Yes, ma'am."

"You're a stubborn soul, Billie Warren, that's what you are, and if I didn't love you so much, I wouldn't lift a finger to help you, scaring me to death with that heart attack."

"Panic attack," Billie corrected.

"Whatever. But that's the least of your worries. When, not if, Bob Norris hears Sadie Byrd was in town and you're traipsing around the state of South Carolina with her. It won't wash. Not with his re-election so close."

Billie ended the call without admitting to Delores that maybe she was right about Bob Norris. The car had idled long enough in Maggie Dalton's driveway to get looks from the neighbors. Billie backed slowly out of the pebbled drive into the street. The gas gauge was nearly full, but they hadn't eaten all day, and if they were headed to the mountains, they'd have to stay overnight.

Miss Sadie touched Billie's arm. "Is there trouble about?"

"No. Everything's fine. We'll drive to Traveler's Rest, find a place to stay, and go see Gert Sampson tomorrow morning."

"What if she's not there?"

"The mountains are pretty. If nothing else, it'll be a nice drive."

As the car rolled down the main drag of Orangeburg, Billie eyed her bare hands and wished she were one of those women who loved jewelry or at the very least wore a nice wristwatch. She scanned the storefronts and pulled the Toyota into a parking space a few doors down from the Pit Stop Grill and killed the engine.

She swallowed hard and opened her purse, sliding her finger into the felt pouch where she kept the sterling silver pocket watch her father got when he retired from the Stanton police department. She wanted to sit with it for a moment, open and close it a thousand times like she used to do when she first joined the force and she was fidgety or nervous. Since then, it had stayed in a pouch in the bottom of her purse, something she never had to worry about because it was always there. Just like her father had always been there for her.

Billie had never pawned anything in her life, never had even been inside of a pawnshop. She'd seen some pretty fancy-looking ones along I-26 near Charleston with bicycles and riding lawn mowers, four wheelers and exercise machines overflowing into the parking lot and wrote it off to a shitty economy. She wondered if the nicer ones might pay better because Snooky's Pawnshop in downtown Orangeburg didn't look too promising. But going back to Charleston meant going back toward Stanton, and, if Delores was right about Bob Norris, that could be risky.

All they needed was enough cash for meals, a motel room, and gas to get back home. When she got back to Stanton, she could draw the money out of the bank and get the watch out of hock when she took Miss Sadie back to Columbia.

Billie opened the car door. "I'll be right back."

Miss Sadie looked at the Pit Stop sign and shook her head. "I'm not hungry; don't think I could eat anything if I was."

"I'm going into the pawnshop."

"Why?"

Billie's stomach pulsed hard as she closed her palm tightly around the watch. She never believed in things like good luck charms, but she'd never gone out on patrol without the watch. Could she afford to pawn away what little luck she had?

"From now until we get back to Stanton, we'll have to pay for everything in cash."

"There is trouble, on account of me."

"Right now, no, and I want to keep it that way."

"I have money."

Billie had forgotten Delores's words until Miss Sadie opened her big Coach bag—*She took a cab all the way from Columbia. Has a pocketbook full of cash.* Billie dropped the worn felt pouch into the bottom of her purse and pointed the car toward the Upstate.

South Carolina is small. From its southernmost point around Hilton Head, to mountain towns like Traveler's Rest that flirt with the North Carolina border, driving time is about five hours. With Orangeburg just below the bellybutton of the state, Billie figured they would be at their destination in two hours, three tops.

Miss Sadie didn't say a word, just stared out the window. At first Billie was glad for the quiet, but questions about her own mother dogged her until she broke the silence.

"You said my mother was good to you, but I never saw her with you, never heard her talk about you."

"She was good to me, and others were, too. They'd give me extra beans or potatoes from their gardens, sometimes tomatoes. Your mama gave me shoes, but they were too small for my big feet, and too pretty to wear. I can't remember but one freezing cold winter when I lived in the Lowcountry. Her and two of her church friends left a coat for me at our old shack, and some extra blankets."

"She never mentioned that to me, but I was little then. Maybe she did and I don't remember."

"From time to time, I would go along that little easement between the houses on your mama's side of the street and the ones behind them to look for Coke bottles to cash in for the money. Your mama figured that out and used to put a little cotton sack with bottles she'd washed out. Sometimes she'd put some hand-me-downs in there or something sweet wrapped up in wax paper. She always hung the bag on a fence picket so the ants wouldn't get in it."

"Ditty bags." Billie nodded and smiled. "Mama made those bags for the USO to send to the soldiers in Vietnam." It was Billie and John's job to stuff the bags with the items the Women's Auxiliary collected at Christmas and on Memorial Day, but Mama made the little cloth sacks all year long. She said it was her patriotic duty.

"I reckon about the nicest thing anybody ever did for me was what your mama did one day. I was big with my seventh, a boy, and it was so hot. She came around back to hang out the wash about the same time I was picking up the bag she'd left for me. She asked me if I wanted to sit a while, said she'd get me a Coca Cola if I wanted. Nobody'd ever offered me anything like that before, you know, to sit and talk like we were neighbors, friends.

"Your mama didn't see Inez peeping over the top of her fence at her like she'd lost her mind, but I did. I took the Coke, thanked your mama, and went on home, but I'll never forget her doing that. She was so good to me."

By the time Miss Sadie finished the story, they were fifteen minutes from Traveler's Rest. Billie was counting on the town having a motel and she was in luck. Just off the highway, there was a strip center pasted to the side of the mountain with a Walmart and an old motel called the Peach Bottom Inn hidden behind a shiny new Cracker Barrel.

Miss Sadie perked up a bit when they walked through the door of the restaurant; she poked around in the gift shop before her meal came and bought an eighteen dollar sock monkey for Little Man that looked a lot like the ones Mama used to make for next to nothing. She came back to the table just in time to order a vegetable plate with corn pone. The waitress smirked and fingered her brown plastic nametag that said she'd been with Cracker Barrel for nine years. "Honey, we've got corn muffins. We don't have corn pone."

Billie wanted to smart off to Phyllis, according to her nametag, put her in her place, but ordered breakfast for dinner instead. It was Amber's favorite meal, and the only one she could cook without asking Billie for help: instant grits and scrambled eggs.

Amber had always had a million questions about what seemed like the simplest things. Sometimes Billie got tired of doing Amber's thinking for her and knew she wasn't doing her any favors. These days, "Read the label" or "Look it up on the Internet," was her standard reply. But pushing the most likely instant grits around her plate, it became clear that Amber wasn't asking questions because she wanted to annoy Billie or even because she wanted answers. Amber wanted Billie to take time to teach her, at least she used to want that. Lately they'd been at odds and Amber didn't want anything from her except gas money.

Billie shoved a forkful of the grits into her mouth that were every bit as mediocre as Amber's. After she took Miss Sadie home to Columbia and got her sorted, she'd get in the kitchen with Amber and they'd cook up a storm.

"You've got that big plate of food, and you're not eating," Miss Sadie said.

Billie forked some eggs and nodded when Phyllis asked if she wanted more decaf. In an attempt to turn the table, Phyllis asked Billie if she could get them to-go cups. "Yes, thanks." Billie took the yellow legal pad page Maggie Dalton had given her out of her pocket and straightened it out on the table. "But can you tell me where this address is? My GPS doesn't have a clue."

Phyllis looked at the paper, then gave Billie an incredulous look. "Don't know what y'all want with Trash Pile Road. That address is just past Johnson's Crossroads. There's a little trailer park back there; don't know what the name of it is; folks here in town call it the Pot."

"Why do they call it that?" Miss Sadie asked.

"Lord, honey, I got tourists in here night and day asking for directions all the time to Caesar's Head, Raven Cliff Falls, but y'all are the first ones to ask about that place. You want to know why they call it the Pot? They got no water out there. You go out there, you best watch where you step." The woman laughed. Miss Sadie blushed hard, picked up her coffee cup, and stared at the fake fireplace in the center of the dining room. "What y'all want with that place anyway?"

"We're looking for a woman named Gert Sampson," Billie said.

The waitress glared at Billie. Without a word, she sifted through the tickets in her apron pocket, slapped the check on the table, and stalked off toward the doorway to the kitchen where a couple of other waitresses stood, waiting for their orders to come out. She said something to the brood who gawked at Billie and then looked away.

"Enough of this." Billie excused herself from the table and headed toward the group. The women scattered like biddies after scratch feed, except Phyllis.

"Ma'am, this isn't a good place for customers to stand. Somebody might run you over."

A burley man was standing just inside the doorway of the kitchen. His shirt had more Cracker Barrel medals than a war hero's; his badge said he was the assistant manager. "Is there a problem?"

"No, no problem, but I'd like to talk with Phyllis when she has a minute."

The big man nodded. "Make it snappy, Phyllis. We're going to be real busy in about a half second."

Billie could feel the woman seething as she followed her back to the table. Phyllis took the white rag out of her apron and dabbed at some tea that had dripped down the side of the Styrofoam to-go cups and then shoved the tip Miss Sadie had left on the table into her pocket.

"What y'all want with me?" she said stiffly.

"Why did you react like that when I asked you about Gert Sampson?"

"She lives on Trash Pile Road because that's what she is," she said flatly. "White trash. Maybe not even as good as that."

Still staring at the fake fireplace, Miss Sadie flinched at the woman's words, but she sat a little straighter. Her eyes seemed to be focused on the propane logs, but she had the same resolve Billie had witnessed at Maggie Dalton's house, a glimpse of the same backbone that had brought the old woman this far.

"So, she's still living?" Billie asked.

"Far as I know. I got work to do. Y'all have a nice day." Phyllis huffed and hurried away.

The sunset would have been a pretty sight if it was backlighting the mountain instead of the Super Walmart. Miss Sadie got a buggy and walked slowly toward the display full of travel-sized toiletries. Just past the STYLE section, Billie rifled through the pajamas until she found a petite small with little blue roses embroidered on the collar for Miss Sadie. She threw it in the cart and started walking toward the checkout.

"You ought to get you something warm to sleep in," Miss Sadie said. "Bet it gets cold up this way at night."

Billie stopped in the middle of the aisle and looked down at her clothes that already looked slept in. She grabbed a pair of $5 sweats off a huge Fruit of the Loom display and threw them in the basket. While they waited in line, Billie called Amber to tell her they would be home tomorrow after they met with someone Maggie Dalton referred them to; she didn't mention Gert Sampson.

"Mama?" Amber said. "I think it's a good thing, what you're doing to help Miss Sadie, but the more I read about this black market adoption stuff, the more I think she'll never see her kids."

"I know, honey."

"Then why are you doing it?"

Billie wasn't altogether sure why she was two hundred and fifty miles from home with an old woman she barely knew. Although, she knew why she'd never told Amber about stealing Miss Sadie's doll. Part of her wanted what every parent wants, for their child never to see the bungling wizard behind the curtain. But Amber was a grown woman now with a baby and a new life growing inside of her. Didn't she deserve to know Billie wasn't the know-it-all Amber thought she was? And was this pilgrimage with Miss Sadie really about penance for a stolen doll?

Billie's answer to Amber's question sounded lame, but it was true. "It just seems right, baby."

———————◆◆◆———————

The hostess led Billie and Miss Sadie to the same table they'd had the day before. Phyllis started their way with coffee and made a sharp detour toward a sweet-looking heavyset woman and said something to her before peeling out toward the kitchen.

"Morning, y'all; it's a great day to be at Cracker Barrel. And they don't pay me to say that. I'm Sheila Kay, I'll be taking care of y'all." She nodded as she took their orders mouthing the words as she wrote them down. "I'll be back with your coffee. Hey," she lowered her voice considerably, "does Phyllis owe you all money or something?"

"No," Billie laughed, "we're just here for breakfast."

"Oh," the woman nodded and raised her eyebrows, "that happens sometimes. Phyllis owes lots of people. She owes me twenty bucks for taking your table, but I'll likely not see it, as she owes just about everybody in here but you."

The woman bounded toward the kitchen with the enthusiasm of a Labrador retriever puppy.

"This Gert Sampson must be a real character," Billie said.

"Do you think she'll help us?" Miss Sadie nodded and smiled as one of the servers poured the coffee.

"Don't know, but it's worth a try."

The small map the motel manager gave of the area didn't give an accurate depiction of how much the topography changed as they traveled down State Park Road toward Gert Sampson's house. The sign they passed said the elevation was just over eleven hundred feet above sea level, but it didn't feel like it. While the town wasn't as flat as Stanton, there wasn't as much mountain to it as Billie thought there would be.

It was a pretty place—hardwoods aflame with color, what the hotel manager had called the peak of season for folks who travel across the state to see the fall leaves and buy cider and fresh-picked apples from roadside stands.

A speck of a town like Stanton before the real estate bust, Travelers Rest was full of gated communities with signs that boasted state-of-the-art facilities and championship golf courses. The ones that touted "luxury mountain homes for pennies on the dollar" reminded Billie of the foreclosed homes on her own street back home.

"Tigerville Road," Miss Sadie said with a sad smile as they passed an outdoor board for a shopping center.

"Have you been here before?"

"No. It just reminded me of Cecil. He was the most gentle soul you'd ever want to meet, went to church every Sunday, but oh, how that man hated the Clemson Tigers."

"If he was a South Carolina fan, I can believe that."

"Said nothing good ever came out of there. I told him he was being un-Christian, that it was just football."

Billie laughed. "No ma'am, it's more than football. I went to South Carolina but was never dogmatic about them. I was just grateful my daddy didn't raise me to be a Clemson fan. I look terrible in orange."

The car came to a crossroad. To the right was Paris Mountain State Park, which sounded a lot better than Trash Pile Road. Billie had thought it was just a nickname for the place, but sure enough a thick row of pines and brush disguised the view of abandoned junkers and appliances beside the road. A little farther down the washboard road, two ancient school busses were parked rear bumper to rear bumper. The exit doors had been removed to make one long living space. A little boy looked out the makeshift curtains and was snatched away by a woman who glared ominously at the Toyota.

Shacks made out of weathered gray wood that looked like it

came from a dilapidated barn were pieced together with building scraps from luxury homes and tucked into the tree line. Scrawny children with expressionless faces, some school age and some toddlers, stopped their play to watch the car ease down the road. There was no mailbox or street numbers to mark Gert Sampson's house, but it was the only real house on the street before you got to the county dump.

The small red brick home was trimmed in what was once white paint that had grayed over the years and was moldy black in places from water stains. The roof was dipped in places like some of the trusses were broken and the shingles had blown off in other places. Cardboard squares patched large holes in the windows. "BEWARE OF DOG" and "KEEP OUT" signs were everywhere.

"This is the place. I'll make sure she's here," Billie said. "For now, just stay in the car."

Billie got out of the car and looked around for the dog. She almost didn't see the huge pit bull peeking out from under the house. The dog stood up, pulled at the chain that was wrapped around one of the footings, and licked his lips but didn't make a sound.

Not all Pit Bulls are bad. Billie's brother John had one that smiled a big toothy grin on command and was terrified of the family's sixteen-year-old tabby. But this one wasn't grinning. His ears were pricked forward; his powerful body pulsed forward, testing the chain. Billie knew from personal experience this kind of pit didn't warn his victims by snarling and barking like a Dobie or a Rottie did. He just shreds them to pieces.

She was glad to see the dog was only following her movements, stretching the chain that looked like it stopped somewhere near the front door. A wiry young girl, maybe fourteen or fifteen pushed the screen door open and stood eyeing Billie. She wore a tight T-shirt that had something written across the bust line and tight jeans unbuttoned all the way to make room for her big belly.

The girl was tiny, almost fragile looking. Billie couldn't tell how far along she was, maybe seven or eight months. "You better get back to your car or I'll have to turn the dog loose."

"This Gert Sampson's place?"

The girl narrowed her eyes. "What you want?"

"Don't want any trouble. My friend and I just want to talk to her."

"For free?" The girl laughed and sat down on the one step porch. The dog laid his head in her lap. "Ain't nothing free, 'cept bullshit and buckshot."

Billie heard Miss Sadie's door open. "Stay in the car," she warned, but Miss Sadie didn't listen, just slipped two bills into Billie's hand. "How far will twenty dollars get me?" Billie asked the girl.

"Pretty damn far." The girl got up off the porch and dusted her behind off. She said something to the dog who took his place in a hole he'd dug under the house. She looked back over her shoulder into the house, then strolled up to Billie, plucked the money out of her hand, and slid it into her pocket. She saw Billie looking at her T-shirt and pushed her chest out a little farther so the "I just came here to DRINK and FUCK . . . and I'm about done drinking" was easier to read. "Is what it is," she grinned.

"You want another twenty?" The girl nodded. "Keep that dog in his place."

Billie helped Miss Sadie up the stoop. The girl threw open the screen door. Before she entered the house, she hid the money in her bra, smirked at Billie, and put her finger up to her lips. Billie nodded and followed her inside.

The faint sweet smell of ether screamed meth lab. Billie didn't see any evidence of one, but she and Miss Sadie wouldn't have gotten this far if the lab was still up and running. The house looked to be four small rooms: a living area, a kitchen, and two bedrooms. Billie didn't see a bathroom.

"Mee Maw. Folks here want to see you. That alright?" The girl called and disappeared into one of the bedrooms. "Give me them things; they're gonna kill you." She came out of the bedroom with a pack of unfiltered Camels, lit one, and blew a big puff of smoke upward like it might form a speech balloon over her head that said, "I'm fourteen and pregnant and smoking with my offensive T-shirt on." She flicked the ashes onto the ancient linoleum floor and winked at Billie. "You need anything else, I'm right here."

The old woman's osteoporosis was so bad, her torso bent like a coat hanger so that her face was nearly in her lap. She angled her wheelchair and wrenched her head to the side so she could get a better look at her visitors. "Who the hell are you?" she rasped. Her long bony fingers searched her neck until they found the hole. She inserted the tip of the cigarette, inhaled deep, and closed her eyes.

"I'm Billie Warren," she said moving closer so the woman wouldn't have to strain to see her. "I'm here with my friend. She knew you when you worked for Mac Dalton."

Gert craned her neck around until she caught sight of Miss Sadie, gulped in enough air to take another puff, and half laughed, half made a chocking rattly sound. "What do you want?"

"We're looking for information about my friend's adult children and thought you might be able to help?"

"Who's your friend?"

"Sadie Byrd," Miss Sadie made sure Gert heard her.

The woman took another puff and looked like she was trying to place the name. Mechanically, she pushed her head away from her shoulders, elongating her neck, and contorting herself to look up at Miss Sadie. A spark of recognition crossed her face, and then, like someone had snipped the muscles in her neck, her face was staring at her lap again.

The woman's shoulders began to heave up and down. The acidic laughter began, followed by guttural coughing, bringing the pregnant teenager to the bedroom door. "You okay, Mee Maw?"

Gert reached toward the sound of the girl's voice, and the

girl went to the bed. She took a long drag on her cigarette and then put it in the hole in Gert's neck. The ember glowed hard as Gert sucked in the smoke. More coughing. The girl snubbed out the cigarette in a saucer turned ashtray and looked at Billie. "Maybe y'all ought to go."

"It's all right. I don't think she remembers anything," Miss Sadie said quietly to Billie, "let's go."

Gert's whole body seemed to expand as she gulped in air. "Oh, I remember you, Sadie Byrd. You were a fertile little thing; one of my regulars. I made some money off of you, I did."

Billie closed the distance to the wheelchair and squatted so that she could see Gert's face, "Do you remember any of the families who adopted her children?"

Gert heaved in a deep breath. "I'll tell you what I remember. Your first one was a boy, with a headful of blond hair." Her lungs rattled as she gasped in air. "Your husband was so excited to get the money that first time, he forgot the Ace bandages I told him to give you." She wheezed several short breaths, laughing. "I bet your tits really hurt when your milk came in and you didn't know to bind them till it dried up." Her eyes rolled hard trying to see Miss Sadie's reaction. Billie was glad Gert couldn't see her from where she was sitting.

"You had more boys than girls. I was always glad for that. Boys cost more than girls." Billie wanted to smash the woman's face in. "You here 'cause you're on some kind of hunt to find your babies? *You sold them, woman.* You got what you God damned asked for. Now get out."

Miss Sadie came closer, standing beside Billie. She bent down low so Gert could see her and put a hand on her humped back. "I always thought if I saw you again, I'd spit in your eye, maybe even kill you, but you're a pitiful sight. You're hard. Dying. You got what *you* asked for, Gert, and may God forgive you."

Miss Sadie raised up, straight and tall, and nodded toward Billie. Gert Sampson was laughing, coughing her lungs up as they filed out of the room. "She's gone die soon," the young girl said matter-of-factly. "Where's my other twenty?"

Billie fished the other bill out of her pocket and handed it to her. "How far along are you?"

"None of your damn business." She lit another cigarette, smiled at Billie, and took a deep drag. The ether smell seemed stronger in the living room than when they first entered the house.

A tiny elbow or maybe a foot stretched against the girl's belly, protruding for a few seconds before disappearing. If the girl was in the family business, or a new family business, Billie wanted to help her, get her away from here—do for this girl what nobody had done for Miss Sadie so long ago.

The girl wasn't skin and bones like most meth addicts, although her bone structure was delicate. Her high cheekbones and tanned skin looked Cherokee, her green eyes Scotch-Irish. Her long chestnut hair was silky, not coarse. Her teeth weren't worn down to the nub.

Aside from the fact that she should be arrested for being pregnant and smoking or being fourteen, pregnant, and smoking, the girl was right. This was none of Billie's business. "Thanks." She handed the girl the other twenty. "Take care of yourself."

The girl threw her cigarette on the front porch and nodded with a cool demeanor that disappeared when a boy got out of a truck parked at the side of the house. Her face lit up and she ran full tilt toward an older sandy-haired shirtless boy with dark eyes and pants that sagged so low, if he didn't keep his legs bowed out, they'd fall off. He let the girl wrap herself around him while he eyed Billie and Miss Sadie with suspicion. "Who are they?"

"They're nobody," she said as she dragged him toward the house.

CHAPTER SIXTEEN

Billie plopped down on her couch, exhausted. Miss Sadie looked equally tired and stone-faced as the reality settled between them; their only hope of finding any of Miss Sadie's children rested in the hands of Judge Harold Norris.

"Can't believe I'm saying this, but do you think the judge would help me find my babies?"

"I don't know. I can ask," Billie said. "I'm sorry this hasn't turned out like I hoped. I really thought we had a shot at finding them." Had Miss Sadie pictured a reunion like the ones in a Hallmark TV special? Something told Billie Miss Sadie had experienced enough rejection in her life to only dream about a guaranteed happy ending.

"It's pretty hopeless, isn't it?" Miss Sadie asked.

"It doesn't look promising."

"I've wanted to see their faces for so long, I don't know how to stop wanting." She glanced up at Billie and shrugged.

While Billie doubted Judge Norris would help them, even if he could, she did owe Deidre Lawson a phone call. Maybe instead of accusing the judge of murdering his daughter, the right play was to ask him what he knew about the adoptions. She grabbed her cellphone and dialed the judge's number.

"Deidre, it's Billie Warren."

"I'm so glad you called." Deidre was silent for a moment. "The judge isn't well, but he wants to see you. How early can you be here tomorrow morning?"

"Be there by seven," Billie said and hung up the phone.

"There's going to be trouble with me here," Miss Sadie said.

Billie didn't answer. She had read through the outstanding warrant; it was valid and clear. But she'd cut out her own heart before she would put Sadie Byrd in jail. The way things were shaping up, she might not have a choice.

Amber tiptoed out of the nursery and closed the door behind her. "I've been online all day," she said as she plopped down on the floor at the foot of Miss Sadie's chair with her laptop. "I entered all your children's birth information, but I couldn't finish some of the posts because I didn't know stuff like your maiden name or your birthday."

"Sadie Louise Byrd." She nodded. "My maiden name was Lawrence."

Amber opened her laptop and pulled up one of the message boards. She entered the information Miss Sadie gave her. "I've been looking at these boards till I'm blind and I still haven't figured out where people come up with all these bits and pieces of information about their adoptions. Most of it seems to come from relatives, but how do they do that? Do they just call a total stranger and say, 'I think I'm the niece you never knew?'"

"Maybe you should give it a rest," Billie said. "You can work on it tomorrow."

"I need to stop; I'm exhausted." Amber bit her lower lip, still scrolling down the computer screen. "But I just can't."

Miss Sadie closed the laptop. "It means a lot that you want to help, child."

Amber hugged the laptop to her chest. "I just can't stop thinking about the things I remember about Little Man just after he was born. I'll have years with him, decades, and you only had your babies for a few minutes."

"I still remember the day each of them was born, what the sky looked like. I remember their little faces, the way they smelled, soft and clean. I may go to glory wanting to know them, how they are now, but I have those moments."

———————◆◆◆———————

The alarm clock blared just as the sun was coming up. Billie threw on a sweatshirt and attempted to comb her hair, which was all over the place, but there was no time to fix it. She grabbed the keys to her car; seconds later, she was backing out of the driveway and headed toward the Norris place.

Sure, Billie wanted to see the judge, but Deidre had said he wanted to see Billie too. If this was a last-ditch effort to throw his legal weight around and have Sadie Byrd arrested, the judge could have Billie charged with obstruction of justice if he wanted to. If that happened, how could she protect Sadie? How could she protect herself?

As she sped down the county road, a delicious selfish thought crept into Billie's mind. What if she had gotten lucky and the old judge had died during the night? Problem solved as far as Miss Sadie's warrant was concerned. But the judge wasn't just the perpetrator in Caroline Norris's murder, he was the only living witness to the adoption of Sadie Byrd's babies. If Judge Harold Norris died before she questioned him, anything he knew about Miss Sadie's children died with him.

Billie floored the accelerator. Chaos. She filled her belly with air and then let it out slowly the way the yoga article she'd read a hundred years ago in *Cosmo* said. She did this several times. Still chaos. She yanked her cell phone out of her bag and dialed the judge's number; a man answered on the first ring.

"This is Chief Warren. Please tell Ms. Lawson I'm five minutes away."

When she passed a Highway Patrol car, the Toyota was doing ninety down the county road that led to the judge's house. The officer must have been asleep or taking a leak because he didn't come after her. The car fishtailed a little as she slowed and turned onto the long gravel drive that rambled up to the Norrises version of Tara Plantation. Two ambulances were parked in front of the entrance but there was no activity outside the house. She pulled alongside one of the ambulances and got out of the car. Deidre Lawson was watching out from the long elegant foyer door and opened it for Billie. "Thanks for coming. We don't have much time."

Billie followed the woman up the majestic staircase. Deidre stopped at a set of double doors at the end of the hall. She looked exhausted and terrified, sad. "I shouldn't be doing this. I'll lose everything, but I can't live with myself if I don't."

"I'm not sure I know what you mean," Billie said.

Deidre leaned her head against the heavy oak doors. Even tear streaked she was beautiful; her hair was perfect, her brown Talbot linen shift and matching shoes were, too.

"Yesterday, Doctor Asbill told the judge—to just—let go." Tears filled her pretty green eyes and spilled down her face. "Since then, he's asked me to call the police—you specifically. I made the mistake of phoning Bob in Washington because I wasn't sure what to do. He said not to call anybody. Especially you. He hopped a plane early this morning and may have already landed. He's coming to stop the judge from talking to you, but this is what the judge wants. He said it was the last thing he'd ask of me." Deidre was fighting hard to maintain her composure.

Billie knew what she wanted from the judge, but the summons to appear before him had her puzzled. "What's this all about, Deidre?"

"I don't know." Deidre attempted to swipe away her tears. "I just know that he didn't rest last night and says he won't rest until he speaks with you." She straightened herself, dabbed at her pretty wet face, and smiled. "He's not my father; I never knew him. The judge and I have just become so close, I couldn't live with myself if I didn't honor his last request."

Deidre opened the bedroom doors. Two nurses were at his bedside, one reading the newspaper, the other putting what seemed like a hundred medicine bottles in some kind of order. The one reading the paper looked up at Billie and nodded politely before Deidre asked the woman to leave the room. She went to the judge, who was raising his hand toward her. It made Billie sick to her stomach when Deidre kissed his palm and then pressed her lips against his forehead.

After what he did to Caroline, to Sadie Byrd, he didn't deserve that kind of love, that kind of mercy. He closed his eyes and smiled.

"Billie Warren's here now, Judge, just like you asked," she whispered. "I'll be just outside the door if you need me."

The judge clasped his hand over Deidre's. "You're such a good girl. I love you, honey." She left the room, stifling her sobs.

He watched her go, then motioned to Billie to sit in the fancy brocade wingback chair to his right. There was a copy of *Leaves of Grass* splayed open on the arm of the chair. Billie picked up the book that looked old enough to be a first edition and put the red grosgrain ribbon bookmark in place.

The judge cleared his throat. His clean-shaven chin quivered. He looked at Billie and then looked away like the guilty soul that he was.

"In all my born days, I never thought I would be . . ."

"Talking to a woman police chief?" Her words came out cordial, respectful. What was wrong with her? "You stumped for me."

The judge cracked the tiniest smile. He coughed fitfully and reached for a cup of water. Billie picked it up off the bedside table and held the hospital straw for him to take a sip.

"They say I may not live to see tomorrow, and this time I believe them."

Even on death's door, the judge's voice had a silky bravado. "My whole life, I've made a living out of the law. When I first began, it was more than that; the law was pure—holy . . ." He stopped and motioned to Billie for more water.

Billie put the straw up to his trembling lips again. For the first time since she entered the room she noticed the overpowering scent of urine and Lysol mingled with the stench of death. The judge took another long sip and waved the cup away.

Before he could start up again, there was a loud commotion downstairs, yelling. Deidre's crying grew louder. Angry footsteps pounded up the grand staircase toward the judge's bedroom, and, before the judge could utter another word, Bob Norris burst through the door with Deidre close behind.

He was red-faced, and glared at Billie before he turned his attention to Deidre. "God damn it, I told you to ignore him."

"I'm not going to ignore your father like you have. He's dying. He wanted to do this."

Deidre stepped between Bob and the hospital bed, but he shoved her aside and marched across the room until he was nose to nose with Billie.

"You need to leave." His fat finger was in Billie's face. "You didn't see anything. You didn't hear anything. You weren't even here. Do you understand?"

"Mrs. Warren," the judge began weakly. "Chief Warren—"

"Dad, shut up."

"Don't talk to him like that," Deidre sobbed.

"Shut up Deidre. I'll deal with you later." He turned to Billie, with a look that was meant to intimidate the hell out of her. "Get out of here. Now."

Billie stared him down like she was a Wild Boy again. As much as she hated the judge for what he had done to Caroline and for the burden he had given Sadie Byrd to carry all these years, right now, she hated Bob Norris more.

"Your father called me, Bob. He's got something to say."

"Leave," Bob screamed.

"I know I should have come forward a long time ago—" The judge began coughing again.

Deidre kissed his head, sobbing. "Don't die. Don't die. Please don't die."

Bob moved closer. His hot breath was in Billie's face, but she would not be moved.

"Caroline—" the judge said. "It was all my fault—I just couldn't believe that she was gone, just like that." The pitch in his voice raised an octave with each word until the last word ended in a sob that rocked his decrepit body.

The look on Deidre's face told Billie that she had known the judge's secret, but it didn't matter. Nothing the judge had ever done could change her heart. He was the father she never had, and she loved him.

"Enough, old man." Bob wrapped his hands around the bedrails and rattled them. "Enough."

"Caroline's blood is on my hands—you should know that." Minutes earlier, the old judge had been eloquent, almost charming, in his closing statement. Now, he was barely lucid. It was as if the same secret that had drawn Sadie Byrd back to Stanton had opened the gates of the jail and sent the prisoner free.

"Help him," Deidre wailed. "Nurse. Help him." She climbed up into the hospital bed, her body convulsing in a mournful sob. Her tears mingled with his. His chin quivered. The light in his eyes was fading fast. "Please don't go," she cried. "I love you."

Two nurses pushed through the grand oak doors with a reverence reserved for the dead. One of them went to Deidre and stood quietly by her while the judge tried to follow the doctor's orders and just let go.

Bob Norris was stone-faced. One of the nurses gave him a look and then turned to Deidre. "I know it's hard, but honey, he is so tired. He'll be in glory soon."

Deidre nodded. She lay her head on the judge's frail body and wept violently while Bob watched his dying father with complete detachment.

"I would appreciate if you would give us some privacy now, Ms. Warren. There's a den down the hall. Wait for me there," Bob said with the coolness of a seasoned undertaker. His aggression had brought out the warrior in her, and she didn't quite know what to do with the extreme swing in his demeanor.

Before she closed the door behind her, she heard Bob ask one of the nurses, "What happens now?" Billie started down the hall, the answer to Bob's words burning.

She remembered asking the nurse that same question when her daddy's circulatory system was shutting down. Billie was barely twenty and still a kid. She wanted to tell the nurse she was wrong. Daddy was hot natured, always had been. But in those last days, he was cold, so cold. He'd wake from time to time like an impatient child on a trip, "Is this heaven?" "No honey, you're still here with us," Mama would say. But their family was his heaven, Billie's heaven. She watched for the rise and fall of the blanket on his chest, overly conscious of her own breath, like she could breathe for him. His sweet blue eyes fluttered open and then closed.

Billie swiped at tears and reminded herself that she was pissed at the judge for a long list of transgressions, the greatest of which had brought Sadie Byrd back to Stanton.

The den had been made over into a lounge for the nurses and paramedics. Coffee was brewing. Pretty coasters were stacked like chips on a poker table. Back issues of *People* magazine, *Woman's Day*, and *Reader's Digest* were neatly arranged on end tables. An older paramedic and a kid who looked too young to be working on sick people sat on a mocha-colored leather couch, watching Kathie Lee and Hoda yuck it up with Kevin Costner on the *Today Show*.

"What is it about that man that he can't button his shirt?" the woman asked the kid like she didn't hear Deidre wailing down the hall. "I saw him on the *Tonight Show* the other night and someplace else, I don't remember, but he can't button his shirt anywhere close to the collar for love or money. Makes him look old, I think. Like an old *Miami Vice* wannabe. Bet he don't have any socks on neither."

The young guy seemed to be zoning out on Kathie Lee, which was kind of creepy. His partner looked up at Billie, gave a half wave, and smiled. "Get you some coffee. There's donuts on the bar, muffins too. That Miss Lawson, she's real good about seeing to stuff like that."

"Thanks." Billie poured herself a cup and sat down at the poker table. The shot of adrenalin that had given her the backbone to go toe to toe with Bob Norris was gone. Sitting down was a mistake. She felt like a fat lazy cop in a donut shop and she wanted to slap herself.

The magnitude of what had happened in the past few minutes should have sunk in by now. Judge Harold freaking Norris had confessed to his daughter's murder, and now he was going to die. In Billie's wildest dreams, she couldn't have asked for a happier ending for herself. But why did she still feel like shit?

The scene she had just witnessed had actually made her feel sorry for the old man. Instead of asking him if Sadie Byrd was Caroline's birth mother and questioning him about Mac Dalton and the adoptions, she'd listened to his broad confession to committing the worst crime in Stanton's history. That was enough of a reason for her to be angry or repulsed by the judge, but she wasn't. Maybe it had something to do with watching her own father die. Maybe it was Deidre Lawson's love for the old man. Hadn't she said she'd risked everything to honor the judge's last wish? Did that mean money or power or Bob's love?

Billie heard the door open down the hall and then close. She heard someone coming toward the den. A dry-eyed Bob Norris walked into the room and poured himself a drink from a decanter on the bar. With his back to Billie, he threw back the drink and stood there for a minute. The smell of expensive bourbon drifted across the room and mingled in the air with the faint scent of cigars that, until now, Billie hadn't noticed.

He pushed the glass toward the back of the bar as if an imaginary bartender might refill it and lend an ear to his troubles. The older paramedic who had been so chatty minutes earlier muttered she was sorry for his loss, then turned the TV off and motioned for the kid to follow her out of the room. Bob didn't acknowledge either of them as they left but did close the door behind them.

He turned to face Billie. Billie studied him as he walked toward the poker table. There was no emotion; although the golfer's tan that the locals often teased him about was replaced by a milky jaundice color. He sat down across from her, dealt her a card face down, and turned up the eight of clubs for himself. He rubbed his thumb across the side of the deck several times before he turned up Billie's second card, a three of hearts.

He flipped an ace of spades on top of his card. Nineteen. Billie had played black jack too many times with the Wild Boys not to do the math. She refused to look at her blind card and pushed them toward Bob.

Bob flipped her card up. "Queen of hearts. Interesting," he said more to himself than her.

Okay, so he wanted to show her that he held all the cards and they were better than hers. She got the damn metaphor.

"I used to do this all the time when I was a kid. Found the instructions in the *World Book Encyclopedia* down the hall in the study. Practiced for hours. Didn't know I was doing anything wrong until Daddy found me and Caroline playing. Being a good Baptist, he beat the hell out of me. Promised I wouldn't be able to sit down for a week, and he was right."

Bob rambled like Billie wasn't there, yet he made sure she was keenly aware of his powerful presence.

"You drew the queen of hearts—I expected as much. You are a very determined woman, but emotional." He fingered the glossy playing card in front of him. "I have the ace of spades—no surprise there. Death—things are coming to a head. Then there's the damn eight of clubs, seems to follow me around. It means trouble—personal troubles."

"Look, Bob, I get it. By some twisted act of fate, you and your daddy got lucky. I can't arrest a dead man for your sister's death. I think you knew about the judge's crime, and did nothing, but I can't prove that."

"It's still quite interesting, you know—the three of hearts." He was still stroking the deck and staring at the cards on the table. "Your three of hearts," he cleared his voice and raised his eyes to meet Billie's. "It means be cautious. In proximity to the ace of spades I'd say it means don't do anything you'll regret."

Billie pushed away from the table and stood. "I'm done here."

He let her get as far as the door. "What are you going to do about Sadie Byrd?" Billie wheeled around and glared at him. "What? You think I didn't know what goes on in your little town? Come on, Billie, you're smarter than that."

"Her husband is dead. As far as I'm concerned, your daddy just closed the case."

"What about the warrant for her arrest in connection with my sister's death?"

"Do you really want to go there, Bob?"

"Maybe."

"Okay. Forget that you're a shoo-in to be re-elected in a little over forty-eight hours. Let's lay this whole ugly mess out there for everyone to see. *Murdering Child Molester's Son Losing Ground in the Polls.* It's been an uneventful election year—hardly any dirt out there. The news networks would eat you alive."

"Watch yourself, Billie. You have a lot to lose."

"Your threats don't scare me, Bob." She was screaming at the Wild Boy inside her to shut the hell up, she had everything to lose. But there was no stopping her. "But you need to ask yourself, do I want my daddy, the judge, to be remembered as a sinner or a saint, because you can't have it both ways."

With a smug look, he sat back in the chair and reshuffled the deck. Billie slung her purse over her shoulder and wished St. Peter would go for a twofer.

The paramedics were on the front porch taking a smoke when she let herself out. The highway patrolman's car she had passed earlier was parked beside the ambulance, waiting to escort the body to the funeral home. Billie recognized the young officer, but he looked so much like the other buzz cut, no necks who worked for the county, she couldn't remember his name.

She slammed her car door hard and hoped Bob Norris heard her peel out of the driveway. Unless he was too busy shoving that three of hearts up his ass.

She was home soon, too soon, and it tore at her gut that she would have to tell Miss Sadie the man who'd murdered Caroline Norris died peacefully, in the arms of forgiveness. And he'd taken everything he knew about her lost children with him.

CHAPTER SEVENTEEN

The strains of an old gospel tune made Billie stop short just inside the carport. Standing in the kitchen, on the other side of the screen door, Miss Sadie looked so much like Mama, Billie could hardly breathe. She was dressed in Mama's housecoat, washing dishes and looking out the window over the sink that overlooked the backyard.

Billie ached to see her mother whole again, watching over her and John. Mamas aren't supposed to get sick. They're not supposed to get old. And they're not supposed to forget you. Not ever.

The gospel singer crooned, "Come to the church in the wildwood." Miss Sadie sang along while Billie's insides pulsed with sorrow, the way they had the day she stole Miss Sadie's doll and all she wanted to do was cry and say she was sorry. So sorry.

The six o'clock bells at God's Hope Nazarene Church had sent all the kids in the park scattering home for supper. Billie walked down Denison Street with a group of boys who were tossing the tattered doll between them like a football while Jamie Beeks gave a play by play of the horrible act Billie had committed. Throughout the day, there had been fleeting moments she thought she could still hear Miss Sadie's desperate cries for the baby doll that was supposed to be a substitute for all the babies that were in her belly one day and then gone for good the next. But when she stilled and listened, there was nothing but the ramblings of her guilty conscience.

Billie wanted to snatch the doll out of midair, run back to the park, and beg Miss Sadie's forgiveness, but she didn't think she could touch the doll again. Instead, she pasted a smug expression on her face and hoped the boys thought she was cocky because the thought of what she did to a woman who was already tormented by the town, by her husband, made Billie want to puke.

She should have just eaten the dog shit Jimmy Malden had offered up.

Joe Jenkins's face was euphoric as he chimed in with his own account of the prank. Billie didn't think anyone could ever be lower than Joe's dad who stayed drunk and beat Joe's mama all the time or Clanton Austin's brother who drowned stray puppies and kittens on a regular basis. But Billie was worse than all of them.

She didn't deserve to walk down the street, pretending to be all proud while the boys patted her on the back like a bona fide hero. She should be down on all fours, raking her bare knees across the ragged pavement that made deep gashes on her legs and elbows whenever the tires of her bike spun out in the fine Lowcountry sand, and begging for forgiveness.

The gang reached Billie's street first; she could feel the tears coming. She hated herself and what she had done, but didn't dare cry in front of the boys. "See ya," she turned, biting her lip, and headed toward her house. "Hey Billie," one of them called. She didn't turn around. "Your prize." The doll hit her square in the back of the head and fell onto the sidewalk. She snatched it up and ran into the house as the boys continued down the street, hooting and hollering over what Pete Johnson had called the best Wild Boys caper ever.

Billie sprinted upstairs and didn't stop until she was in her bedroom. She took a piece of Blue Horse notebook paper out of her three-ring binder and sat down at her desk. She wrote "sorry" on the paper, centered in the middle of the page, making sure her script was perfect. She swiped the tears away from her eyes and stared at the word. It was so small and looked like the page was swallowing it up, the way Billie had been swallowed up by her fear of being alone, by her need to belong.

She crumpled the page up and threw it into the trashcan. Billie pulled the box of stationary out of her desk. Her aunt, the one who didn't have children, had given it to her when she turned six. She dusted off the top of the box and slid the satin ribbon off. The pages were soft pastel-colored, mostly pink, and looked tie-dyed. At the top of each page was a hot pink peace sign. She messed up four pieces of stationary until she finally got one right. This time "sorry" was in all caps and underlined twice.

She went through the box of girly toys relatives gave her for her birthday and Christmas until she found what she was looking for, then sprinted back down the stairs and out the back door. "You're already late for supper," Mama called, up to her elbows in dishwater at the kitchen sink.

Billie ran toward the park with Miss Sadie's doll tucked up under her shirt and didn't stop until she got to the bench the woman always sat on. Billie slid the doll out from under her shirt and laid it on the bench. She put the note on the doll's cloth belly, but decided it would be best to put the note under the doll in case the wind picked up. Fat black clouds rolled across the sky. The thick summer air smelled more like the paper mill twenty-five miles from Stanton than it smelled like rain.

She tore open the package showing a happy blond girl in ringlets with her Bonnie Baby doll. The package claimed it "Looks just like a real baby bottle!" Of course it wasn't a real baby bottle, but neither was the tawny-colored vinyl doll with molded blond hair still in the box at the top of Billie's closet.

Dolls were creepy. Especially Miss Sadie's with its eyes painted open and its mouth in a permanent O. Maybe Billie should have given her the Bonnie Baby she never played with as well. Maybe she should have given her all of the dolls Mama kept in hopes that Billie might change her ways and become more girly. But Miss Sadie loved this doll, clung to this doll.

Before today she'd never seen Miss Sadie put the baby down like it was a toy. She always cradled it or held it against her chest; she rubbed little circles on its back like Billie had seen new mothers do, but she never put it aside like it wasn't real. Not until she tried to help Skip Johnson when he pretended to be injured.

Her belly was big again, and she'd struggled to get up from the park bench. She always seemed fragile and childlike, always smelled of baby powder. Billie wondered if she was okay. What if stealing the doll had upset Miss Sadie so much it had hurt the baby she was carrying?

Billie wished Miss Sadie was still at the park. She'd tell her how sorry she was and give her the letter and the gift. She looked at the note one last time and rubbed her thumb across the hot pink peace sign before she put it back in the envelope. This would have to do. But it would never be enough.

At the dinner table, Billie pushed her food around on her plate until Mama put the back of her hand on her forehead and declared her well enough to eat the spottail bass Daddy had caught for supper. The coleslaw that was loaded with Miracle Whip was optional. They all chatted about their day, Daddy about his fishing with Jimmy's uncle, Chief Malden, and Mama about her coffee klatch. John contributed to the conversation with wisecracks aimed to snap Billie out of her guilt-ridden trance and when that didn't work, Daddy leaned across the table and tilted her chin up.

His big hands were rough and warm and with the slightest smell of the fish he'd cleaned earlier. He had the kindest face and had a trick he always did with his thick brown eyebrows, waggling them in rapid succession until she burst out laughing. But she couldn't look at him. If she did, she'd confess everything and nobody in their right mind at that dinner table would ever love her again.

"Somebody do you wrong, sweet pea?"

She could hear the smile in Daddy's voice, the same voice that he used around the horses he never bought at the Saturday auctions *they went to. The same soothing voice he used when their German shepherd got hit by a car and died in his arms. Billie shook her head and pushed back from the table so fast the chair toppled over. She ran upstairs to her room and threw herself across her bed and sobbed hard into her pillow.*

Billie's mind played the cruel trick it always did in those first few seconds she saw her mother, when Billie could pretend she wasn't sick, the MOMENTS before her mother looked at her blankly and asked, "who are you?" Miss Sadie was completely unaware of Billie's presence, completely unaware she was playing the part of Mama.

Billie could barely hear Miss Sadie's pretty alto voice as she washed each dish, then bathed it under the trickle of rinse water. "There is nothing so dear to my childhood as the little brown church in the vale. There she sleeps close by in the valley, lies the one that I loved so well, / She sleeps, sweetly sleeps 'neath the willow. / Disturb not her, rest in the vale."

Miss Sadie noticed Billie, dried her hands on a dishrag, and opened the screen door. "You're home."

Billie's head nodded slowly. "Go back to the sink." Her voice was raw with emotion as she closed the screen door. "Go back to the sink. Please." *Wash dishes. Sing again and let me stand on the stoop in the carport forever.*

"What? Child, you're crying."

Billie touched her cheek and looked at her fingers. Her face was wet with tears that had spilled down her neck.

"Come tell me what's wrong." Miss Sadie motioned Billie into the kitchen and set a cup of coffee on the table at Billie's place. "Is it your mama? Is she okay?"

Billie crossed the threshold into the kitchen, sat down at the table, and took a long draw of coffee. "No, ma'am." She swiped at her eyes with her shirtsleeve, looked Miss Sadie in the eye, said the words, then looked away.

"I know. Heard about the judge on the radio a few minutes ago." She sounded relieved, but maybe that was what Billie wanted to hear.

"I went to his house this morning." Billie could barely breathe much less talk. The tears wouldn't stop. "He confessed—to killing Caroline—and then he died." She laid her head down on the table and sobbed. Sweet gentle hands rubbed her shoulders.

"It's alright." Miss Sadie repeated the words again and again, like saying them would make it so.

Billie raised her head and looked at her. "I'm so sorry there's no justice. Not for you. Not for Caroline."

"There is justice from God."

"But you came here—"

"I came here to make things right so I can see Jesus. I suspect the judge called you out to his house to do the same."

"I hope he burns in hell." Billie's words came from her heart, but after seeing the broken, penitent old man die, they didn't seem right. Who was she to dole out justice? She had her own sins to confess.

"The Bible says sin is sin," Miss Sadie said. "That's hard for us to understand, but that's the way God works. I didn't come here to see the judge go to jail, child, I came here for myself and for Caroline."

"But what happened to her wasn't your fault."

"Not doing anything was my sin."

Billie looked away and then laid her head back down on the table. It was Billie's sin, too.

◆◆◆

The dream was real, so real. Billie was in Mrs. Pilot's third grade class, in the reading circle made out of desks with the rotund sadistic teacher in the middle. Mrs. Pilot kept a yardstick beside her chair to whack children on the tender part of their legs if they stammered or their attention wandered. Billie had never been whacked.

But that word. She always stumbled over it. It was in the paragraph she would be forced to read aloud like the rest of the inmates. It was easy, her brother John had said, any dummy could say it. She sounded it out in her head. Al—pha—be—ti—cal. She didn't even know what the passage in the *Weekly Reader* was about. Her turn came. Her voice came out smooth, and confident, something about the Library of Congress in Washington, DC. Almost to the end. Any dummy could say it. Right?

The sting of the yardstick woke her up. Her head snapped back from her crooked arms on the table. She wiped the drool from her chin. She'd slept hard, so hard she felt hung over, or maybe she felt the full weight of everything hanging over her. Miss Sadie had replaced Billie's coffee cup with a glass of tea. The clock on the microwave said it was after noon.

"You were so worn out," Miss Sadie smiled, "I wanted to put you to bed like the little one. But I didn't dare wake you."

Amber came into the kitchen and kissed Billie on the temple. Until recently, Amber had never seen Billie broken, and Billie knew that was wrong. Of all the things she'd tried to teach Amber, life skills, she'd called them, probably making Amber feel like *she* was in the reading circle, Billie had never taught her daughter it was okay to break. As far as Billie was concerned, it was just okay for everybody else, not her. But now, it seemed trite to say, "Amber, come sit down and let me tell what you need to know to undo the last nineteen years."

"Mama, are you okay?" Amber forced a smile, eyebrows raised slightly, screaming, *please, say yes. Please say yes.*

"No." The truth rattled Billie to the core.

Miss Sadie excused herself and Amber sat down across from Billie and reached for her hand. The look on her face said, *But you HAVE to be okay.*

"Amber, you and Little Man, my mother, Cole, y'all are everything to me."

"I know that."

"I've had so much on me lately, I just feel," Billie could barely get the word out. "Crazy."

The word seemed to sting Amber, another unintended consequence. "Mama, you're not crazy."

"Yes, I am. I hurt inside, so bad, I hope you never know what this feels like. And yet I know you already do."

The memory of Amber's suicide attempt hung between them like a limp, black sheet. The baby had cried night and day. Amber was weepy all the time, which didn't play well with Billie's exhaustion. There'd been a fight that day before Billie stormed out the door to go to work. When her shift was done, she was so tired, she didn't cruise by the Row to unwind like she usually did and was sound asleep when the phone rang just after two in the morning. Mama's sitter said Mama had somehow gotten up by herself and had fallen. Billie spent that night and most of the next day in the emergency room, returning home just in time to shower and dress for work.

From the carport, she could hear Amber crying again. What was it this time? Amber had seen a post online . . . some girls comparing notes on Tyson Cantrell notes in intimate detail; Amber was hysterical. Billie was tired. She didn't think. She didn't want to admit that Amber's postpartum depression was real. Dangerous. Billie was physically and emotionally exhausted when she told Amber the same thing she told herself to get by. "Get over it."

"How?" Amber had whined.

"Do whatever you have to do." And she did.

After Billie left, Amber called Abby to take the baby for a while. When Billie found her daughter, she had a belly full of muscle relaxers and was barely breathing. Amber was lucky, the doctors had told Billie. The Flexeril that had been in the top of the medicine cabinet was six years old and had lost most of its potency, "otherwise," the doctor had said, "this could have ended badly."

"I'm sorry, Mama." Amber was coming to, crying. "I'm sorry for everything."

Now, Billie's own apology sputtered out, desperate to fix her life, Amber's life. "I don't want you to look at me and think I'm some kind of superwoman who knows everything because I'm not. I ache for my mother, but she's never going to be the way she was. I love Cole, but I'm so screwed up, I can't let myself have him."

And she was a horrible mother. What had she taught Amber? It was more than okay to reject the very things that were best for her just like Billie had, from chocolate and Cole Sullivan, to everything in between. She had ignored herself and tended to the rest of the world like it was a requirement, a badge of honor.

"It's okay, Mama." Amber's huge blue eyes brimmed with tears. She pressed her hands against Billie's cheeks like she did when she was little and was trying to *make* Billie listen to her. "You're the best person I know."

Billie shook her head, unable to believe that, not even for a minute. "I'm so sorry I haven't always said it, made you feel like it, but I'm so proud of who you are."

Amber's smile was thin, but not mocking, like Billie's might have been if she were in Amber's place. "All I ever wanted was to be like you."

CHAPTER EIGHTEEN

The sun had not been up long when Billie awoke. She was still exhausted and only remembered bits and pieces from last night. Amber had put her to bed and tended to Billie like she was sick, bringing her hot tea and chicken and stars soup, the same things Billie prescribed for Amber when she was out of sorts. The last thing she remembered before she fell asleep was Amber spooning up behind her, her arm wrapped around Billie's middle.

From down the hallway, Billie heard hushed voices and then Amber's muffled giggle. Best guess, Tyson had stayed over in the nursery with Amber, and he was trying to dress and sneak out before Billie was awake. "Shhhhhh," Tyson whispered. Little Man began to stir. "Da Da Da!" Another giggle. Billie heard the nursery door open and then close. She didn't have a robe on but was presentable in her T-shirt and pajama bottoms.

"Tyson?"

He stopped dead in his tracks. "Yes, ma'am?"

"Come here a minute, please."

He stood in her doorway, eyes downcast, braced for the

sermon Billie preached the last time she caught him with Amber. "I'm taking Miss Sadie back home to Columbia today to settle her son's estate, and it might take a couple of days. I'd appreciate it if you would look in on Amber and the baby, stay here—if that's okay with you."

Tyson nodded and gave her that Tom Cruise grin that said he knew she'd get used to having him around—eventually. "Sure." He stood there for a minute, maybe waiting for another miracle and then left, most likely to buy a lottery ticket as soon as the Gas-N-Go opened because Billie Warren hadn't been nice to him in a long, long time.

"Sorry I didn't ask if he could stay over." Amber strolled into the hallway looking radiant in her white terry bathrobe.

"Are you sure you're up for another road trip?" she asked warily.

"I'm fine. How about you?"

Amber sat down on the bed, grabbed a throw pillow, and hugged it to her chest. She was positively beaming and quite obviously head over heels in love with Tyson Cantrell. "I'm good; never sick in the morning like I was with Little T—thanks for asking Tyson to check up on us. I know it meant a lot to him, Mama. It means a lot to me."

"You're growing up." Billie pushed a feathery strand of blond hair behind her daughter's ear. "Getting married."

"I really love him, Mama, and he loves me and Little Man so much, and feels so bad about what happened before. He says he's going to spend the rest of his life making it up to us," Amber said. "I know you think we're too young to know what we want, but we're not. We just want to be a family."

"Da Da Da," Little Man squealed on cue.

Amber hurried to the nursery and brought her treasure into Billie's room. She threw back the comforter and handed the baby to Billie before she climbed into bed, pulling the covers over their heads. Little Man wiped the morning sleep from his eyes and laughed.

Billie apologized for the pitiful breakfast she'd set on the table. "It's just fine—what I normally eat at home," Miss Sadie said as she shook some Special-K into a bowl. "At least the coffee's decent." Billie poured two cups and gave one to Miss Sadie. "I thought we would go by Mama's this morning before we head out to Columbia."

"Are you sure you feel up to this?" Miss Sadie asked.

"I'm not going to lie; yesterday was a hard day, but I'm fine now." She looked reassuringly at Miss Sadie. "No dizziness. No pain." Billie's first lie of the day. Seeing Mama every day was a painful but sacred obligation.

"All right then. I did want to visit with your mama before I go. And that Nan. I really like her."

Billie drank another cup of coffee while she waited for Miss Sadie to finish up in the bathroom. She made a quick list of things Amber needed to do over the next few days. At the top of the lists she had made for Amber lately, Billie had written *JOB—get one*, but she didn't do that this time. In her best chicken scratch, she left a simple grocery list. She started to write some words of wisdom, but drew a heart with little x's and o's instead. Checking her wallet, she found zero cash—no surprise there. She wrote out a check for fifty dollars to the Stanton Piggly Wiggly and figured what Amber didn't spend at the Pig on groceries, she could use for pocket money.

Miss Sadie was taking her time in the bathroom, which gave Billie a minute to call her good friend who was also the solicitor for Penny Gifford's case, Jane Kreeble. "I thought I'd be leaving a message. You never answer your phone before nine," Billie said.

"I started working out. I absolutely despise it, but Bo and I are going on a cruise next month. So, here I am pulling into the gym parking lot at seven-fricking-thirty in the *gawd* awful morning."

"Got a second?"

"I take it you're calling to speak with the D.A. and not your friend."

"Pretty much. What'd you have in mind for Penny Gifford?"

"Good God, Billie, nobody wants this one to go to court. Considering Mr. Gifford's history and Penny's spotless record, I offered her a year's probation and six month's house arrest to be served at a women's shelter."

"Jesus, Jane, she'll have a record."

"Even if he needed to be shot, Billie, Penny Gifford did attempt to murder her husband. While we at the solicitor's office secretly do a happy dance when somebody like Mr. Gifford takes it in the ass, courtesy of his victim, it is by definition attempted murder."

"What did Penny say?"

"That she'd think about it. Frankly, I think she's enjoying her time away from the son-of-a-bitch."

"I can't argue with that."

"So, you called because you thought I was going to offer that poor abused woman life in the slammer? You know me better than that, Billie Warren."

"Just checking, that's all."

"So how's Cole?"

"Why does everybody always ask me how Cole is?"

"Oh, I don't know, because he's brilliant and gorgeous? Because you have this little undertone in your voice that screams, *I need to get laid?* Maybe it's a huge undertone screaming in a little voice, I can't tell. But, as we like to say in my business, facts are facts."

"And I thought *I* was the lousy friend."

"Well, when was the last time you got some?"

Billie's face blushed hard; she felt the thinnest smile tugging at her lips. "Shut up."

"I bet there are cobwebs down there, thick scary ones."

"You're terrible."

"Yes, I am, but if I can find the perfect man at fifty-four, I am bona fide living proof that you can too. Hell, you and I both know you already have the perfect man, you're just too damn stubborn to admit it." Jane's car door slammed. "My advice to you, get yourself laid by a certain tall, dark, and hot as hell artist and have a little faith in me next time."

"Thanks for the tip," Billie said and ended the call.

Billie ran a comb through her hair and brushed her teeth. Looking at herself in the mirror, she looked tired and felt every one of her forty-nine years. Abby and Jane were always fussing at Billie to get ahead of the inevitable curve and invest in anti-aging stuff. They e-mailed Billie *affordable* substitutes for the products they bought for hundreds of dollars for just a tenth of an ounce.

One thing she had noticed, back when she'd slept with Cole, was the corny fact that she glowed. Whether it was the mind-blowing sex or just curling up on his chest to sleep, Cole was her secret that had far exceeded any promises made by any magic beauty potion. He erased her fine lines. He brightened her skin. He made her look and feel younger.

She threw a black Samsonite overnight bag on the bed and stuffed a pair of jeans, a night shirt, two Gap T's, and a cotton blouse that looked good with the khakis she had packed. Billie never wore much make-up, but decided she might give the Clinique bag full of samples Amber had given her a try and tossed it in the bag. Her pajamas puddled onto the floor and she slid into a pair of black chinos. Amber had actually hung up Billie's knit shirts when they came out of the dryer, which was a shocker. Billie pulled on a white polo and smiled to herself when the tail of the shirt didn't go very far past her waistband. Amber may have learned to wash and fold, but she was definitely challenged when it came to reading the laundry instructions.

"Are you ready to go?" Billie asked.

"To go home? Yes, ma'am," Miss Sadie nodded and followed Billie out to the car.

The few times that Billie had carted Miss Sadie around Stanton, she had gone out of her way to avoid the park, which was kind of hard since it was smack dab in the middle of town. Billie put the car in gear and headed for the shortcut that passed through the center of Norris Park.

Miss Sadie didn't say anything. The silence seemed unmerciful, but given Billie's own history, she figured she deserved it. She wanted to confess to stealing Miss Sadie's doll, to explain, to apologize for something that on the surface seemed insignificant. But to Billie, and maybe to Miss Sadie, it wasn't.

Bright orange cones and signs warned that there was tree work being done on the great live oaks that lined the street that dissected the park. Billie thought about taking one of several detours that would lead to Mama's house, but continued on toward the roundabout at the south end of the park. A short Hispanic man waved a caution flag and motioned to Billie to stop while a large limb was being pruned away from the power lines.

There was nobody behind Billie. She could have easily backed up and taken Fulton Road or Hengst Street and bypassed the park altogether. The town was so small that almost any street could eventually get her to Mama's. But there she sat with the Hispanic guy eyeing her. God, was he flirting? If he knew what she'd done here in this very place, he wouldn't be flirting. He'd be giving her the finger or at the very least, a dirty look, and Billie would have deserved it tenfold.

"Miss Sadie, there's something I need to say—" Billie stopped short at the look on the old woman's face. Seeing the park had jogged old memories, crushing memories. Billie hoped the whine of chain saws and the growl of the chipper would filter out Billie's confession. She hoped Miss Sadie was one of those elderly folks who just smile and *pretend* to hear what's being said.

"A long time ago—I did something that has bothered me to this day. I know it's stupid, I was just a kid. But it was terrible, and it hurt you." Billie didn't know the man was waving her through until he rapped his knuckles on the hood of the Toyota.

Miss Sadie smiled. "I believe that man wants you to move on," she said.

Billie eased the car past the workers and turned left at the roundabout just past the street where Mama lived. She pulled into the driveway, switched off the engine, and turned to face Miss Sadie, to give a full accounting of herself.

But Miss Sadie spoke first. "You know, Billie, there are so many bad things that I remember as clearly as if they are happening this very second, and there's so much more that's gone and forgotten. I rest in the mercy of what's forgotten. What you have to tell me, I don't need to know. What you have to tell me, I forgive you."

"But—"

"I'm ready for some peace now, child, and I don't believe I'll come by that if I don't accept God's grace from the things I don't remember. You've been so good to me, a blessing. That's all I know, all I need to know."

Billie's nose stung like she was nine again. She needed to know if Miss Sadie had found the note and the pitiful gift she'd left to atone for stealing the doll. Maybe then Billie could stop atoning. But reminding Miss Sadie of what happened in the park so long ago was as selfish as the act that got Billie into limbo in the first place. She whispered a simple thank you and let Miss Sadie keep her peace.

Nan met them in the driveway, doled out hugs, and announced that Mama was having a little better day—not raging, but still in Neverland. Billie bristled over the word *better*, that just didn't happen to folks with the big A.

The three women walked into the house quietly like Mama was asleep even though she was sitting at the kitchen table with Inez. Nan had rigged Mama's chair at the breakfast table with the ties from a couple of chenille bathrobes that crisscrossed Mama's chest to make a seatbelt.

"I think she likes to sit up," Nan said, pushing a wisp of hair away from Mama's slate gray eyes. "And lo and behold if she doesn't seem to respond to *Wheel of Fortune*."

"Well, she ought to. Me and Aida's been watching it most every night for I don't know how many years," Inez snorted. "How're you?" she said to Miss Sadie, like it was an effort to be hospitable.

"Fine, thank you. Would it be all right if I sat down and talked to Miss Aida?"

Inez gave a stiff nod without the least bit of appreciation that Miss Sadie had asked for permission. While Billie was listening to Nan go on about her own prognosis for Mama, her attention was focused on the women at the harvest gold Formica dinette.

"I know it will kill John to put your mother in a home," Nan said under her breath. "But she needs so much care, that's the best place for her."

Billie's eyes widened at the word *home*. She looked at Nan and shook her head, thankful that Inez's hearing wasn't what it used to be. Nan mouthed sorry then rambled on about Mama's medication and the article Inez had told her about that said Alzheimer's patients respond positively to music.

At this point, Billie stopped listening. She saw Miss Sadie pick up Mama's hand and hold it for a while. Miss Sadie leaned over the table and whispered something in Mama's ear, prompting another snort from Inez who clearly still did not like Sadie Byrd. For an instant, Mama's eyes turned from a murky gray to the beautiful blue color her mother had passed on to her. And then, just like that, they were back to a dull gray.

"I've got to get your mother up and change her," Nan said.

"Yes, sure," Billie said. "We need to get on the road."

Nan gave Billie a squeeze. "Don't worry about a thing, Billie. Inez and I are holding down the fort here and Amber's a grown woman. She can take care of herself."

"Thanks again for doing your thing," Billie said.

She watched as Miss Sadie cupped Mama's hand in hers and smiled at her before getting up from the table. "Bye now," she said to Mama and then Inez, who rolled her eyes and looked at the placemat she was fingering.

The connection between Mama and Miss Sadie was undeniable. Maybe everything Miss Sadie had said about knowing Mama was true, but how could that be? Mama wore her heart on her sleeve and couldn't even keep Christmas presents a secret. Yet, it seemed the two women had known each other.

While Billie was curious about the relationship between Mama and Miss Sadie, more than anything, Billie wanted to know what Miss Sadie had said to Mama that brought her back from Neverland, just for a moment. Billie couldn't help but wonder, even worse, hope, that she could string those same words together over and over. Spin them into a minute of clarity, an hour.

Billie started the car and headed toward the interstate. On her way out of town, she passed by the post office, looked up in her rearview mirror to make sure nothing was coming, and did a 180.

Miss Sadie looked puzzled. "Is everything all right?"

"I just need to make a quick stop before we get on the road."

Billie pulled into the back parking lot of the Stanton Post Office and was grateful to see Harry Bennett's car. There were no customers yet, just a couple of cars that belonged to postal workers who wanted to get a jump on their day.

"I'll be right back," Billie said as she got out of the car.

She walked past the post office coffee klatch in the break room in which a heated discussion about the latest episode of *The Bachelor* was taking place and pushed open the door to Harry's office. The walls of the cinderblock room were plastered with motivational posters like the ones Amber bought at the book fair when she was in elementary school. One had a terrified-looking kitten clinging to a bar with his front paws, his body dangling in midair. HANG IN THERE was written in great big pink letters below the kitten. A peppy little number from *The Little Mermaid* played on a small boom box.

"Knock knock."

"Hey." Harry looked genuinely glad to see her. "What are you doing here?"

"Just checking in."

"Are you okay? My neighbor works at the ER, so I heard what happened with your heart attack."

"It wasn't a heart attack. Just a little shock that sent me reeling, actually it was a big shock—Amber's pregnant again."

"But you're okay?"

"Yes, but that's not why I dropped by, Dr. Phil."

"You want to know if I've been to Gun-Mart."

"Something like that." She could see that he was wounded. In truth, she hadn't really planned to stop by, hadn't prepared a speech. But something niggled at her as she drove past the post office, and she'd rather be safe than sorry.

"Everybody has a right to own a gun, you know. Says so right there in the gall darn Constitution of the United States." Harry sounded pissy. Maybe that was a good thing and he was finally moving past the first stage of grief. Or maybe not—after all, he seemed more pissed at Billie than at his ex-lover.

"I just wanted to make sure you were okay, Harry."

"What? Were you worried I'd go all postal on you?"

"Look Harry, I'm tired of telling you what you already know. You're a good man. Just be yourself and have a good time and Mr. Right will come along. And if he doesn't—then so what? You've had yourself a really good time."

He straightened some papers, put an oversized rhinestone paperclip on them, and tossed them into the out box. "That's easy for you to say. You have Cole. He's beautiful and nice. And you know what, Billie? He sticks. There's a lot to be said for that."

"Yes there is, but if you spend the rest of your life holed up in your house or this office, you won't find that, Harry."

"Why can't I have a man like Cole?" He looked like he was going to tear up. He smiled again. "Why can't I find a man like you?"

Billie laughed, "Just give me the damn gun so I can sleep tonight."

Harry looked like he was contemplating his next move. He gave Billie a slight nod, got up, and walked briskly out the back door of the building and into the parking lot to his ancient Chevrolet sedan. He unlocked the door, dumped the contents of an Office Depot bag onto the floor, and put a nicked-up Beretta into the bag before he ceremoniously handed the bag to Billie.

"I met a guy, at that big pawn shop by the interstate on the way into Charleston." He beamed. "He's real cute and sweet, works in the gun department."

She raised her eyebrows. "And you bought a gun because?"

"It was his first day on the job and he hadn't sold a thing. Besides, it was worth it—he gave me his number."

She peeked into the bag at the pitiful excuse for a gun that was so old and uncared for it would be a miracle if it worked, but she wasn't taking any chances. She made sure the safety was on, wrapped the bag around the gun, and headed to her car.

"Glad you're taking it," he called after her. "It'll give me a good excuse to buy another one."

CHAPTER NINETEEN

A black SUV a few cars back followed Billie onto the interstate just outside Stanton. Whenever she and Amber made a road trip, there was always that one car, usually with Ohio plates, loaded down with stuff from a week at the beaches near Charleston, that seemed to follow them. Billie would stop for gas or food, the Ohio car would do the same and somehow, they still ended up passing each other several times along the way.

In the lead, Billie couldn't see the plates, but was reasonably sure it wasn't from Ohio, since there was no plate bolted to the front of the vehicle. For a little more than two hours, Billie kept an eye on the SUV. Maybe it was just her being suspicious, but it seemed the SUV was keeping an eye on her too until it disappeared and she felt silly for being paranoid.

Miss Sadie had been asleep almost the whole way and began to stir. She wiped her mouth with the back of her hand as they passed an outdoor board. "Piggy Park Barbecue," she read aloud. "We're almost to Columbia."

"Yes ma'am." Billie glanced up in the rearview mirror for the

SUV. Still nothing. "We have to stop somewhere and get some lunch. Do you like Piggy Park?"

"I used to until I heard that the man who owns the place gave out pamphlets that said the black folks were better off when they were slaves. I told my Cecil that I wasn't going to set foot in that place again, no matter how good the barbecue was."

"Don't blame you," Billie said.

She followed the GPS directions into the city, then down a pretty street in the trendy Shandon area. The car passed under a bright yellow canopy of fall leaves created by huge pin oaks on either side of Beaumont Street. Miss Sadie's small honey-colored bungalow stood out like a sore thumb among the stately limestone and red brick homes that looked like Martha Stewart and *Southern Living* magazine had teamed up to restore them to their original glory.

The hairs on the back of Billie's neck prickled as she pulled into the driveway and killed the engine. Coming back to Stanton just after her son's funeral had been difficult for Miss Sadie, telling what happened to Caroline almost did her in. How would she survive walking through the door of the tidy bungalow knowing her son wasn't there, and never would be? Miss Sadie's chin quivered hard as she looked at the house. "He was such a good boy, my Cecil," she whispered. "He was always so good to me. I just can't believe he's gone."

"I think about Amber and the baby, and I can't even imagine what you're feeling." She patted Miss Sadie's hand and looked at her with all the reassurance she could muster. "I know this isn't easy for you; we'll sit here as long as you like. We can drive around the block a million times. Whatever you need until you're ready to go inside."

Miss Sadie nodded and took a small pack of tissues out of her pocketbook and pulled several out. While she collected herself, Billie assessed the homes on either side of the bungalow. To the left was a large limestone Tudor-style with a perfectly manicured lawn and shrubs and every Fisher Price toy in the state, spilling out of the backyard and into the front. Heavy curtains were drawn tight in all the windows of the stately red brick Georgian home on the right. It was equally as well landscaped as the Tudor, but too much shade from the pair of large oaks in the front yard made the grass sparse.

Two unread newspapers were on the porch steps of Cecil Byrd's home. His yard was neat and landscaped in such a way that there was no grass to cut. Delicate bracelets of waist-high azaleas encircled three large oaks whose leaves had turned the brightest yellow but had yet to fall. Waxy green camellias full of buds outlined the little house, promising a colorful late autumn.

The house itself was modest. Red-checkered curtains hung in a window on the carport side of the house; maybe that was the kitchen. An old tin Sunbeam bread sign was nailed up on the wall of a storage room connected to the carport. Funny how those old ads, like the Sunbeam bread girl or the little Coppertone blonde, could always bring a smile to Billie's face.

Miss Sadie took in a deep breath that slipped back through her lips in a sigh. "I'm ready now."

"Are you sure?" Something didn't feel right, but Billie couldn't put her finger on it. Miss Sadie's son was dead; there was nothing right about that. She thought about Amber. Was this what it would have been like if Billie hadn't found her in time? Would she have ever been able to go back to the home they shared? What if she'd had to raise Little Man by herself? What if she never saw Amber's face again? She pushed the thoughts away and tried to focus on Miss Sadie. "I'm in no hurry; take all the time you need."

"Guess it's not going to get any easier—just sitting here. This is my home and sooner or later I have to walk through the door and face facts. Cecil is gone." She closed her eyes and muttered a brief prayer before she handed Billie the house key. Miss Sadie laced her fingers in Billie's and the two women walked slowly up the walkway to the friendly red front door.

Miss Sadie said the key was stubborn, and it took some doing until it unlocked the door. Billie's gut tightened as she turned the knob. This wasn't right. It would never be right. She tried to push the door, but it wouldn't budge.

She looked at Miss Sadie. "Looks like this one's stuck. Maybe we should try the side door."

"It's never stuck before."

Billie pushed hard against the door, and it budged three or four inches. One look inside and her heart began to pound, sending adrenaline rocketing through her body. Overtones of the same headiness that had swept her away toward the anxiety attack threatened. She took a deep breath and blinked away the darkness. *Breathe damn it.*

She squinted hard, refocusing on the sight on the other side of the door. Upholstered furniture was slit open, its stuffing littered the room like feathers from an errant pillow fight. Knickknacks were smashed to bits. A small ornate secretary was upended and broken in two. Books littered the ground and the lever to the fireplace damper had been ripped off and was lying on the floor in a pile of soot. The part of the kitchen that could be seen from the doorway looked as if somebody had played fifty-two-card pick up with its contents.

Billie hurried Miss Sadie back down the steps and to the car.

"What's wrong? Aren't we going inside?" Miss Sadie asked.

"Somebody has broken into your house."

"Why would someone do that?" Miss Sadie was trembling. "Shouldn't we call the police?"

Billie opened the glove box and took out Harry Bennett's gun. She slipped it out of the Office Depot bag and pulled back the slide. Great. No bullets.

"I'm pretty sure whoever did this is gone. Just to be on the safe side, you stay in the car and keep the doors locked. My cell phone's there on the console. If I'm not back in a couple of minutes, dial 911 and press the green button. Got it?"

Miss Sadie picked up the cell phone and nodded hesitantly.

Billy ran up the sidewalk and onto the small concrete porch. She rammed her shoulder hard into the door, pushing it open just enough to go inside. The gun scanned the living room and what she could see of the rest of the house. Miss Sadie's things that lay broken on the floor crunched under her feet—framed photographs, crushed and broken Precious Moments figurines, a fancy green cut glass candy dish.

She scanned the entrance to the kitchen before she darted into the room. No sign of anyone. She turned the light on and started down the short hallway. There were four doorways, three of them closed. Billie didn't like this worth a damn. She pressed her back against the side of the first door and pushed it open with her left hand—nothing but the bathroom. The door to the medicine chest was standing open, but its mirror was shattered. A little plastic doll with a crocheted southern belle gown that had once served as a toilet paper holder was smashed and lay in a puddle of shampoo on the floor.

She continued checking the bedrooms, but her gut told her whoever had done this was long gone. She walked back through the house. All clear. The back door was unlocked. She had entered the house at 12:00; it was 12:05 now. She slid the gun in the waistband of her jeans, closed the front door behind her, and walked quickly to the car. Miss Sadie looked relieved to see her but was still very upset.

"I was so worried. I just prayed and prayed the whole time you were in that house."

"This doesn't look like a bad neighborhood. Are break-ins common?" Billie said, not wanting to ask the question she was sure would wound Miss Sadie.

"No. Never. We've lived here for thirteen years. Who would do this to my boy's house?"

"Do you know of anybody who had something against your son? Maybe a co-worker? An old girlfriend?"

"Everybody loved Cecil." Miss Sadie was crying hard. "*Everybody.*"

Billie held her breath for a minute and then let it out slowly. "Miss Sadie, this isn't what I think, but when the police get here, they're going to ask you—Was your son involved in any illegal activity? Drugs? Gambling?"

"No. Cecil was a real good boy."

"They didn't take the cash on your son's dresser or the jewelry in your bedroom, but they were definitely looking for something."

"But what? Cecil didn't do anything but go to work and come home. He went to the football games when he could get a ticket, but he mostly just stayed home. He didn't take any medicine, no bad drugs. For goodness sake, he was Baptist. *He didn't even drink.*"

"Well, somebody tore your place up looking for something. If they'd taken things, I'd say they probably saw the death notice and looted the house for what they could get. But they didn't take valuables that were in plain sight."

Less than half an hour after Billie made the call, two policemen arrived. Billie introduced herself as a cop from Stanton, but not the chief of police. One of the policemen cleared off a place at the kitchen table and up-righted two chairs. He asked Miss Sadie to take a seat. She obliged, although still visibly shaken, and said she would answer their questions as best she could.

Billy made sure Miss Sadie was okay and then joined the other cop's partner as he poked around the house for clues. "It's kids." The tall cop shook his head as he closed Cecil Byrd's bedroom door. "I guarantee you; it's kids. Worse yet, it's probably a bunch of rich kids. They do shit like this all the time, and their mamas and daddies get them out of trouble because they know the DA or the judge. They probably live right here in this neighborhood."

"Kids," Billie said, "seems to me if it was a bunch of kids, they would have taken the money and the jewelry."

"Kids get bored and do this kind of thing. Now I'm not saying this kind of vandalism happens all the time, but it's not unusual."

The cop stepped over an overturned lamp in the hallway.

"Really?" Billie asked incredulously.

"Well, you're a cop. What do you think?"

"I think—" Billie's cell phone interrupted the conversation. She glanced at the display. Amber. She excused herself and stepped out onto the front porch. "Hey. I—"

"Mama." Amber was gasping for breath between sobs and sounded like she was going to hyperventilate. "He—he—he" If Tyson Cantrell had gone back to his wandering ways, Billie was going to make him pay big time. *"He-lp."*

Billie stopped breathing. Little Man let out a scream and was sobbing hard.

"Amber, what's happened?" More sobbing, "Come on, baby, *breathe.*" Billie's throat tightened. Her skin felt like it was on fire, and the baby elephant that had sent her to the emergency room a few days ago was tap dancing on her chest. "Okay now, slowly. What's wrong?"

"He—"

"Stay with me. Take a breath and tell me what's wrong." Billie walked farther from the house and out of earshot. *"Amber."*

Amber let out a wail that sent chills ricocheting through Billie's body. "The house. Somebody tore up our house—and"

"Amber, has something happened to the baby?"

There was no answer. She was crying harder now.

"Is the baby okay? Are you okay? Oh, God. *Amber, answer me.*"

"Yes—but—they were here."

"Who, Amber?"

"I don't know. They taped a picture—a Polaroid to the mirror of a man—holding him."

"Amber, who was holding the baby?"

"I don't know—his face is out of the picture. Oh, God, Mama, they could have done anything to him. They could have taken him; they could have *killed* him."

"Amber, are you hurt?"

"No. I wasn't—here. Miss Marsh's dog got out—the baby had just gone to sleep. I thought it would be okay to leave him—a black SUV had hit the dog and drove off. Miss Marsh was so upset. I couldn't have been out of the house for more than twenty minutes—Oh, Mama I'm so sorry, I was just trying to . . ."

"Help. I know, but you have to listen to me. Look at the photo. Do you recognize anything about the man? A scar, a tattoo, anything about his clothing? Anything at all, Amber. *Think.*"

"He's a big man. White. He's wearing the kind of vest Daddy used to wear when he went hunting with Grand Pa. A rifle on his shoulder."

Camouflage. Smart. Billie's house was at the end of a cul-de-sac and backed up to an open field that was a hunting preserve. With deer season in full swing, hunters walked through the yards that backed up to the field every day. Nobody would think twice about armed men perched in shrouded deer stands that dotted the edge of the open field, a hundred yards apart.

Amber was getting cranked up again. Billie had to calm her down to get more information out of her so that she could figure out what in the hell was going on.

"Come on, Amber. Stay with me. If I'm going to help you, you need to get a grip and think. Is there anything else that you remember, anything else that I need to know?"

"There's a phone number on the back of the picture."

"Did you call the police?"

"You are the police," she sobbed.

"Did you call Tyson?"

"No, just you."

"Give me the number on the back of the photo." She was terrible with numbers; she repeated the phone number three times as she put it in her phone. "Okay, listen carefully. I don't know what the hell is going on, but you take the baby and get the hell out of there now. Can you calm down enough to drive?" The high pitch whine turned into sobs again. "Honey, listen to me. You have to get yourself together, for yourself, for the baby. If you can't drive safely, call Tyson on his cell and have him pick you up. Go to his house and stay put. I'm leaving Columbia now. Take your cell phone and stay with Tyson until I get back to Stanton. Okay?"

"Okay."

"I'll be home in about two hours max, but you get the hell out of there now. Hear?"

"Okay." Amber sounded a little calmer, like she was trying hard not to flip out again.

"I'll call Jimmy Malden. Just get out of there now. I'm on my way."

CHAPTER TWENTY

A massive streak of heat flashed through Billie, as Amber's cry for help echoed in her brain. Her head began to pound, at odds with her rapid-fire heartbeat. *"Breathe,"* she hissed. The beautiful November day began to dim and then go black. She was falling—at least she felt like she was. Was she going to faint? She leaned into one of the live oaks in Cecil Byrd's front yard, her back sliding down the massive trunk until she was squatting.

The muscles in her thighs throbbed hard, struggling to force more blood to her heart and then her brain. She shook her head. *Get a grip.*

She should have called Jimmy straightaway, but she dialed the number Amber had given her instead. As the phone began to ring, her heart froze and then beat wildly out of control. *Pick up, dammit!* It rang eight times and then disconnected itself. She punched in Jimmy's cell number, but, before she hit the Send button, her cell phone rang. She looked at the caller ID—*UNKNOWN NUMBER.*

"Hello Billie," the voice slinked through the phone with a

chilling calmness. "I guess I don't have to tell you not to call the cops."

"You son-of-a—"

"Oh, that's right," he laughed. "Like Amber said, you *are* a cop."

She looked around to see if the perp was standing nearby. "If you lay a hand on my family—"

"I already have." Complete silence reinforced his point. "Now, it's my turn to talk, Billie. Understood?" More silence. "Good. I want you to call your daughter and tell her to stay put with the baby—alone. No phone calls, no contact with anybody but you. Tell her to keep the blinds up."

"Don't—"

"You're in no position to tell me what to do, Billie."

"Please. Don't hurt them."

"Unfortunately, the police are going to be at Mrs. Byrd's home for a while. After they leave, find the cell phone duct-taped to the bottom of the desk in Mrs. Byrd's bedroom. Retrieve it and call me back on that phone in fifteen minutes. Just hit the Send button, the number's already been programmed in the phone." Silence. She was sure he had disconnected. "And Billie, when you speak to Amber, be sure and tell her it wouldn't be a good idea to try to leave."

"You touch her and I'll—"

"She's such a pretty thing. Even through the scope of an assault rifle."

Billie sucked in her breath and hated herself for feeling paralyzed by fear. The predator was saying something. Oh God. What did he say? Her heart pounded in her ears. She felt numb, yet every inch of her skin was on fire. "Oh, and while I'm thinking about it, be sure and tell your daughter she looks good in pink."

Billie had fifteen minutes. She looked toward Miss Sadie's house to see if the officers had seen her knocked to her knees by the predator's call. The top of the taller policeman's head was barely visible over the wooden privacy fence in the back. He and his partner were still talking to Miss Sadie.

Billie pressed the home button on her call list and prayed that Amber was still alive.

"Mama? We're okay." She sounded better, like her survival instincts had kicked in. "I-I'm walking out the door now."

"NO! Amber, wait."

"Wait? Why?"

"Have you called anybody besides me?"

"Tyson. He didn't answer. He's in class, so I sent him a text message."

"What did you say?"

"I told him to come ASAP. He texted me back and said he would be here as soon as he got out of class."

Billie closed her eyes. "Amber, what color are you wearing?"

"What the hell does that have to do with anything, Mama? We have got to get out of here."

"Just tell me what color your shirt is. It's important."

"Pink. Why?"

Billie died a little more inside. "Amber," her voice was hoarse at first. "Listen to me. Whoever took that picture of the baby is watching you. I know this is going to be hard, but you're going to have to stay in the house and not call anyone until I can fix this."

"Oh God." She was crying again.

Little Man joined in screaming at the top of his lungs. Above the crying, Billie could hear the distinctive crash of the metal blinds against one windowsill and then another.

"Amber! Listen to me. Open the blinds." Amber stopped short and the baby did too. "Are you listening to me?" She was whimpering now, most likely nodding. The baby started up again. Billie could tell by his cry that Amber was bouncing him on her hip in an effort to silence him. "They said you have to keep the blinds open. Lock the windows and deadbolt the doors and text Tyson. Tell him whatever you have to tell him but tell him *not* to come."

She was sobbing again. "I'm scared, Mama. I need him." Billie swiped at her eyes. "I need you."

"No, baby, you can do this. Don't call anybody and don't go set foot outside that house until I figure this out."

Billie thought of her teasing Nan the last time she had visited Atlanta because Nan was obsessive about using her high dollar alarm system and double checking to make sure the doors were locked, even when John was home. Nan had turned right around and taken the opportunity to fuss at Billie for being crazy enough to leave her house unlocked, even in a little town like Stanton.

Nan. Mama. Inez. She refused to go there, to think that maybe their lives were threatened, too.

As impossible as the situation seemed, logistically it made sense that someone could make Amber a prisoner in her own home. Between the shrouded deer stands overlooking the back-yard and the vacant houses a few yards away, all the exits would be easy to cover. Billie had seen what a deer rifle with a scope had done to the teenager who was accidentally shot during deer season a couple of years ago. She trembled at the thought of what an assault rifle could do to Amber. To the baby.

"Stay calm." Billie said it as much for herself as she did for her daughter. "Stay put. You can do this, Amber. I love you. I'll call you as soon as I figure this out. I promise." She disconnected, took a deep breath, and started toward the wooden gate.

"I just can't believe that there are children who would do such a thing. Cecil was always nice to everybody." Miss Sadie looked sad, hurt. She shook her head and toddled off toward a yellow climbing rose that had long since outgrown its trellis.

"She'll need a copy of this for her insurance company." The policeman tore off a yellow duplicate of the police report and handed it to Billie. "I was just telling Mrs. Byrd that someone will be here in about five minutes to dust for prints. Doubt we'll find anything we can use. If these kids are from this neighborhood, they won't have a record. Rich folks have friends in the right places."

"Yes, that's what your partner told me," Billie said and followed the officers to the front yard. "Thanks for coming. I think the best thing for Miss Sadie is to get out of here and let the insurance company clean up this mess. Here's my card if you need to get in touch with her. I wrote my home phone number on the back."

"Chief, huh?" the stocky policeman said and smiled like it was some sort of joke.

"I need to run into the house and get her cell phone before we head out," Billie said.

"Don't—"

"This isn't my first crime scene," she said. "I know not to touch anything."

An unmarked sedan pulled up to the curb and a pretty auburn-haired woman got out of the car. She gave the officers a little wave and opened the trunk to retrieve her case. "It's our lucky day, Roy. They sent Angie to do the dusting." Both policemen fell all over themselves to get to the woman's car.

Billie walked up to the front porch and entered the house nonchalantly before sprinting down the short hallway to Miss Sadie's bedroom. She dropped to her knees. Her fingers moved across the underside of the desk until she felt a smooth metal object. She yanked it lose, shoved the no-frills flip phone into her pocket, and ducked out the back door before the policemen and the investigator came through the front.

"Let's get out of here, Miss Sadie, and let the police do their thing."

The old woman raised her head and looked crushed to the core. Billie glanced at her watch; seven minutes had passed. She helped Miss Sadie up and walked her to the passenger side of the car. Billie hurried around and got into the car. She backed slowly into the picturesque street and headed toward the next intersection. After barely coming to a complete stop, she hung a right out of the neighborhod and sped up until they reached a Kroger grocery store they'd passed on the way in. Billie pulled into the parking lot and took the burner phone out of her pocket just as it started to ring.

"Two minutes to spare, and you got Amber to raise those blinds. Very good, Billie." He let out a contented sigh.

"Who *are* you?" she growled.

"Does it really matter?"

"Tell me who you are."

"Are you a good listener, Billie?" He paused. "Dead silence. Good, I like that because a lot of people are counting on you. My associates did a fine job tossing your house, but they didn't find what they were looking for at Mrs. Byrd's. I'm sending them back as soon as the police finish up to look again."

"What do you want?"

"Obviously, I haven't found what I'm searching for. I'll be honest; it hasn't been a good day. Seems I keep running into dead ends at every turn, and that isn't good for me. Or you." He seemed to be taking great pleasure in baiting her, but Billie refused to get sucked into his game any more than she already was. "Mrs. Byrd has something that I need, a letter in a white linen envelope with no return address. It has a burgundy wax seal on—"

A letter? A freaking letter? Billie tried to listen, but her mind was racing toward the worst possible conclusion: Her life. Miss Sadie's life. The lives of Amber, of the baby were at the mercy of the United States Post Office? *Shit.* He continued to talk. Oh God, what did he just say? She shook her head in an effort to expel the paranoia that was zinging around inside her like a pinball machine gone mad.

"So, in the meantime, go to the State House. There's a Confederate monument there. Do you know the place?"

"Yes." Twenty-seven years ago, Billie was a student in Columbia and knew it like the back of her hand.

"I know the place."

"With her house tossed, not to mention her son dead, I expect Mrs. Byrd is a little rattled. Use the time I'm giving you to talk to her about the letter." While he paused, Billie heard another male voice and highway noises in the background. "She doesn't own a cell phone, but when this call is over, you'll need to toss your phone and the burner phone into the trash. And that pathetic gun as well."

How did he know about the gun? Had he followed her to Harry Bennett's? Had he followed her to Mama's? Her heart began to pound faster. Needle-sharp pains raced up the back of her neck and were drawn to her head like a magnetic pincushion. He was talking again—what was he saying? Oh, God.

"It should take you about ten minutes to get from the grocery store parking lot you're in to the State House; I'll contact you there. Make sure Mrs. Byrd stays with you. Oh, yes. I'm afraid there won't be any more contact with Amber for a while. But you can imagine how upset she is, how much she wants all this to end and soon." He chuckled, and the call disconnected.

Billie scanned the nearly empty parking lot. Two mothers with little ones were putting groceries in their cars and chatting like they knew each other. The Wonder Bread man was filling a cart to take into the store, and an old man with a navy blue Kroger apron on was gathering up stray grocery carts. She bristled at the thought that whoever was doing this was watching her every move. Even worse, they were watching Amber and Little Man too.

Her body jolted as the phones hit the steel drum with a deafening clanking sound, effectively severing the lifeline that connected her to Amber and the baby. She wanted to scream, to sob. She wanted to claw the predator's heart out of his chest. Instead she stuffed the Office Depot bag with Harry Bennett's worthless gun down under a wad of plastic bags in the trash, then wiped her shaking hands on her shirt.

Billie Warren—mother, cop, Wild Boy, was officially helpless. And she was losing her mind. Even with the advent of the anxiety attacks, Billie had always been a card carrying Timex woman, who like the famous watches, "took a licking and kept on ticking." But the memory of Amber's sobs, of Little Man's pathetic cry drowned out any hope of logical thought. She didn't have the first clue as to what she was going to do. She wasn't even sure she remembered the predator's instructions.

When she got back in the car, Miss Sadie put her hand on her arm. "Are you all right, child?"

Billie closed her eyes and shook her head. What in the world was she going to tell Miss Sadie? Could the old woman handle the truth? Could Billie afford to tell her anything but the truth?

"It's not my business who you were talking to, but I hope everything's fine." Miss Sadie shook her head. "There's a lot of badness in the world, like what those kids did to my boy's house."

"It wasn't kids," Billie's voice was hoarse. "They wrecked my house, too."

"What in the world—?"

"Somebody was looking for something, a letter addressed to you. It has a wax seal on it—a burgundy wax seal."

"They tore up my house for a letter? From who?"

"I don't know, but whoever did this is threatening to hurt Amber and the baby if we don't give them what they want."

"Dear Lord."

"Do remember getting a letter like that?"

"No. But I didn't stop the mail before I left for Stanton. Usually, if nobody is home for a couple of days, one of the neighbors will get the mail. Cecil used to do the same for them all the time, especially Lana, she's the neighbor with the little children. If she didn't pick the mail up, Grace Martin or her husband, Tom, might have."

Billie started the car and turned toward a main thoroughfare that would lead her to Sumter, the street that ran in front of the State House.

"What are we going to do?" Miss Sadie's voice trembled.

"Whatever they tell us to, until I can figure this out."

After two passes around the grounds, Billie was lucky enough to score a parking space that was fairly close to the monument. A school bus went by, full of noisy children. A boy in the back, who looked to be maybe nine or ten, looked at Billie, grinned, and gave her the finger. Any other day she might have laughed at the exchange, but not today. She cupped her hand under Miss Sadie's elbow and helped her out of the car.

"Where are we going?" she asked.

"The State House."

"Don't we need to go to Lana's house and see if she picked up the mail?"

"The man on the phone said he was going to contact me here," she said, opting out of telling Miss Sadie that the bastards were going to toss the house again.

Billie guided Miss Sadie toward the monument that was directly in front of the State House. Until this year, the monument with its Confederate flag flying high above it was a sore spot to the majority of the state. But the flag was also cherished by a bunch of rednecks and a small group of powerful men who claimed the flag was an homage to history and had nothing to do with hate.

Less than a month after the horrible shootings by some idiot racist at the Emanuel African Methodist Episcopal Church in Charleston this past summer, the governor removed the stars and bars from the monument.

True to form, Columbia was nearing ninety degrees on the cloudless early November day. Billie didn't know if the legislature was in session because the grounds were all but deserted. Billie and Miss Sadie sat down on one of the three benches on either side of the flagless monument to the Confederacy. Miss Sadie was quiet, which was good because Billie needed to think, to twist and turn the events and the conversations with the predator around like a Rubik's cube until something made sense.

What was Cecil Byrd hiding? Did he have some kind of secret life that brought this kind of trouble to his doorstep? Or had trouble come looking for Cecil, only to find that he was already dead? And the letter? *Nobody* writes letters anymore. There had to be some common thread, something Billie was missing.

An attractive woman with dark chocolate skin sat down on the bench beside them. She pulled a Bible and a sketchbook out of her canvas bag and rummaged through the bag until she found a thick drawing pencil that looked like the kind Amber had used in kindergarten.

The woman looked at Billie and smiled before turning her attention to the monument. Billie looked up at the memorial; how odd, she thought, that this woman of color would want to sketch this monument to a South that had enslaved her ancestors. Could she be delivering the next message?

The woman didn't say anything, just continued her work. She must have sensed Billie was watching her. "I like the State House," she said, without looking up. "It's nice here."

Billie's smile was thin but polite. She noticed that the artist was shading an object onto the page, but she couldn't tell what it was. She looked around the general vicinity of the monument but didn't see anything other than twenty or so showy monuments and masses of century-old oak trees that dotted the west side of the State House grounds. The object began to take shape as the woman's pencil rubbed across the paper. She cocked her head to the side, looked at her drawing, and then showed Billie. The woman had sketched the monument in the shadow of a rugged cross.

Any other day, Billie would have told the woman that she was a wonderful artist. She would have asked her if she had had any formal training, and maybe asked her if she was familiar with Rennie Patterson, Carol Murphy, or some of the other fine artists who lived at the Row. But today she said nothing and prayed to God with all her might that if the woman wasn't a messenger, she would hurry up and leave. Otherwise, the predator might not make contact.

The woman must have thought she had offended Billie because she packed up her Bible and sketchbook and walked across the lawn to one of the monuments Billie remembered from a field trip when Amber was in the fourth grade.

Oh, God. Amber. Sweet Amber. And the baby. Little Man, her sweet little boy she took care of when Amber was in the hospital. Billie felt her nose and her eyes sting. What if she lost them? A cell phone chirped. Billie followed the sound to the bench next to hers, felt around under the slats, and yanked another burner phone from under the bench. She sucked in a deep breath and answered it before it rang again.

"Hello, Billie."

"I want to talk to Amber. Now." Her voice was demanding, maybe too demanding. "Please." Silence. Tears. God, she was scared and angry. So angry. "Who *are* you?"

"Let's see, my associates can take out your daughter and grandson in a matter of seconds, and I have a deadline to make for my client. Do you really want to waste time asking me stupid questions you know I'm not going to answer?"

"Look, I talked to Mrs. Byrd. She doesn't know anything about the letter you want."

There was a long pause. Billie's heart was beating so hard it reverberated in her ears.

"That's unfortunate."

"Wait!" Billie shouted in desperation and then quieted her voice. "I can find it. I will get it for you. It just may take some time. Please—"

"With the right motivation, I'm sure you can."

The line went dead. Bastard. Billie tried to reconnect, but got a fast busy signal. She tried again. Nothing. The shrill ring of the cell phone in her hand nearly made her jump out of her skin. She answered the call.

"Mama!" Amber was sobbing hard, gasping for air. "There's—there's two men in the deer stands across the field, they have their guns pointed—at me. One of them called me on the pho—phone and said not to move until he told me to or he would ki—kill—"

The line went dead before Billie could say anything and then immediately rang. "Amber? Amber?"

"Not Amber," the bastard said. "Poor girl, she's lying face down on the floor, afraid to move after she tried to sneak out of the house. She won't try *that* again."

"If you hurt her . . ." Hot silent tears streamed down her face. God, she needed to do something, anything to save her family. She needed that letter. Maybe by the time she found it, she'd have a plan. Right now, she was this maniac's gofer, and she was in no position to bargain.

"If I hurt her, you'll what?" Silence reinforced his point. "Amber's fine. For now. You have my word. The gentlemen watching her will call her and tell her she can get back to the baby. I'm sure she'll be glad for that, and you, Billie, should be well motivated."

"What happens when I give you the letter?"

"All of this simply goes away."

She didn't believe that for one second.

"And if you don't find the letter—well, we won't talk about that right now. Better to stay positive, don't you think?"

"I'll find it. Just don't hurt them.

"I'm sure you will. We're all done at Mrs. Byrd's house, and I'm sad to say we didn't find what we were looking for. Find the letter, Billie. If you want to see your daughter and the baby alive, find that letter."

CHAPTER TWENTY-ONE

No matter how loudly Billie's brain screamed at her to snap out of her stupor, she felt like she was back in the cocoon. It was nice, kind of like the one that surrounded her the day of the anxiety attack. Insulated by thick, soft, cotton, street traffic was barely audible and the monuments, the State House, even the sun hanging low over the trendy Vista area looked too brilliant, too real, like she was watching the world through one of those HDTV's.

"This is my fault," Miss Sadie said solemnly. "It's all on account of me."

Miss Sadie's words cut through the haze and yanked her back into the moment. "I never should have gone back to Stanton."

"Don't say that." Billie helped Miss Sadie up from the bench. "We'll figure this out. It will be over soon."

"And Cecil? God rest his soul, I just can't believe all this has anything to do with him." She continued walking toward the car, staring straight ahead.

Billie's legs felt like lead as they headed toward the car, her head thick from the heady cocktail of the adrenaline high that started with Amber's cry for help and the numbness from the anxiety attack that didn't seem to have an end. That someone could kill Amber and the baby? It was crazy. Surreal.

Miss Sadie seemed oblivious to the sky parade of starlings packed into overbooked formations, heading farther south for the winter. She was rambling, something about being worthless, *always* worthless.

"Don't ever say that," Billie said hoarsely. She looked at the woman and shook her head. The layers of cotton batting that had insulated Billie, giving her respite from the horror of what was happening, of what was at stake, were falling away, awakening the warrior inside her. "This is not your fault."

"Dew always said that about me, especially after Caroline died and I went completely crazy. For most of my life, I believed it deep down, even when Cecil was so good to me. I didn't deserve his mercy then, and I don't deserve God's mercy now. I'm sorry I brought this on you and your family. I should never have gone to Stanton, should have just gone on to Jesus and taken my chances that he would forgive me for what happened to Caroline."

When Miss Sadie had arrived in Stanton, Delores had commented more than once that Miss Sadie was as polished as a new penny, which was a nice way of saying she was a far cry from the bedraggled town crazy that roamed the streets forty years ago. Now her veneer was fading like invisible ink, giving way to a haggard old woman who was undeniably worse from the wear of a pilgrimage to set things right.

"Honest to Jesus, I don't know what any of this is about," she said wearily.

"I know you don't." Billie looked at the clock on the dashboard. "It's almost six o'clock; let's just hurry back to your house, find the letter, and be done with this." She tried to sound confident, but the ordeal was bearing down hard on Billie, too, casting long shadows of doubt on the world outside her precious cocoon.

As Billie pulled into the driveway at Cecil Byrd's house, she couldn't help but notice Lana Peterson. Standing by her standard issue minivan, she was strikingly beautiful. Her hair was a rich auburn color, and she had the body of an aerobics queen or, more precisely, a young mother of three wild little boys. Her chubby bald baby with the pink headband Velcroed to her head was straining to get out of the car seat while the three boys played chase, using Lana's body for interference.

When most women would be tempted to cuss at the boy's rough play, Lana freed her giggling baby and then held her up like a prize over the friendly mêlée, laughing all the way toward the arched front doorway of her stately limestone home. One of the boys yanked on her crisp white cotton shirttail and pointed to Billie's car. Lana jiggled the key until the front door of the grandiose old home opened and the boys charged in.

"That's little Sydney," Miss Sadie said as Lana walked toward them with the baby bouncing on her hip, her tiny fingers holding onto the V of Lana's shirt. "She's so precious."

Lana went right to Miss Sadie. "Hey there," she said, "let me hug your neck."Billie guessed it was out of habit that the baby went to Miss Sadie too. Lana laughed as she handed the little bundle over. "Gosh, we've missed you. The boys have been checking every day to see if you were home yet, and look, Sydney missed you, too. How are you doing?"

Miss Sadie held the baby close and then smiled through dark sad eyes as she handed Sydney back to her mother. "I reckon I'm as fine as I can be."

"The day of the funeral, when I came back from picking the boys up from school, I went next door to check on you. But you'd already gone." Lana looked like she wanted to say something else, maybe ask questions, but decided against it. "It was a beautiful service."

"Yes, child, it sure was," Miss Sadie's voice trailed off.

"I'm Billie Warren." Billie extended her hand, which Lana ignored as she hugged Billie.

"We're real big on hugging around here—especially friends of Miss Sadie's."

With the business at hand, Billie was taken aback, stiff. The bubbly, perfect mom must have sensed something wasn't right; when she pulled away, her polite thin smile made Billie think maybe Lana knew something, suspected something.

From the outside, there was no evidence the house had been ransacked. Had she heard anything or had the pillagers waited until she left the house? Billie guessed by her friendly demeanor that Lana didn't know, and it was best to keep it that way. "Miss Sadie came to stay with me for a few days until she was ready to settle her son's estate. I'm here for moral support."

"Billie's been a real big help," Miss Sadie said.

"Oh." Lana's suspicious look said she wasn't completely convinced that Billie's intentions were good. "That's really nice of you."

There was an uncomfortable silence. Lana shifted the baby to the other hip.

Miss Sadie said, "Lana, honey, did you get my mail while I was gone?"

"Yes, ma'am. Let me put the baby down for the evening, and I'll bring it right over. Oh, I almost forgot, I have two casseroles in my freezer that some ladies brought by for you after you left. They're from your Sunday school class."

"Miss Sadie's so worn out, and you have your hands full with the kids," Billie said. "If it's okay, I'll just come over now and take the mail and the casseroles off your hands."

Sydney rubbed her eyes on cue and kicked her chubby little heels hard against her mother's hips like she was spurring a pony. "Poor Sydney, it's way past her bedtime. I was shopping most of the day and had parent–teacher conferences tonight at school. With the boys in three different classes, I think we were one of the last to leave," Lana said. "Give me an hour to get the kids settled in and check on dinner. By then I'll have Miss Sadie's things together for you."

An hour? Shit, Billie didn't have an hour. She started to press the issue but decided against it. "Thanks, Lana."

It didn't seem possible that the house was an even worse mess after the police sifted through the wreckage, but it was. Billie up-righted a pretty Queen Ann's chair and eased a pitifully sad Miss Sadie into the seat. She knew the old woman had endured too much, and seeing her son's house turned upside down again had robbed her of the color she'd had a few minutes earlier while she held the baby. She was unsteady. Trembling.

"I think I need to lie down," Miss Sadie said.

"They cut the mattresses to shreds, the couch cushions, too. Let me see what I can put together." Billie poked around in the debris until she found a couple of quilts and spread them over the tattered couch. "It might not be too comfortable, but try to get some rest."

Miss Sadie nodded and sat down on the couch, her tired face lined with worry. "But we have to find that letter."

"You try to get some rest, and let me worry about that."

It was twenty till eight when Billie locked the house up tight and headed next door to Lana Peterson's. The stately Tudor home seemed eerily quiet and not at all like the circus it had been earlier. Billie knocked quietly on the kitchen door and waited. Before she could knock again, Lana opened the door and invited Billie into the rambling homey kitchen that smelled like rosemary, sage, and the unmistakable aroma of homemade bread.

"I've got a late dinner going—stew. My kids wouldn't touch it; they're all about spaghetti and chicken nuggets, but Rick loves it. I made bread to celebrate his abandoning the No Carb diet." Billie laughed politely and noticed five boxes of cereal sitting by the pantry. Lana smiled and blushed. "Poor guy's been so crunch deprived, but come breakfast, he can crunch till his heart's content."

She stacked a small canvas bag on top of two frozen casseroles in Pyrex dishes and handed them to Billie. Billie set the casseroles down and sifted through the mailbag. No letter with fancy sealing wax.

"That's just today's mail. I'm sure the Martins picked up Sadie's mail while we were out of town. Grace left a message on my machine that their daughter had finally had her baby. I know they were planning on staying for a while to help her out. It's her first."

Looking around the spotless house, Billie knew the answer before she asked. "Lana, is there any chance some of Sadie's mail might have gotten mixed up with yours?"

"I don't think so, but I can look more thoroughly after I tuck the kids in. They're upstairs in bed reading now. Their school is having a competition to see who can read the most books. Clayton's teacher said he was padding his numbers; I'm sure he's not looking forward to that discussion before bedtime." Lana laughed and continued. "So, this letter must be important to Miss Sadie." She sifted through some envelopes on the desk in the kitchen Inbox, then tossed the letters back in the box and straightened them. "Sorry."

Billie thought of the wax seal, how unusual that might seem to the boys. "Any chance one of the boys might have picked up some of the mail?"

Now, the adorable perky housewife was insulted. She smiled politely and told Billie in an equally polite tone that the boys have never had the least bit of interest in the mail. "They don't go anywhere near the mailboxes; they aren't even allowed in the front yard unless Rick or I am out there. We have too much traffic around here."

Billie thanked Lana and tried to smooth things over, complementing her on her home and how beautiful the children were in a photograph displayed in a little silver frame on the kitchen windowsill. Lana graciously accepted. "I've got plenty of stew. Would you and Miss Sadie like some? There's plenty of bread, too."

Neither Billie nor Miss Sadie had had a bite to eat since their pitiful breakfast. "None for me, thank you. But Miss Sadie might be hungry."

Lana chose a large cherry red ceramic bowl from a cabinet shelf and ladled the thick stew into the bowl. She took the loaf of bread out of the machine, set it on a thick chopping block, and sliced a large hunk that was meant for two. "Let me get you something to carry all of this in."

Billie wanted to dart out the door so that she could plan her next move, but waited instead. Lana returned from her butler's pantry with a plastic crate that held the casseroles, the mail, and the gracious dinner.

"I hope you find what you're looking for," Lana said.

"So do I." Billie thanked her and started down the kitchen steps.

"Billie, if it's really important, I know that Grace always pays one of the Barton kids to feed the cat and water the plants. They live two streets over and would have a key."

"Thanks, Lana."

———◆◆◆———

Billie waded through the mess and set the crate on the kitchen table she had righted earlier. She didn't have to look at Miss Sadie to know that she was sawing logs, but there was no reason to wake her. Billie started in the living room, sifting, straightening, looking for any clues the perp might have left behind and wondering what kind of mess Cecil Byrd had gotten himself into.

There was nothing out of the ordinary in the living room or the kitchen. The medicine cabinet beside the refrigerator had three bottles of Tylenol and a lot of over the counter drugs. Three of Cecil's prescription bottles with fill dates from over a year ago were full of pills that had never been taken. Crestor, Toprol, Lisinopril—all for high blood pressure and cholesterol. The contents of the refrigerator looked like a heart attack in a box; the five-pound bucket of lard in the pantry would have made Inez proud, but would have totally blown her theory that rendered pork fat had never killed anybody.

A check of the bathroom across the hall from Miss Sadie's bedroom was equally as fruitless as the other two rooms. Billie replaced the contents of the linen closet that had been emptied out on the floor and couldn't help but notice the perfectly folded sheets that looked like they'd been ironed, like Mama used to, even after the advent of permanent press sheets.

She moved across the hall to Cecil's room and turned on the light. Even all jumbled up and trashed about, it was easy to tell the place had been rather sparse but neat. He'd kept his room clean, and it appeared someone had caught the dust before it hit the floor. His closet was full of khakis and golf shirts and what looked like two pairs of Sunday pants and two dress shirts, one long sleeved, one short. A file full of bank statements was dumped on top of his shoes. Billie sat down on the floor, cross-legged, and glanced over several of them, concentrating more on the ones from recent months. It looked like all Cecil's bills were on bank draft; there were no large deposits or withdrawals. His paycheck from the South Carolina Health Department was automatically deposited into his account on the 15th and the 30th. Doing the math, Billie figured he made fifty-four thousand dollars a year give or take.

His bookcase bed looked like a throwback from the 1970s except that it had been ripped apart. Novels were scattered across the gutted mattress, all thrillers except for a yellowed copy of *Love Story* and a well-worn autobiography of Ali McGraw. The glass on a framed, black-and-white glossy of the actress was busted; someone had ripped the photo in half to see if anything was hidden behind it. There was a sticker on the back with a purchase date that indicated Cecil had bought the photograph on Ebay a couple of years ago and on the front of the photo, the actress had presumably scrawled—*To Roy. Love means never having to say you're sorry. Ali McGraw.*

The investigation into what Cecil was involved in had yielded nothing other than the probability he had a thing for the star of the movie version of the blockbuster novel. Billie took one last look around and glanced at her watch. It was nearly nine.

Miss Sadie was still resting, her face was relaxed, peaceful; an old Bible whose cover had been ripped off was tucked close to her chest. Billie eased into Miss Sadie's bedroom and looked at the jumble of precious things and clothes flung about. She tried to be quiet, continuing to look for anything that might give her a clue, even though her gut told her that a man like Cecil Byrd would never have hidden anything somebody else wanted this badly in his mother's room.

"Did you find anything?"

Miss Sadie's words startled Billie. "No, ma'am. But as best I can tell, this doesn't have anything to do with Cecil."

CHAPTER TWENTY-TWO

The hollow ticking of the kitchen clock fueled the debate in Billie's mind. Should she risk getting arrested and break into the Martin's house? She'd checked out the window decals that adamantly declared the home was protected by Phantom Security, so getting busted was a certainty.

Billie called the kid Lana said was watching the place. The girl's mother said that she was at a dress rehearsal for her school's production of *Grease*. She went on and on about the early buzz for her daughter as Rizzo and how this had given her daughter's hopes and dreams a bent toward studying acting and voice after graduation instead of her intended major of animal husbandry.

"Wren puts so much of herself into her role, she will be completely spent and worthless tomorrow when it's time to go to school. She texted me around eight, when they took a dinner break, and said she wouldn't be home until after eleven. But I think it'll be worth it, don't you?"

"Excuse me?" Billie could not listen to the woman babble on

another second. Out of sheer desperation, she put Miss Sadie on the phone.

"Nadine, I really need to get my mail tonight; there's a letter I need and . . . my daughter's got to be back at work tomorrow," Miss Sadie looked up at Billie. "No, you never met her. She lives in the Lowcountry. Yes, it is real nice of her to help out. Well, all right—okay. Thanks anyway."

After Miss Sadie ended the call, Billie stared at her for a moment, unable to speak. Bits and pieces of memories from her childhood raced through her head. Had John been right when he had teased her? Was Billie one of "Crazy Sadie's" babies? Had Mama and Daddy traded Coke bottles for her? No. Billie looked just like her mama. But her nose was identical to Miss Sadie's, and they had the same skin tone, sort of gold, sun kissed compared to Mama, who is as fair as alabaster. Damn it, Billie didn't have time for another bombshell. Distraction was her enemy. Still, a part of her was reeling from Miss Sadie's words; Billie couldn't help but wonder—*Are you my mother?*

"I shouldn't have lied," Miss Sadie said sheepishly before Billie could say anything. "God, forgive me. I just couldn't think of what to say to make her stop talking."

The question gnawed at Billie with bone splitting force. That Billie's slender face was just like Mama's, her mama's. She had small hands, like the ones folded penitently in Miss Sadie's lap, and the same dusting of freckles Billie had tried to scrub off the few times she played dress up in Mama's clothes a hundred years ago. But the freckles, like Miss Sadie's, never washed away.

As she reached toward Miss Sadie's downcast face, the burner phone rang slamming through the building blocks that were forming into something; but what? "There's been a change, Billie. I have something more pressing; the deadline has been moved up."

"But I can't get into the house next door until after eleven o'clock, maybe midnight."

"Break in."

"It's wired."

"You'll just have to do it and be quick about it, or—"

"Okay. I'll do it. Just, please, let me talk to Amber. I need to hear that she's okay. Please."

"For now, you'll have to take my word that she's fine. Just get the letter and meet me at the municipal parking garage off Assembly Street. Head for the top level. Get out of your car and wait for my instructions. You have one hour."

"But—"

"Really, Billie, I don't have time to toy with you anymore. *Just do it.*"

"But what if—"

"I never pegged you as a what-if-kind-of-girl, Billie. Me, I'm an I-wonder-kind-of-guy. For instance, I wonder what it sounds like to hear a baby's skull split cleanly in two."

"*Stop. No.*" She was terrified, shattered into a million pieces.

"I wonder what it sounds like to hear his mother convulse from pain from seeing her baby die before her eyes and then gratefully welcome the taste of cold steel in her mouth to stop that pain."

"*I'm sorry. I'll do it. Just please. Don't hurt them.*"

His voice was getting louder with each taunt. "Tell me Billie, do you think her pretty teeth would chatter on the barrel of the gun? Could anybody stop her from pulling the trigger?"

"I'll do it. I'll do it. Just don't—"

"You're in no position to give orders," he was screaming at her. "I have a deadline to meet. If you want to see your daughter and her baby alive, you'll get the letter. Now."

The line went dead. The Imperial Empress of the Wild Boys stood there with the phone pressed hard against her ear. She had to stop crying, to stop trembling. "We don't have time to wait for the Martin girl to get home." She swallowed hard. "I'll have to break in and hope I can find the letter before the police respond."

"What happens if you don't?" Miss Sadie asked.

She would be locked up, and Amber and the baby would be dead. A chill careened down Billie's spine. "I can't think like that. As soon as I get back, we'll need to find this guy and give him the letter."

The shrill whistle of the tea kettle called, making Billie's stomach plummet like a falling elevator. Miss Sadie rummaged through the wreckage on the kitchen floor until she found two cups that were unbroken. One was a well-worn University of South Carolina mug that Billie thought must have been Cecil's, the other was a tacky Pedro's South of the Border cup that looked like it had never been used. Miss Sadie rinsed them out in the sink.

She seemed rattled by the obvious answer to the question she had asked Billie. "I'll make some tea," she said. "Tea would help, don't you think?"

"Yes, Miss Sadie. Tea would be fine." And then she leaned toward the old woman and kissed the crown of her head. "I'm so sorry about everything—your son, the house. I'm going to fix this. Everything's going to be okay."

The kiss, the whole scene in the kitchen, seemed surreal as Miss Sadie poured the steaming water over the tea bags. The sharp herbal twang of lemongrass wafted upward with the potency of smelling salts. What in the hell was Billie going to do? She wished she had a shot of the old Gray Goose to settle her down.

The night air had grown considerably colder. Her rubber soles made a deafening squeaking sound against the blanket of dampness that covered the thick Saint Augustine grass. Billie slipped through the hedge of tall red tip shrubs that surrounded the backyard and approached what appeared to be the laundry room door.

Looking inside, there was no evidence of motion sensors with small red LED lights like Nan's security system. Still, the windows could be wired. The double doors next to the laundry hamper were open. A streetlight shone in the leaded glass of the front door. Billie could see down the hall into what she guessed was the foyer. There was a hall table, but she couldn't make out much else. It was near the front door, a good place for a lazy teenager to drop the mail before she opened a can of cat food and locked up. The doors had dead bolts.

The spigot outside under the small laundry room window could give her a leg up. If she was lucky and Grace had left the window unlocked, she would have a shot at getting in. Billie hurried down the steps and stepped on the spigot, pushing hard with one leg until her fingertips grasped the edge of the brick windowsill. She dug in hard, fingers pulsing, throbbing as she pulled herself up on her elbows, her feet dangling into the nothingness far below. She braced herself on one arm and pushed hard against the window with the other. It refused to budge. She smacked at the base, in case it was stuck, but it still wouldn't move.

Her feet searched in vain for the spigot to brace herself on the climb back down. She would have to jump and pray the curse of her bum ankle wouldn't follow her to the ground. *Shit!* The pain scorched through her right leg awakening an old injury that started all the way back in high school and had plagued her ever since. Face down in the wet grass, she writhed around in pain, her hand over her mouth to stifle her scream.

When she finally opened her eyes, a green blur was staring at her. She blinked hard, trying to focus. It was a frog with a golden crown, like one of those tacky plastic ones she had seen in catalogs vendors still sent Mama even though she hadn't ordered anything from them in ten years—the kind that are so tacky, they're overlooked by thieves trying to break into a house. Billie limped to the squatting frog and turned it over. In the less than generous light, she studied its backside, then pushed in the small button on the frog's belly and a thin plastic door opened, yielding a small brass key.

"Thank God for Lillian Vernon," Billie whispered. She got on her knees and made a lame attempt to stand. Her tortured ankle was swelling, making her shoe too tight and her foot tingle. She needed to walk off the pain, but she wasn't even sure she could stand. She scooted across the wet grass on her butt until she got to the black wrought iron railing that led up to the laundry room door. She hobbled up the stairs like a three-year-old and leaned her head against the glass.

Fingerprints. The thought was trivial compared to what was at stake. Her fingerprints were in the state's database. If the alarm triggered and the police came, they would find her prints on the laundry room window. With that thought, she put the brass key in the deadbolt, used her shirttail to grip the knob, held her breath, and opened the door.

Nothing. She felt around the jamb and then opened the laundry room window and checked for a sensor. Apparently, Phantom Security was just that. And the only defense the company provided was a facade produced by a dozen or so conspicuously placed vinyl stickers and two yard signs.

Billie hobbled down the hall that made a straight line to the entryway door and the foyer table only to find a beautifully carved wooden bowl and a half dozen or so frames with family pictures and one prominent eight-by-ten of a stately looking Irish setter. Just off the hallway, she found the kitchen, which was immaculate and did not have a desk. Billie opened and closed several drawers. Still no letter.

She limped back into the hall and opened a large oak pocket door. A massive mahogany desk glowed under the light that streamed in from the street lamp out front. This was too easy. Fear replaced the intense pain from her ankle; it prickled up the back of her neck as she approached the desk. What in the hell was she going to do if and when she found the golden goose that would free Little Man and Amber? Could she stifle the cop inside of her long enough to give the coveted letter to a phantom who had all but promised her a happy ending? After everything that had happened, did she really believe that there was such a thing?

But there it was, pretty as you please, right on top of the desk—a thick envelope made out of expensive-looking paper addressed by hand to Mrs. Sadie Byrd.

Billie ran her hand across the paper; its texture made it seem as old as sin itself. "Just get the letter and go"—she said the words out loud, hoping that they would propel her toward her—deadline. God, she hated that man and that word he had purposefully woven into their conversation over and over again as if Billie needed to be reminded that he had the power to alter Billie's life forever. The pain from her ankle radiated up her thigh and her taut stomach, making a beeline for her brain. She snatched up the envelope and hobbled down the hall and out the back door.

Car keys, purse, Miss Sadie. Get the hell out of here and over to the parking garage. Billie climbed the steps to Miss Sadie's house, leading with her good leg to get her to the top. She hesitated before she opened the front door. There were voices; two, distinct voices. Maybe a TV or a radio had miraculously survived the looting. Just to be on the safe side, Billie stuffed the letter into her waistband and, for the billionth time today, wished she had her gun. She pulled her shirttail down to conceal the letter and pushed the door open.

"Hello Billie."

"Deidre?"

CHAPTER TWENTY-THREE

Miss Sadie didn't seem to have a clue that sweet, pretty Deidre Lawson, who was sitting beside her all ladylike with her legs crossed at the ankles, had the nose of a gun pointed at her. The silencer was barely noticeable under the classy hobo bag that matched the damn woman's shoes. Deidre set her jelly glass of hot tea on the TV tray between her and Miss Sadie and dabbed at her mouth like she had just aced the etiquette class Billie flunked when she was ten.

"Miss Sadie, why don't you go lie down again and rest a bit while I talk to Deidre."

"No, I think it would be better for her to stay right here," Deidre said, watching Billie's face as she nudged the barrel of the gun from its hiding place.

Miss Sadie gasped and went white as alabaster. "What in the world?"

"It's okay." Billie tried to sound reassuring. "I've got this." But that was a lie. Billie wasn't in control of anything, much less Deidre Lawson, wielding her firearm with the confidence of a seasoned professional.

Deidre put her finger to her lip and gave Miss Sadie a menacingly polite look that said, Shut up. Please. "Billie, I'd appreciate if you would put your gun on the floor. I can barely think with those things around."

"Looks like you're doing just fine to me," Billie said.

"They make me nervous. Your gun." She motioned to the floor.

"I don't have one," Billie wished she was lying.

"Billie? What's going on?" Miss Sadie asked.

Deidre cocked her head to the side and motioned for Billie to prove it. Billie lifted her shirt up and turned slowly.

"Good. I'm guessing that letter in the waistband of your jeans is the one letter I'm looking for."

"You found it!" Miss Sadie said. Billie nodded.

"Hand it to me—slowly," Deidre said.

"But we need—" Billie shot Miss Sadie a look that stopped her midsentence.

"Not as much as I do. Hand it over, Billie."

"I can't give this to you." Billie said. "I won't."

Deidre pushed the gun into Miss Sadie's side. As it was, Miss Sadie looked scared, now the look on her face was reminiscent of the one she had when Billie had stolen her doll. "You all seem like such reasonable people, Billie, and I truly don't want to hurt anybody."

"I can help you, Deidre. Tell me who's behind this," Billie said. "If we work together—"

"That's not possible."

"Look, my daughter and grandson are being held—"

"Hostage." A single word, and Deidre's cool demeanor melted away. Her Cover Girl skin was pale and gaunt; tears glistened in steel blue eyes that just seconds ago had exuded the seasoned coolness of a gun moll. "God damn him," she hissed, then wiped her eyes with the back of her hand. "I have to get out of here. *Now.*" Angry tears streamed down her face. "Give me the goddamn letter."

"Who's behind all of this, Deidre?" Billie demanded, holding the envelope out as an enticement. "Who in the hell has me breaking into a stranger's house and you running scared and threatening to kill people?"

"Oh, God, if he knows, we'll never get out of this alive." She was melting down, her whole body convulsing with fear and anguish. "I have to get to my sister before he does."

"Who are you running from? Is your sister in trouble? Let me help you, Deidre."

"I need that letter. Now." The gun went eerily steady and was pointed at Billie's head. Billie had no doubt Deidre would hit her mark if she fired. "Give it to me now, Billie, or I swear to God I will kill both of you."

Since that first terrifying call from Amber, Billie had watched every second tick off the clock with blinding speed. Her sole purpose for drawing breath was to secure the safety of Amber and the baby. With Deidre in the same boat as Billie, and despite all her threats, Billie's instincts told her Deidre might be a crack shot, but she wasn't capable of murder.

Billie walked over to Miss Sadie and helped her out of her seat. "Sit down," Deidre gulped through tears. Miss Sadie looked at Billie with complete trust, or maybe it was her complete trust in God that allowed her to walk toward the front door with Billie. "Please. Don't make me do this." Deidre sobbed. "He'll kill us."

Billie and Miss Sadie headed for the door and didn't stop until they were in the car.

— ◆◆◆ —

The glowing green digits of the dashboard clock screamed at Billie as she pulled into the entrance of the unattended municipal parking garage. She could hear her own heart beat pounding. 10:38, she was already late. In her mind, she rehashed the man's instructions. The car snaked up the ramp and stopped near the designated spot on level three at the opposite end of the elevators. Billie scoped out the place. No phone, no fire alarm in plain sight, nothing she could use to save the world.

He's late, she thought, unable to breathe a sigh of relief. What does that mean? What if it was too late—oh, hell, what if he's been here and gone? What if Amber—the thought paralyzed her, suffocated her. She could not allow herself to think like that. She would not allow herself to believe that her greatest fear had been realized.

She rifled through the glove box for something to use as a weapon. Anything. She always fussed at Amber for keeping her car like a garage sale junkie's and wished she were no different. The Camry manual, an insurance card, the registration, and two breath mints. She shoved everything back into the box and closed it. They were still the only car on the parking level.

"We have to get out." Billie helped Miss Sadie out of the car and walked to the opposite end of the garage. "We're supposed to wait here."

They heard the service bell signaling the elevator's arrival to the third floor. When the door opened, Billie fully expected the bastard to be in there, but the car was empty. Nothing to do now but wait. She had no phone. She had nothing except the letter Deidre thought she could kill for.

God, she needed a weapon. The tire iron in the trunk of the car. Sure it would be useless against real bullets, but at least it was something. She looked around to make sure they were still alone, hurried back to the car, and popped the trunk. She yanked the small L-shaped iron out from under the pristine floorboard, slammed the trunk shut, and shoved the long end into the waistband of her baggy chinos where her gun should be. She felt every inch of the cold steel across her lower back and down her right leg.

She had no plan, all she had was hope that there'd be one stinking moment that might finally go her way.

This part of Columbia was as dead this time of night as it would be at three or four in the morning; and there was just enough background noise from the bars and restaurants in the nearby Vista to play tricks on Billie's mind.

An explosion rocked the parking garage. Billie was far enough away from the designated spot to see a car burning a block away. A handful of adults, maybe students, were standing around the car; seconds later, fire trucks from the Blanding Street Fire Station came roaring to the scene.

The noise from the sirens reverberated off the concrete ceiling and the walls of the empty garage, so that Billie didn't hear the black Mercedes slinking its way up the ramp until bright lights completely blinded her. In the glare, he looked like a tall black blur getting out of the sedan and walking straight toward her. She couldn't see his face but she knew without a doubt it was him. "Nice diversion."

"Sorry I'm late." He sauntered over to her like she was harmless. She didn't recognize him, but the smug look on his face matched his voice. "The letter?" He said almost in her face, his breath hot on her cheek. Miss Sadie clutched Billie's arm with surprising force; Billie could feel herself trembling.

Bile crept up in her throat as she handed over the one thing that, up until now, had kept Amber and the baby alive. She had nothing to bargain with now, nothing to save anybody's life, much less her own.

He slit open the envelope with his thumb and flipped through the pages. "Very good." A few seconds passed, and almost as an afterthought, he patted her down. "Really?" he laughed as he tossed the tire iron on the floor. He flashed Billie's own gun at her—or more precisely, Harry Bennett's worthless gun and grinned at the firearm that looked as shiny and new as it did when it was made. "Much better, don't you think? And fully loaded."

He steered Billie and Miss Sadie back to the Toyota. "Get back in the car."

She'd gone along with all of this because she believed there'd be a way out. Shit. He was going to kill her and Miss Sadie and there was nothing she could do. Miss Sadie didn't have a chance and if she or Billie ran, they were both dead, which meant Amber and Little Man—oh God, what if they were already dead? What if those bastards had killed her babies? The monster's cell phone rang. He nudged Harry's gun into her back and answered it.

"Everything's good. Hope things are on your end too." His nonchalance made her stomach pulse hard. She wretched. With nothing in her stomach, little more than water and bile came up. "Ready to wrap things up?" The volume on his phone was turned up enough to hear the man on the other end's clipped answer. "Yes."

"Good. I don't care how you take care of things; take your time if you want."

"What about the baby?" the man asked. Billie's heart skidded out of control. Her knees began to go weak. She started crying, quietly at first, then full-blown sobbing.

The bastard said something. Oh, God, what did he say? If she wanted to get out of this alive, she had to get a grip. If Little Man and Amber were dead, what was the point?

"Just make it neat." He ended the call. "Get in the car." He nudged Miss Sadie toward the passenger side. Miss Sadie obeyed. "You too." He motioned for Billie to take the driver's seat.

Damning anger bubbled up through the helplessness that had paralyzed her most of the day. And what would she have to show for her submissiveness? The words were on the tip of her tongue—"What are you going to do, shoot me?"

Four dead bodies. If it were her, just her, she wouldn't be in this situation; she would have taken her chances. She would have been bolder, maybe even smarter. But there had been other lives hanging in the balance, making it impossible to think straight, impossible to do anything but submit.

When she did nothing, he opened the car door and pushed her onto the seat, and, to her surprise, handed over Harry Bennett's gun.

"There now. A good clean shot. I'm sure you can manage that," he said coolly, his gun pressed hard against Billie's temple. "If you kill the old woman, I'll call my men off your pretty daughter and her son. If you don't, everybody dies. But you won't let that happen, Billie." His voice had changed from cool and businesslike to sadistic.

When Billie did nothing, the buzz cut, no neck grabbed her chin and forced her to look at him. He looked like he had walked straight out of a Terminator movie. "I know you better than you know yourself, Billie Warren. You're always valiant, always saving someone. Something. *Shoot her.*"

"*NO.*"

"Do it child." Miss Sadie wasn't crying anymore; her voice was gentle, calm. "I'm ready to leave this earth, to see my boy."

"No," Billie growled at the perp.

"Don't be stupid," he hissed, "You can save your daughter. Your grandson."

"Shooting you won't save anybody," she said to Miss Sadie.

"Goddamn it, shoot her," he roared.

"I'll be damned before I go out the way you want." She dropped the gun on the floorboard and looked at the bastard with the coolness of a Wild Boy. "You and I both know nobody's going to survive this. So go ahead and kill me."

"You don't know that," he spat. The need for her to be hysterical, helpless rolled off him.

He jammed the gun into her temple. She turned to face him. The barrel pressed hard against the middle of her forehead.

"No," Miss Sadie gabbed Billie's right arm. "Please child. No."

"Last chance." His smile was thin, tight.

Billie looked him dead in the eyes. "Fuck you."

The shot that rang out through the garage was as deafening as Billie's scream. Blinded by tears, Billie gasped for air between sobs. "Noooo," she cried and waited for the second bullet that would inevitably pierce her skull. The body made a hollow thud as it slumped across Billie's lap. Everything went black. Where was the bright light? Where was heaven? She needed to find Amber and the baby. And her daddy. She wanted to see his face again, to hear him laugh and tell jokes. Maybe that's what heaven was.

"He's dead," Miss Sadie stammered as Billie came to. "I tried, but I couldn't push him off of you."

Billie shoved the body off her and onto the concrete floor. She wiped her eyes in disbelief as Deidre knelt down by the bastard. The same hands that had been steady enough to take him out with a single shot, shook wildly as she checked the body for a pulse. "They have my daughter and her baby," Billie convulsed again into tears. "They're going to kill them."

Deidre didn't reassure her that everything was going to be all right; she didn't say Jack shit, just handed the man's gun to Billie, then took the cell phone he had used to order the kills. "Your man is dead. Call of your dogs now." She cleared her throat, maybe so her voice would stop trembling. "*I* have the letter now. If you don't, you'll be reading about it on the news crawl in a matter of minutes.—Test me and your life as you know it is over." She ended the call and slid into the back seat of the Toyota. "Let's get the hell out of here."

The tires squealed as the Camry made its way to the exit ramp. "What if there are more like him?"

"It wouldn't be the first time Bob Norris has underestimated a woman, but I don't think he would send more than one man to take care of the two of you. That doesn't mean there won't be more if we don't get out of here."

"Where to?"

Deidre rattled off an address, and Billie peeled out onto the street.

CHAPTER TWENTY-FOUR

Deidre made a call on her cell phone and spoke in code as Billie sped toward the address she'd given her. "No, Kate, stay there. I'll find you," she said and ended the call. She tore open the letter and spread the pages across the back seat before taking several pictures with her cell phone.

When she was done, she returned the pages to the envelope and lay her hand gently on Miss Sadie's shoulder to get her attention before handing her the envelope. It looked small, innocuous, and yet Billie and Miss Sadie, even Amber and the baby had almost died because of it.

"You should have this," Deidre said. "The originals; they're yours."

"Mine?" Miss Sadie took the envelope with the pages Deidre had copied but looked puzzled.

"Judge Norris," the words caught in Deidre's throat. "He wanted it this way. I know it doesn't change what happened, but he was truly sorry for everything. He—" She stopped for a moment. "Even though he did some terrible things, I believe he was a good man. I loved him in spite of those things."

"He wrote this *to me?* Why?"

"At the time I didn't know why—I just knew it was extremely important to him. Two days before he died, he begged me to mail it to you, and I did it without any idea of what was in it. "The day you came out to the house, Billie, after Bob broke in and sent you out of the bedroom, the judge told Bob about the letter. In it, he said that he'd finally absolved himself and that Bob should, too. That he'd sent a letter to Mrs. Byrd. None of that meant anything to me until I overheard Bob's phone conversation ordering the person on the other end of the call to get the letter by any means necessary. That was when I knew I had to find it before he did."

"But why?" Billie asked.

Deidre was quiet for a moment and continued. "For the last two years, Bob started coming to Stanton less, a lot less, and when he did, it was always for some photo op with his father. He rarely had time for me and when he did, it was more my idea than his. I knew there was somebody else, not his wife. At the time, I was desperate, trying to hang onto him the only way I could.

"As soon as I found out I was pregnant, I realized how stupid I'd been. I knew Bob would never accept the baby. When I couldn't hide the pregnancy any more, I took a leave of absence, had the baby, and stayed with my sister here in Columbia. My daughter was three weeks old when I got the call that the judge had taken a turn for the worse. My sister kept the baby, and I went to be with him.

"I showed him a picture of Olivia; I thought it would make him happy. But he was terrified for us. He said Bob would kill both of us and made me swear to him that I would never tell Bob about the baby."

"Dear child," Miss Sadie whispered.

"The judge must have known I didn't believe him because he told me about Janice Browning, Bob's college sweetheart."

Billie had been a freshman in high school when the College of Charleston coed was bludgeoned to death. The police had called it a robbery turned murder.

"The day they found Janice's body, the police showed up at the judge's home to question Bob. Instead, the judge talked to them, dismissed the idea that Bob was capable of murder, and personally vouched for him. Janice's expensive engagement ring had been taken and a silver locket she always wore was gone too. The judge said it was obviously a burglary gone bad. The police agreed and the case went unsolved.

"After the judge told me about Janice, he insisted I leave before Bob came back to Stanton, but I couldn't leave him there to die, not without someone who truly loved him by his side. When I refused, he told me Bob had always had high aspirations, and the baby and I would be no different from Janice."

"Jesus, Deidre," Billie said, "You're a smart woman. How'd you ever get mixed up with a guy like Bob in the first place?"

"I've always been attracted to powerful men; seems I'm really good at picking the wrong ones," she said. "It's funny, when Bob exiled me to be with his father, I was devastated. I grew up in the foster system, so it felt like he was sending me away, to another home. I never had a father, so I couldn't believe how quickly I grew to love the judge—how very precious he became to me."

Billie shook her head and glanced up in the rearview mirror to see Miss Sadie's reaction to Deidre's adoration, but the old woman's face was passive.

"After he died, I was surprised that Bob stayed around to help out. He said that people would be coming by to pay their respects and that it would be nice to make the house back into a home instead of a temporary hospital. The staff and Bob and I worked all day; it was good—it helped take my mind off the grief and emptiness I felt.

"Toward the end of the day, Bob became tense—almost frantic. I thought it was because I was still there and his wife was coming in for the funeral. I wanted to get away from him, so I went up to the attic to put some things away.

"Alone, with the judge's things—I felt closer to him. I was putting some things into a trunk when I saw a small wooden box he had kept by his bed. I noticed it wasn't locked anymore. When I opened it, an antique silver locket was inside. I opened the locket and saw a picture of Bob with a pretty dark-haired girl. I knew then that he had murdered Janice Browning.

"Before I could take the locket or the ring as evidence, Bob came in and saw the box. He didn't know I had seen what was inside. He was relieved, and took it.

"After seeing the locket, there was no doubt that the judge's concern for me and the baby was justified. I had no idea what was in this letter, I just knew that it was addressed to you, Mrs. Byrd, and I had to find it before Bob did. It was my only hope."

"I never thought one of my own would take another life," Miss Sadie said sadly.

"Bob Norris was one of your kids?" Billie asked, shocked.

"I'm as sure of it as I am that Caroline was mine."

Billie's hands gripped the steering wheel hard. That bastard had threatened to take away everything she held dear, and if she hadn't died in the process, she would've wished she was dead. "The person you called, Deidre, when you saved my family. That was Bob?"

"Yes," Deidre said quietly.

CHAPTER TWENTY-FIVE

The marquee of the Embassy Suites hotel read SC Democrat Party Election Headquarters. Billie pulled into the packed parking lot and parked on the curb. "You sure about this?"

"Bob's across town waiting to give his acceptance speech," Deidre said before Billie could ask any questions. "He wouldn't dare set foot in this place tonight."

She opened the door to get out of the car. Billie grabbed her arm. "Your phone."

Deidre gave her the cell and hurried into the hotel. Billie fumbled with the keypad until she heard the call go through.

"Amber?"

"Mama? Oh, God I hadn't heard from you in so long. I thought you were—" Amber's words dissolved into a wail.

"Are you okay, honey? Did they hurt you? Is the baby okay? Please, don't cry. I'm fine; Miss Sadie is too."

"Mama—he's out there. I can feel him watching us," she whispered. "He's going to—"

"Nobody's going to hurt you, Amber. We got the bad guys."

She said, praying Deidre was right.

"You got them?" She sounded like she'd swallowed tears all day for the baby's sake, then fell apart, barely able to catch her breath.

"Shhh. It's over, baby. I promise." Little Man chimed in screaming so loud, Billie was almost shouting to be heard. "Amber, listen to me. I'm going to call Sheriff Malden to send a squad car to pick up you. You stay at his office until I get there. Understand?"

"Mama, are you sure it's okay?" Billie opened her mouth to reassure her daughter, but Amber's words came through the phone before she could say anything. "I thought I'd lost you forever, Mama. I love you. I love you so much."

"I love you too." God it was killing her to hear Amber so scared. She swiped at her own tears. "Now, wait for Jimmy to send a car for you. Call me at this number if something doesn't look right."

"DON'T hang up. Mama, please."

"I'm sorry, baby." Billie squeezed her eyes shut. "I have to go now, but I swear to you, everything's going to be okay."

Billie ended the call and dialed the Charleston County sheriff's office. "Billie Warren calling for Jimmy Malden; it's an emergency."

Seconds later, Jimmy laughs into the phone. "Emergency? What? Did the only stop light in Stanton quit on you?"

"Jimmy," Billie cut him off quick. "I need you."

"What's wrong?" he clipped.

"Send a car over to my house to get Amber and the baby."

"You want to tell me why?"

"I don't have time right now, but I need this, Jimmy."

"I'll go myself," he said, canning the sarcasm for the first time since she had known him.

Billie ended the call, picked Harry's gun off the floorboard, and ejected the magazine. The bastard wasn't kidding—it was loaded with shiny gold bullets.

"Are you okay?" she asked, keeping her eye on two men in a white panel van a few cars over.

"What if something had happened to that precious baby, or to Amber? You ought not to have taken any chances back there. You should have done what he said."

The van finally pulled out of the parking lot, headed toward the interstate. "Never," she said softly, the word almost catching in her throat. "Deidre says we're safe, but I'd feel better if you were in the backseat with her."

She scanned the cars in the parking lot as she helped Miss Sadie into the back. All she could think about was flying down the interstate to Amber and the baby, but she wanted to get Deidre to a safe place. Billie owed her that much. She owed her everything.

And she wanted to see Mama.

Shit. Nan and Inez were there, too. Had they gone through the same hell Billie and Amber had gone through? Were they all right? Were they alive? Billie punched in Mama's number and held her breath.

"Nan?" God it was good to hear her voice.

"Hey, you," Nan gushed. "How are things going with Miss Sadie? Are you all having any fun because we sure are. Abby's been over here all day, playing cards, and keeping us girls in stitches."

Billie couldn't speak. She just listened to the voices in the background, savoring the sounds of Inez and Abby playing Bullshit, cackling at the top of their lungs.

"Billie," Nan said. "You okay?"

"Everything's fine. Perfect. I'm headed home."

"Well, I better go. You know Abby cheats like hell. Have to watch that girl every stinking minute. See you tomorrow?"

"Tomorrow." Billie ended the call. An hour ago, she had a gun to her head and was sure there was no such thing. She swiped away her tears and glanced up in the rearview mirror to see Deidre hurrying back with a baby carrier draped in a bright pink blanket.

She strapped the carrier in and gave Billie the address for a private airfield before she fell to pieces. Billie drove toward the west side of town, keeping an eye for the white panel van, for anyone who might be following them, but the streets were characteristically empty.

Miss Sadie laid a reassuring hand on Deidre's shoulder. Deidre wiped her eyes and pulled back the blanket for Miss Sadie to see. Billie glanced up to see Miss Sadie Byrd beaming at the little one.

Deidre draped herself over the carrier and slept the fifteen minutes it took to get to the private airfield on the outskirts of Columbia. There were a few cars in the parking lot, some were very old and looked like they had been there for years. The rest were black SUVs that looked like standard issue law enforcement vehicles. "We're here," Billie announced as a thoroughly disheveled Deidre raised her head. "I'll help you out of the car."

Deidre ran her hands through her thick blond hair. She fumbled with the seat belt buckle until it clicked, releasing its precious cargo. A man in a dark suit opened her door and greeted her while another spoke into his radio and gave the pilot the order to prepare the jet for takeoff. A look of relief crossed Deidre's face when the engines of the jet began to hum.

The men looked like the Secret Service guys in the movies in nondescript dark suits with nondescript faces. "Miss Lawson," one of them said reaching for the carrier. Billie thought it was odd that after everything Deidre had been through tonight, she handed the Babies-R-Us carrier overflowing with pink blankets to him without reservation. The two men flanked her while eyeing the landscape ominously.

"Thank you." Deidre offered her hand to Billie, then Miss Sadie.

"No—thank you," Billie said, "I owe you everything."

"I'm so grateful for what you did for us," Miss Sadie said. "I know you're going to be a good mother."

"I hope so," Deidre said.

"Of course you are. You risked your life for your baby."

"Mrs. Byrd, I don't know what to say to you. Olivia and I have to go away. Maybe for good."

"Then you say goodbye." Miss Sadie's eyes glistened with tears. "Do you think—would it be okay? Can I hold her before you go?"

The man holding the carrier had been patient enough and was ready for this Hallmark moment to be over. "We need to go, Miss Lawson."

"Just a second," Deidre said firmly. She knelt down and unbuckled the buckle.

"Miss Lawson, this really isn't a good idea. My orders are—" Deidre shot the man a look that stopped him in midsentence.

The cold night air nipped at the tiny baby as her mother lifted her out of the warm carrier. As she put her in Miss Sadie's arms, the little one grunted and snuggled into her grandmother, making the three women laugh for the first time in what seemed like forever.

Miss Sadie kissed the child's tiny hand. "She's special, you know. They all are."

CHAPTER TWENTY-SIX

Billie glanced into the rearview mirror, maybe a little too much, watching the darkness for headlights. To be safe, she should have put the gun back in the glove box, but it was easily accessible, tucked away under her seat.

"What does that red light mean?" Miss Sadie asked, pointing at the dashboard.

Billie had no idea how long the fuel light had been on.

While Amber had turned reading the needle and stopping for gas just before her Civic hiccupped into the BP station into an art form, Billie never let the Toyota's tank get below half full.

"Means we need gas."

It went without saying as Billie pulled into a lone truck stop along I-26 that she wouldn't have stopped unless she was forced to. The way the day had gone, it made perfect sense every pump was occupied. She weighed the idea of trying to find a less busy station down the road, but the gas gauge was too far beyond the ominous E.

Billie ran her debit card through the slot on the pump and pressed the buttons that answered questions that seemed utterly ridiculous after all she had been through today. Did she want a receipt? No. Did she want a carwash? No. Did she want to buy a Pepsi and look under the cap to see if she had won a—hell, no! Finally, the gas began to fill the tank. Exhausted, Billie set the trigger of the nozzle on auto fill, dug her fists into her lower back, and stretched.

She opened the door. "Hopefully, this is our last stop until we get home. Can I get you something?"

She shook her head. "Would it be too much to ask for you to read this to me?"

"Sure," Billie nodded and got into the car.

"You know, before, I didn't want anything to do with this letter, but now I think I need to know what that man had to say to me."

Billie opened the envelope, pulled out three sheets of expensive linen paper, and steadied her hands. Even though the danger was over, her heart beat fast. She needed to know what was in the pages that Bob Norris was willing to kill for.

Dear Mrs. Byrd:

Looking back through the scope of a long life, memories come unfiltered and raw. I do not see the good other folks tell me I did but rather a never-ending parade of crimes against God and man.

I committed great sins with little or no thought to consequence, in a manner that was as natural as breath. Consequences were for the guilty who came before me in the courtroom and for innocents like you, Mrs. Byrd, who craved the protection of the law but never knew it.

Billie looked up from the letter. Miss Sadie was wringing the leather handles of her purse the way she had the first day she came into the Stanton police department to report Caroline Norris's murder.

"Are you okay?" Billie asked. Miss Sadie nodded. "Do you want me to go on?" She nodded again.

I manipulated the law to insulate myself from paying my due and for this alone, I know that I will never see the face of God. But

I have seen your face in my dreams for over forty years now and will continue to see it throughout these last days.

Out of my own shame, I will not call out to God and beg for mercy I do not deserve. But a declaration of guilt is due before I leave this world, a full accounting before death comes for me.

For years, Mac Dalton presided over the South Carolina Bar with the same sense of entitlement that I presided over District and then the State Supreme Court. Yet both of us amassed a large part of our considerable fortunes peddling newborn flesh and using information derived from those sales for personal gain.

I am sure there will be little comfort in knowing there were many women like you, and yet I cannot name one of them. I bartered and sold their babies as I did yours. One woman, I recall, produced fourteen children. Hundreds of babies were taken from their mothers of whom the vast majority did not initiate the sale but rather were coerced or bullied into signing away their parental rights.

By now Miss Sadie had stopped wringing the leather; her eyes were fixed on the pages in Billie's hands. "In my heart, I didn't believe it when Polly Herron and Maggie Dalton said there were more women like me, but it is real."

"Yes, it is," Billie said.

"They were like me—" her words came out just above a whisper.

Billie continued on, glancing up at Miss Sadie as she read.

My barren wife and I were blessed with two of your children. Bob was just three hours old when Amanda held him in her arms and declared he was the finest son she had ever seen. Even though Amanda was sickly, she was a good mother who loved her children as much as anyone can.

It may seem rather cruel for me to tell you that Caroline was supposed to go to an affluent family in Charleston. I took her home with me instead, hoping that Amanda's joy would sustain her a little longer, but my dear wife's cancer had spread so, she didn't see Caroline's first birthday.

Oh, how I wish that I had placed Caroline in their arms or more fittingly, left her with you, but I did not. I know with great certainty that good begets goodness and that evil begets evil, but it is surely the good who suffer from this truth. I cannot tell you why my son, Bob, raped and murdered his sister.

"But I saw—" Miss Sadie stammered.

Billie read the next few paragraphs to herself. "I know, but this makes sense."

You were not as well hidden as you thought that day I carried my precious Caroline's lifeless body out of the thicket. I knew you thought it was I who took her life, and I let you think that for fear of losing the only child I had left. When your husband confronted me, I scoffed at the very idea that he would hold a Norris accountable for anything, much less rape and murder. I did this fully knowing that your husband was accusing the wrong Norris.

"Oh, my Jesus. A *boy* did that? *My boy?* He was all of eighteen then."

The color was drained from Miss Sadie's face and her hands shook fiercely.

"Look, we don't have to do this now. We can wait until both of us have had some rest," Billie said as she refolded the pages.

"I don't know if I can ever sleep, knowing that one of mine did such a thing." She shook her head, then looked at Billie. "You don't think the judge is trying to put this off on Bob, do you?"

"I don't know. After everything that's happened tonight, my gut says the judge is telling the truth. It seems like he cared enough to try to set things straight before he died."

"I want to hear the rest." Miss Sadie nodded like she was trying to convince herself.

Over the years, whenever my past revisited me, my blood ran cold wondering what could have driven such a young boy to commit the worst of crimes against his own sister. Many times, I dropped to my knees and begged God's forgiveness as I now beg for yours, although, I do not know if there is forgiveness for such things.

I believe my children would have been better off had they stayed with you. Maybe Bob would not have gone on to kill again. I did not see him commit the act myself, but in my heart I know that he murdered his college sweetheart, Janice Browning. But with me as his alibi, the police were easy to manipulate; the coroner who was beholden to me never released the fact that Janice was six weeks pregnant.

I take no solace in any part of my confession. I imagine, Mrs. Byrd, that you have been tormented by bits and pieces of the truth for many years, and now you know it all. I hope that in your last days, you will find comfort in my sorrow for these truths I have proclaimed.

Sincerely,

Judge Harold R. Norris

Billie folded the letter and put it back in the envelope before getting out of the car. She returned the nozzle back in its cradle and then got back in. Her first instinct was to crank up the engine and floor it all the way home to Amber, but she was worried. After everything that had happened, the added weight of the judge's words seemed to have worn Sadie Byrd down beyond the nub.

"Do you think we're safe," Miss Sadie asked.

Billie took a quick look around the gas station. Nothing seemed out of the ordinary. A young couple was trying to quiet their little one who started crying as soon as they cut the engine off to get gas. A handful of people in gray uniforms, maybe day laborers, chatted in the parking lot, drinking convenience store coffee. A petroleum truck was making a delivery in one of the bays.

"Between the election and all the media attention, at the very least, Bob's distracted." Miss Sadie nodded, but looked like Billie's words were a pitiful consolation.

"I keep asking you if you're okay because I don't know what else to say," Billie said. "I guess it's stupid to think that anyone might have the right words to—"

"The judge wrote that for Caroline, you know," Miss Sadie said. "Maybe when you think of her now, you can have some peace."

CHAPTER TWENTY-SEVEN

Billie wasn't sure whether it was the hour, or the fact that it was almost time for the highway patrol shift change, but she flew home on the flat interstate that stretched from Columbia toward Charleston and then home. Miss Sadie didn't say much. She stared out her window, nodded off occasionally.

As weary and raw as Billie was, all she could think about as she ticked off the calculations between the mile markers and landmarks she passed was that she was going home. First stop, the highway patrol office that was twenty miles from Stanton. She imagined that Little Man would be sacked out and that all the officers would be fawning over the fair damsel, Amber.

Her heart revved as she took the exit. Tyson's parked car at the entrance of the sheriff's department told her that Amber couldn't do without him another minute. She pulled into a parking space and glanced at Miss Sadie. Even with the gravity of the judge's confession, Billie couldn't help but feel jubilant. They had walked through the fire together and nabbed the bad guy in the process—well one of the bad guys.

With the baby attached at her hip, Amber pushed through the double doors of the building and ran to meet her. Billie was dizzy with exhilaration as she wrapped her arms around Amber and her precious Little Man.

Tyson must have helped Miss Sadie out of the car because the three women were now a mass of arms and tears. He stretched his arms around all of them and kissed Billie on the forehead. "She told me," his voice quivered. "You saved them."

"She did," Miss Sadie said. "And I'll tell you right now, if I had my choice of saviors, she would be right behind Jesus Christ. And another thing—"

"If this happy reunion goes on much longer, I'll have to start charging." The look on Jimmy Malden's face said that Amber had told him as much as she knew about what had happened. "You look like shit, Chief Warren. Get some rest and stop by for some coffee tomorrow. You got some 'splainin' to do."

"Thanks, Jimmy."

"You owe me," he said and strolled back into the building.

Amber came up for air from the happy throng, "Mama—" She squealed when Little Man put the death grip on her long, blond hair. "Cole called a hundred times today, but I didn't answer. After Tyson got here and I stopped crying—well—I called him a few minutes ago."

"Amber!"

"I had to call him, Mama; he was crazy worried. He said he finally got through on your cell and some guy answered and said he had fished your phone out of a trashcan. He wanted to meet you here, but I told him you would meet him at his house."

Before Billie could say anything, Little Man nearly toppled out of Amber's arms reaching for Miss Sadie. Everybody laughed. Miss Sadie took the baby, held him close, and kissed the top of his head the way she had Olivia's. With his arms wrapped around Amber, Tyson grinned at his son. He closed his eyes and nuzzled Amber's neck like he knew now how truly precious she was.

"I'll take them home—Miss Sadie, too." Tyson wasn't asking for permission. "First thing tomorrow, we'll get the house put back together."

Something inside Billie needed to see Amber and the baby tucked in bed. She needed to walk Miss Sadie through the front door and help her to the guest room where she would check in on her during the night. But the look in Tyson's eyes said that he really was ready to step up and care for his family.

"Thank you, Tyson." Billie said.

"I love you, Mama." Amber threw her arms around Billie and held her tight.

Billie kissed her cheek. "I love you, too, baby. I'll be home soon."

Tyson had a hard time contorting his tall lanky frame into the back seat to strap in Little Man. He said something about trading in the Trans Am for a four door. Amber got into the back seat with the baby, and Tyson helped Miss Sadie into the passenger side. He looked at Billie like he wanted to say something, like maybe he wanted to apologize *again* for being such a royal ass to Amber. Instead, he just gave a slight wave. "Thank you." He whispered with a reverence that came from almost losing the most precious things in his life. "Thank you."

Billie got back in the car and cranked up the engine. She put her Don Henley CD in and then turned it off before it started to play. She'd had enough of "The End of the Innocence."

She let the road take her toward the marsh, and the Row. Though the moon was a few days past full, it still played brilliantly across the fingers of water that laced in and out of clumps of sea grass anchored onto muddy oyster beds. The music of the Row called to her, the ruts of the dirt road swayed her body, setting it to a different rhythm.

Though it wasn't unusual to see the artsy folks up late, it was well after two in the morning and every house was dark, except for one. When he saw her car, he ran to her. She barely stopped the car, and had not turned off the engine, before he threw open the door and pulled her into him.

"Thank God, you're okay," he said. "I thought I had lost you for good."

Billie closed her eyes. She'd thought the same about him, too, many times, but especially tonight when she was sure she was going to die. She held him as tight as she could, claiming him, surrendering to the love she had for him.

The tears wouldn't stop, and she was tired, so tired of being the strong one, of trying to save Amber's world and Mama's world, and oh, God, that whole thing—that really had happened with Deidre and Miss Sadie.

She had earned the right to let herself go a long time ago. Now, she was giving herself permission.

She had no recollection of Cole picking her up and carrying her in the house. She remembered him laying her on the bed, remembered pulling him down beside her so that he spooned up to her. At this point, Abby would have written in a torrid love scene, but Billie was too exhausted and fell instantly asleep.

When she awoke, it was almost 8:00. Cole wasn't there. He had cut some camellias and put them in a vase next to a handmade pot that was warm with lemongrass tea. She poured herself a cup and read the handwritten note on top of his iPad. *DON'T GO ANYWHERE. I have no food in the house. When I come back, we'll have great food and phenomenal sex. Love, Cole.*

Billie grabbed the iPad. She sipped her tea and tapped the screen to see the election results. Her heart sank when she saw Bob Norris smiling, waving triumphantly to his supporters. Disgusted, she tapped the screen again to see the related stories. The next headline that popped up made her heart race:. *Janice Browning Murder Investigation Reopened.*

She put the mug on the bedside table and knifed up to read the story. The first paragraph touted new evidence, and said Janice's parents had given the district attorney's office permission to exhume the body. Most importantly, it proclaimed to the world that Bob Norris was the last person to see her alive.

Deidre had gotten the judge's letter into the right hands. Billie toasted her with a sip of warm tea as she lay back down and pulled Cole's pillow into her chest. She breathed in its earthy clean smell. Outside the floor-length windows, the fence post people played hide and seek in the thick fog that crept out of the inlet and onto the cool November ground. The sun was itching to break through.

She heard his car in the driveway. The creaking sound of the ancient screen door set her heart racing. By the time he set the groceries on the kitchen counter, she was dizzy. His keys landed in the brass bowl he kept on the kitchen counter.

He moved down the hall, like he thought she might still be sleeping, then stopped in the doorway with a bunch of flowers and a shiny gold box.

She rolled out of bed and flung herself at him. "Are those chocolates?"

"Grocery store Godivas," he smiled, "and irises."

"My favorites." It was good to hear herself laugh, to hold him close. "I love you, Cole."

He held her at arm's length, his eyes searching her face. It wasn't the first time she'd said those words to him. He read her with the same intensity he used when he was creating something beautiful and then scooped her up. She heard some of the stems of the irises break. Amethyst-colored petals with kisses of yellow fell to the floor strewing the path to the bed.

She silenced the voices in her head that told her to hold back. She was tired of going to the edge of everything, including loving Cole, and keeping a safe distance. She wanted him so badly, but the words wouldn't wait.

"I'm here, Cole," she whispered against his lips. "I'm here and I love you. Forever."

Please enjoy a preview of *A Peach of a Pair*
by
Kim Boykin

A stand-alone novel of betrayal and sisterhood

A PEACH OF A PAIR

I

Thursday, March 26, 1953

"Mail call," old Miss Beaumont bellowed into the commons room, and a flock of girls descended on her like biddies after scratch feed. Except for me. Normally, I would have been right there with them, clamoring for news from home. But since Mother called right after the tornado hit last month to say everyone back home in Satsuma was still in one piece, there hasn't been a single word from anyone. Not even Brooks.

It was bad enough that Hurricane Florence blew through in September and smashed much of Alabama to bits. Six months later, just when everyone was getting a handle on putting my hometown back together, a tornado roared through, undoing

Satsuma all over again. And while I wanted Miss Beaumont to bellow my name, I was sure the folks back home were too busy with the cleanup to write.

On good days, the silence was unsettling, and on bad days, it turned my stomach inside out. But I knew better than to complain.

Three and a half years ago, I'd been dying to get out of *the armpit of Alabama* to study music and accepted a full ride to the most exclusive women's college in South Carolina. Funny how, back then Satsuma, even Alabama herself, seemed too small for me. Now, all I can think about is moving back home, and it won't be long, just eight weeks till graduation.

I missed my mother and Sissy like it was the first day of my freshman year. And if I let myself think of the very long list of the people I love who have stopped writing me since those awful catastrophes, I would never stop crying. And Brooks. Loyal, faithful Brooks, who loved me enough to let me go away to college, saying he would wait forever if he had to for me to be his bride. The thought of how much I loved him, missed him, made my heart literally ache with a dull pain that left me in tears.

I was sure Brooks was working himself to death, helping rebuild Satsuma, because that's the kind of guy he was, always building something. At Christmastime, he proposed, a promise without a ring, but a promise from Brooks Carter is as certain as my next breath.

Miss Beaumont called the name of one of the catty girls who are jealous of me because I am the only 'Bama belle at Columbia College. Maybe in the whole state of South Carolina. She cut her eye around at me, waved three letters, relishing the fact that I had none. My roommate, Sue, had one clutched to her chest, praying for more as hard as I've prayed for word from home. Something. Anything.

Sue had badgered me to call home. Collect. I knew my family would accept the charges, but I was afraid of the news that must be so terrible, nobody could bring themselves to call the pay phone in my hallway. So I waited for letters. I craved them as much as I dreaded them.

Since I went away to college, Mama and Sissy, who just turned nineteen last month, have written me every week, sometimes twice a week. Nana Gilbert and Grandma Pope wrote just as often, always slipping in a newspaper clipping from home, sometimes a dollar bill, whenever they had it to spare. With nineteen cousins who are all tighter than a new pair of shoes, I could always count on letters from them. One day I received twenty-two, a record at the college; it was better than Christmas. And Brooks, my beloved one true love, his letters were always like Christmas and the Fourth of July rolled into one.

Brooks loves and knows me better than anyone. He should; we'd been sweethearts since the fourth grade. While it has been a little rough with my studying music and education here in Columbia, and him back home in Satsuma, Brooks has been the most wonderful, understanding man in the world. Of course when I got the scholarship, he wasn't at all happy, but he knew I was working toward our future. Me a teacher, maybe even a church pianist too, him running the feed store his daddy left him.

Lots of girls here have diamonds and are getting married the moment they graduate. But Brooks and I are waiting until next summer. He said it would be a good idea to get a year of teaching experience under my belt before we're wed. He's always so sensible like that, forward thinking, which I am not.

"Sue Dennis," Miss Beaumont yelled. Sue snatched the letter from her and cocked her head at me, reminding me to be hopeful. But I knew there would be nothing for me, not until Satsuma was put together again. And it must be bad back home, much worse than Mother let on for the news from home to have stopped altogether. As awful as that was, the worst part was knowing in my heart why.

I shook my head at Sue and forced a thin smile.

"Nettie Gilbert," Miss Beaumont called like the world had not just ended. I kept my seat on the kissing couch in the common's room. Sue jumped up and down for me, squealing, but for the life of me I couldn't move. She grabbed the letter from Miss Beaumont's withered old fingers and flew to my side.

"It's from Brooks," she gushed. "I just know it is."

But I knew it's wasn't. Mother's letter-perfect handwriting marked the front. I turned it over to see the flap she always sealed with a tiny mark, *xoxo*, but there was nothing. Someone was dead, their long obituary folded up inside. Someone so precious to me, no one, not even my own mother, could bear to break the news to me.

"Open it," Sue said. She'd already read her first letter, from her beau back home in Summerville. Her face was still flush. Sometimes we read our letters to each other, but lately, she'd kept the ones from Jimmy to herself since she visited home last. Even though their June wedding was right around the corner, I suspected they did the deed the last time she was home, and her letters were too saucy to share.

On the last night of Christmas break, I'd wanted to go all the way with Brooks and would have if Sissy hadn't fetched us from the orange grove. We'd taken a blanket there to watch the sunset. It was a perfect night. As crisp as a gulf night can be in December. The perfect time, the perfect place, but Sissy, who could never leave Brooks alone, insisted we play Parcheesi with the family. When I protested, all it took was a *Mother said* from her, and Brooks was folding up the blanket, putting it back in the knapsack along with my chance at becoming a woman.

"I'll be at your graduation before you know it," he promised when I gave him a pouty look. "And next summer, you'll be my June bride," he whispered like it was naughty. His breath sent chills down my thighs and made me hate Sissy, just a tiny bit.

At Christmastime, I saw the devastation from Hurricane Florence firsthand, but after the tornado roared through Satsuma a few weeks ago, I knew it was much worse. When I'd called, Mother had sworn everyone was okay. But I knew if something were wrong, if someone were terribly injured, she'd try to keep a tight lip, at least until I graduated. Partly for me because she loved me, and partly because I would be the first on both sides of my family to get my degree.

Mother had tried college, and then got married the summer after her freshman year. But I also know part of my mother was still angry at me for going so far away when I could have gone to 'Bama, which did *not* have a decent music program.

"Come on, Nettie, read it," Sue chided. But my heart refused to let my hands open the letter; I passed it off to Sue as she drug me back to our room.

"Sit," she ordered, pushing me gently down onto my bed. "You're being silly. It's something wonderful, I'm sure of it," she gushed, reaching for her letter opener. She slit the top of the envelope, pulled out a small white card, and offered it to me again.

Tears raced down my face, my neck. When I pushed it away, a sheet of lined notebook paper folded into a perfect rectangle escaped from the card and fell to the floor. Sue snatched it up while scanning the card. Her smile faded, and her face was ghostly white.

"Oh, Nettie," she whispered, unfolding the letter from my mother.

"It's Brooks, isn't it?" She nodded. "Oh, God."

I threw myself across the bed, sobbing. Brooks was dead. I would never see his beautiful face. Hear his voice rumble my name. Feel his arms wrapped tight around me, making me feel adored. Safe. Loved. The life that we'd planned would never amount to anything more than just words whispered between two lovers.

"Nettie." Sue lay down beside me, stroking my hair. "My sweet Nettie, you need to read this."

I couldn't. I buried my face in my pillow. She whispered how strong I was, how life wasn't fair, how very sorry she was my heart was broken to bits, and held me until I was all cried out. After I don't know how long, I shook my head and looked at her. "I just can't believe Brooks is dead."

Sue gnawed her bottom lip the way she did when she was taking a test. "He's not dead, Nettie." Her hand trembled as she put Mother's letter in my hand. "He's getting married."

"What?" I jerked the page away from her, and the card fell onto my lap. Neat white stock with two little doves at the top. Mother might have been a farmer's wife from Satsuma, but her well-worn etiquette book sat atop the Bible on her bedside table. And as far as Dorothy Gilbert was concerned, they were one and the same. Except the invitations weren't sent out months in advance. They'd been done so quickly, they were not even engraved, and the wedding was four weeks away.

Brooks's name should be below mine, but it was below Sissy's—Jemma Renee Gilbert, glared at me, *cordially inviting* me to her wedding. Worse yet, *the parents* of Brooks and Sissy were cordially inviting me too.

"This must be some kind of a sick joke," Sue whispered. "How can they do this to you?"

She read my mind and uttered the words I could not bring myself to say. How *could* they? *How could Brooks?*

My hands trembled so hard it was difficult to read the impeccably neat handwriting.

Dear Nettie,

It might seem cruel to send this letter along with a proper invitation, but I couldn't bring myself to call you, and I wasn't given much notice regarding this matter. I also know you well enough to know you would have to see the invitation to truly believe it. Although I do regret not having enough time to have them engraved.

I'm sorry to be the one to give you the news about Brooks and Sissy. I love you, Nettie, and I love your sister. I'm not condoning her behavior or the fact that she is in the family way, but you are blood. You are sisters. No man can break that bond, not even Brooks.

There's money and a bus ticket paper-clipped to the invitation. I've checked the schedules. You should be able to leave Columbia on Thursday the week of the wedding after your morning classes and get back by Sunday night. I know how you hate to miss class, and if you are also missing some wonderful end-of-the-year party, I'm sorry. So very sorry.

But the milk has been spilled, Nettie. Come home and stand up with your sister. She needs you. She's a wreck, and it makes me worry about the baby.

Just come home.

Love,
Mother

ABOUT THE AUTHOR

As a stay-at-home mom, Kim started writing, grabbing snip-its of time in the car rider line or on the bleachers at swim practice. After her kids left the nest, she started submitting her work, sold her first novel at 53, and has been writing like crazy ever since. Her books are well reviewed and, according to RT Book Reviews, feel like they're being told across a kitchen table. She is the author of *Echoes of Mercy*, *A Peach of a Pair*, *Palmetto Moon*, and *The Wisdom of Hair*. While her heart is always in the Lowcountry of South Carolina, she lives in Charlotte and adores hairstylists, librarians, and book junkies like herself. You can keep up with Kim at KimBoykin.com and follow her at facebook.com/authorkimboykin.

CPSIA information can be obtained
at www.ICGtesting.com
Printed in the USA
FFOW05n0524240816